The Ecumenopolis

Page Turner

The Ecumenopolis

Psychic State Book 4

Published By: Braided Studios, LLC

https://braided.studio

ISBN: 978-1-947296-12-1

A special thanks to my Patreons

Poets

Elan L.

Michael S.

Praisers

Annabelle P.

Don S.

Emma L.

Julie H.

Kate L.

Mayson R.

Michael D.

Trisha A.

Troy N.

Sherpas

Adrian S.	Kristopher C.
Alex B.	Larissa R.
Alex V.	Lil F.
Allen H.	LylahJay
Andrea	Matt W.
Anthony M.	Michael C.
Avery F.	Miggity M.
Chris C.	Mr. Fox
digitalmumbling	Peter P.
Edith M.	PiXi S.
Elizabeth	Randall K.
Emma R.	Ricky W.
Georg	Robert F.
HEY M.	Samuel T.
Hillary J.	Scott L.
Jackie	Sean R.
Jay R.	Sharon M.
Jitesh M.	ShiniWolf
KaffeKnot69	Stephanie W.
Kat	Sunshine W.
Kirsten J.	Terry M.
Kit L.	Tiana S.
Kristi C.	Wesley E.

Other Supporters

Alicia M.	Jeana O.
Allyson L.	Jenny B.
Amanda N.	Jim B.
Amy	Jim H.
Andrew B.	Joann C.
Anna C.	Jonathan .
Ashley M.	Jonathan W.
Baron P.	k k
Benjamin P.	Kacey H.
Beth C.	Kate S.
Bethanie L.	Katherine f.
Bex	Katherine G.
Bionyx	Kathleen D.
Brandon C.	Kayla
Brendan B.	Kris B.
Brian M.	Kristen W.
Brian M.	Krystal S.
Cassildra	Lady M.
Chelle	Lani D.
Chris D.	Lauren M.
Christina B.	Leah R.
Clarita D.	Lily H.
Coleman S.	Lisa T.
Dallas S.	Lucee R.
Daryl	Maria S.
Dasmine J.	Marion L.
Delmariel .	Maureen S.
Edward W.	Menachem C.
Endre H.	Michael H.
Giovanni i.	Michael W.
Grace	Michelle M.
Greg	Nekola S.
Gunter G.	Nick
Imbri	Nicki K.
J. Scott	Patti P.
James A.	Paul V.
James H.	Pepper H.
Jason D.	Pete J.

Other Supporters

Philip C.
Philipp D.
polymerase
Pour V.
Riki S.
River F.
Sara D.
Sarah D.
Sasquatch N.
Shakespeare_28

Sherri
Tamara W.
Tay W.
Ticia B.
Tina N.
Tris S.
Trisha T.
Tyler J.

For everyone who has ever been cursed by knowledge

Ecumenopolis
from Greek:
οἰκουμένη (oecumene), meaning "world",
and πόλις (polis) "city,"
thus "a world city"

The hypothetical concept of a planetwide city.

Good Scientists Know They Don't Know Everything

May you live in interesting times.

-The Chamberlain Curse

"If you tell anyone about this, Penny, you're dead meat," Amarynth Watson said, not making eye contact. She glared out the window of the luxury sedan transporting them to Penny's doctor's appointment.

"My lips are sealed," Penny replied. "Anyway, you have dirt on me, too. Take, for example, the whole point of this trip."

Amarynth grunted assent. "I just don't want it getting around. That's all."

"Don't want *what* getting around, Am? That you have money?"

"Yeah," Am said, "or that my mother does anyway."

"You do have to admit it's kind of funny. After all those times you made sure that people knew you weren't one of *those* Watsons..." Penny let her voice trail off.

Amarynth didn't take the bait. She just let the sentence sit there, incomplete.

"Well," Penny continued, "you *were* one of *those* Watsons."

Amarynth frowned. "Not really."

"Oh, sure, right, not really," Penny said, gesturing around her. "Then how do you explain this?"

"I mean, I am technically one of *those* Watsons," Amarynth explained, "but Mom's the black sheep of the family."

"Even black sheep ride in style," Penny observed, "provided they strayed from a fancy flock anyway."

"*Penny*," Amarynth said, with more weight behind her voice. It was a plea, an entreaty, a gentle request that she stop talking about the subject.

Penny got it. She nodded. "Understood," she said. She fidgeted in the obscenely plush seat.

The vehicle pulled to a stop. The tiny window between the driver and passenger compartments slid open.

"We have arrived, Ms. Watson," the driver called back at them.

Penny gripped her door handle.

"No, Penny, wait a second," Am advised her.

Penny jerked her head back in Amarynth's direction just in time to catch the driver opening the door for Amarynth. He took Amarynth's hand and guided her onto the curb outside of the medical center. Then he beckoned to Penny to scoot over. Sighing, Penny acquiesced. As she moved her body over the leather seats and took the driver's hand, she felt very much like a beached mermaid struggling over a rocky outcropping.

How do you ever get used to having people wait on you? Penny wondered. It wasn't natural. Some might consider it to be an honor, she supposed, but it was awkward.

It made Penny glad that she hadn't stayed at home, that she'd committed so deeply to the illusion of being an orphan and had run headlong into the hardscrabble existence of a PsyOps agent. Even if that decision meant growing apart from the family she'd once been a part of, at least she hadn't become one of those helpless people who needed others to wait on her, whose entire reason for living seemed to revolve around being reminded that they were better than people who weren't as fortunate. Who, frankly, weren't as lucky.

"How do you get used to living like this, Amarynth?"

"I try hard not to," Am replied.

There were so many other questions that flooded Penny's mind. Why had Amarynth joined PsyOps in the first place? How did her powers work? Why did she always seem to know things she shouldn't? And why couldn't she explain how she knew?

But all those questions were pushed out when Penny saw a giant symbol looming over her. It was a vertical line joined to a horizontal one at a perpendicular angle, forming an upside-down T. Below this inverse T were two additional horizontal lines parallel to the first, each one shorter than the last. All of this was encased in a circle.

Until quite recently, this design had been used primarily as a symbol for grounding in electrical applications. It still was, as far as Penny knew. But another usage had been sweeping the Psychic State, as the Grounded Temple, a new religion, had decided it would work beautifully as their religious symbol.

That didn't seem safe to Penny, but so far, the State had allowed it. It would probably take a tragedy for things to change, someone mistaking a religious icon for a legitimate grounding symbol and frying themselves in the process.

Really, Penny thought, people would be better served if they responded to the Grounded Temple as they did any other potentially lethal element, like an electrical current. And she indeed found herself frozen in place at the sight of the symbol, viewing it as dangerous.

Amarynth studied her friend's face and followed her sight line to the hospital building bearing the symbol.

"Where are you taking me anyway?" Penny said weakly.

"Don't worry, Penny," Am said. "We're not going over there, to the Temple Hospital. I just had the driver drop us here to be discreet. Dr. Clark's office is over in the medical mall."

"You're lucky I'm not Karen," Penny said, referring to her romantic and work partner. "She'd run in the other direction."

Karen's father Augustus Cross had been the one to found the Grounded Temple, and Karen wasn't shy about calling the group a cult. Among many other unattractive qualities, the Grounded Temple was notoriously psychophobic. Dealing with those kooks was an intuitive's worst nightmare. "I'm tempted to run myself," Penny admitted.

"I'm not delivering you to a cult, Penny," Amarynth reassured her, sighing. "C'mon." She led the way to a row of nondescript offices on the other side of the parking lot.

They rode in silence in the elevator up to the suite for Skinner Women's Health. The doors opened and spilled them into an expensively appointed medical office.

"Geez," Penny said. She shot a worried look at Amarynth. "I hope they don't expect me to pay upfront."

"Don't worry about it," Amarynth replied. "I've got this."

They approached the reception desk together. "Hello, I have Penelope Dreadful in for a 10 am with Dr. Clark," Amarynth explained. She slid a thin black card across the desk.

The receptionist picked it up. She whistled. "Bella Watson, huh?"

Penny shot Amarynth a suspicious look. Some black sheep.

Amarynth nodded. "I'm Amarynth," she explained. "Her kid."

"Normally, we require cardholders to be present," the receptionist began, "but considering your mother's condition..."

Amarynth nodded. "I'm used to acting as her agent."

The receptionist clacked loudly on her keyboard, hesitated, and then nodded. "Yeah, it says so here. Designated agent: Amarynth Watson. Do you have some ID?"

Amarynth nodded. She opened her wallet again and extracted two cards. The first one Penny recognized instantly. It was an employee identification card for PsyOps, the Department of

Psychic Operations. Like Penny's, it was emblazoned with a Green Star designation, an indicator that she was using her intuitive powers in service of the government. As far as official statuses went, being a Green Star meant more freedom for a registered psychic citizen but also more responsibility.

Of course, the unregistered intuitives were the freest of all. But they also lived in fear of being discovered.

Penny expected Amarynth to present her PsyOps card to the receptionist, but Am put it away. Instead, she presented another card to the receptionist rather quickly, so quickly that Penny almost didn't see it. But she did.

Amarynth was carrying a second identification card, one that was standard issue for Psychic State citizens who called themselves "normals," the back-formation a constant reminder that intuitives were considered aberrant and deviant.

And it was this second ID card that the receptionist took from her. She began noisily entering the information on it into her system.

The receptionist nodded. "Okay, we're good to go. You and your..."

"Friend," Amarynth offered.

"You and your friend can take a seat. They'll let you know when they're ready."

"Thanks," Amarynth said.

She and Penny sat down.

"Why do you have a normal ID card?" Penny asked.

Amarynth sighed. "It's a long story."

"You have a lot of things that you shouldn't have," Penny said.

Amarynth bristled at this. Same uncomfortable topic all over again.

"Black sheep, my ass," Penny muttered.

A door at the far end of the room swung open. "Penelope Dreadful," a woman in scrubs called into the waiting room.

Penny rose. "Is it okay if I bring my friend with me?" she asked the medical assistant.

"Sure, honey, whatever you need," the medical assistant replied.

Penny beckoned for Amarynth to follow her.

Klaxon Clark, MD, wore lilac scrubs. She had strawberry-blond hair and ruddy skin that trended perilously close to the same color as her hair. There was nothing conventionally attractive about her, but when she smiled it felt like the sun had just come out.

"I'm glad Bella sent you my way," the doctor said. "Klaxon Clark." She extended her hand to Penny, who was too dazed to shake it.

"Thank you, Dr. Clark. I'm happy you could see us on such short notice," Amarynth replied. "My friend needs your help."

Dr. Clark nodded. "I figured. First things first, she's definitely pregnant." She scratched her forehead. "I'm at a loss to explain how this happened, however. The medical records you sent over clearly indicate that she was sterilized when she joined PsyOps, just like every other new intuitive on the force."

Penny nodded.

"Unless the records you sent me were forgeries," Dr. Clark said calmly.

Amarynth shook her head violently. "Not at all. What would be the point of that?"

"Indeed," Dr. Clark said. "I was able to pull up imaging studies from your last hospital stay, Ms. Dreadful, and your pelvic scans confirm the same thing. You were sterilized."

Penny nodded, wincing a little at the memory. It wasn't exactly a pleasant experience, the time she'd been to the hospital. The whole ordeal had been massively annoying. She'd been injured working a case for PsyOps, and she knew the entire time she was fine, but her supervisor Martin Meek had insisted she get medically cleared out of an abundance of caution.

She wasn't surprised there were pelvic scans in the records. She'd been poked and prodded so many times during that brief visit that she suspected the hospital had enough information now to clone her.

"Who's the father?" Dr. Clark asked.

Penny shrugged.

"How many men have you been sexually active with over the past year?" the doctor asked her.

"None," Penny replied.

"I'm sorry?" Dr. Clark said.

"I've never had sex with a man," Penny said.

"So you're saying you're not sexually active?"

Penny shook her head no. "No, I'm not saying that. I *am* sexually active, just not with men. I have two long-term partners, but they're both women."

The doctor looked to Amarynth for confirmation, who nodded at her.

"Your female partners don't produce sperm, do they?" the doctor pressed.

Penny shook her head. "No, and not that it matters, but they're both sterilized as well. We all work for PsyOps. Same mandatory procedure."

Dr. Clark frowned. "How do you think you became pregnant if you didn't have procreative sex?"

Penny looked to Amarynth.

"Don't look at me," Amarynth said, throwing her hands in the air.

"It's hard to explain," Penny said.

An understatement, Amarynth thought. Even though Amarynth had grasped it intuitively and knew that it was the truth, it still didn't make a whole lot of sense to her.

"Well, try," the doctor prompted.

"I went on an interplanar journey," Penny began.

This statement was rewarded with a raised eyebrow from Dr. Clark, but the obstetrician remained silent as Penny continued.

"I'm not... from here. I'm not originally from Earth. This is just one plane of existence, but there are many others. Whatever sterilization procedure I had here protected me from pregnancy on Earth, but I recently went back home to another plane where I wasn't protected. A plane so fertile that new life can spontaneously happen without sex. I don't know if there was a humanoid father that I encountered in some casual way who managed to passively impregnate me using a method I didn't recognize — having spent my adolescence on Earth —or if the plane itself is the father of my unborn child or if... if I'm both the mother and the father. All I know is that I'm pregnant, and I'm scared. Because I don't know what to do."

Penny turned and looked at the wall, feeling profoundly embarrassed. It sounded dumb to her as she said it, even though she'd been the one to live through it.

Dr. Clark was silent for a moment. "I'll admit it's a wild story," she finally said, "and with such a wild story and a psychic mother claiming to be an extraplanar being, well… many of my colleagues would recommend psychiatric referral in this case."

Penny frowned at the wall.

"I suspect that's why Bella sent you to me, however. Because I'm not like those other horribly judgmental folks. The way I see it, it doesn't matter if your story checks out. The treatment is the same, after all. You're pregnant. Whether you're pregnant for the reasons I'm used to or for highly unusual ones that I've never heard of, I'll still treat you the same way. And anyway… a good scientist knows that they don't know everything. They can't possibly. It's important to be in touch with knowing what you don't know," Dr. Clark said. "It's important to realize you might not know everything."

Penny turned to face the doctor, feeling a bit relieved.

"You have options," the doctor said. "There's termination of course. That wouldn't be so hard to accomplish at all. Now, we wouldn't want the procedure to take place within Psychic City of course. There are too many people here who could easily turn you in to the State. It wouldn't be safe to do it in Skinner. Not in Watson either. But drive a little outside of the city, just a few hours or so, and you'd be just fine. There are a ton of places where you could have a procedure, and no one would have to know about it. There's nothing between Bosque and Skinner," Dr. Clark said. "I used to drive all the time from Skinner to Valdez, the entire five hours, since I was working down there." She shook her head. "Nothing. And anything that is there is always twisted somehow. Out in Saguaro, it's even worse. Nothing but tumbleweeds. Weird ones, too. I don't know how anyone lives in the spaces between the cities. These days it's hard enough living in the cities as it is. Especially for someone like you."

"Oh, it's not so bad," Penny replied, more out of courtesy and a desire to be polite than anything else.

Dr. Clark tuned into her motivation instantly. "You're a good girl. Never let anyone tell you anything different."

Penny smiled.

"You could also carry the pregnancy to term," Dr. Clark said.

"You mean keep it?" Penny said.

Dr. Clark nodded. "You'd need to get regular antenatal care of course. I'd monitor your progress and make sure you and the fetus remained healthy."

"That sounds expensive," Penny said.

"Don't worry about that," Amarynth interjected.

"Am," Penny said.

"Hey, you're family now," Amarynth said. "You're practically my half-sister-in-law."

Penny grinned, stifling a giggle. Viv, Penny's other work and romantic partner, was still grumpy about finding out that Amarynth, her professional frenemy, had the same father that she did. "I suppose you're right," Penny replied.

She turned to Dr. Clark. "But won't you get in trouble?"

"In trouble?" Dr. Clark said.

"For treating a pregnant intuitive and not reporting it to the State," Penny offered.

"Now why would I do something like that?" Dr. Clark replied.

"That's exactly what I want to know," Penny said.

"Well," Dr. Clark said, "it's a good thing I don't see a pregnant intuitive in front of me. Good thing all I see is a woman who needs my help. The State can go to Hell for all I care."

Penny blinked at the doctor in disbelief. "Good thing," she repeated back to the doctor, bewildered. "You're a saint," she added.

"No," Klaxon Clark replied, "not a saint. Just an MD." She grinned. "But I like to think I'm a damn good one. And more importantly, I'm one who doesn't judge."

Am smiled. "I think I'm starting to understand why my mother recommended you."

After she'd dropped Penny off, Amarynth instructed the driver to return to her mother's house. It would be good to thank her in person. It wasn't easy for new patients to get appointments to see Dr. Klaxon Clark — and it had been brilliant of her mother to suggest the physician and gracious of her to arrange the visit.

As the car pulled into the grand porte-cochere, Amarynth felt her stomach tighten a little. It was a reflexive response. Bella Watson's estate was lovely and well appointed, but once upon a time, it had been a place that Amarynth could not leave.

When she was a little girl, her mother's agoraphobia had imprisoned them both.

That was of course a different time. Many years had passed. Amarynth had gotten more freedoms as she aged — had become a sort of errand girl for her financially well off but socially anxious, shut-in mother. But a slight part of Amarynth never quite forgot how small and claustrophobic her childhood had been once upon a time — and that slight part of her didn't hesitate to speak up about it.

Never mind that, Amarynth thought, steeling herself. She exited the car, walked into the house, wound her way up to her mother's study, where her mother was perched next to a large window, spying on the neighbors — or, as her mother liked to call it, "observing" them.

Amarynth expected to hear a description of their goings-on, perhaps acted out with wild gesticulation — a staple of every visit with her mother.

This did not happen this time. Bella spun around in her chair to face Amarynth. Her eyes widened.

"Why didn't you tell me that you're suspended from work?" Bella Watson said. "Did you think I wouldn't find out? I may not get out much, but news travels to me. You know this. You had to know that I'd find out sooner or later that you got suspended."

Amarynth shook her head. "I wasn't keeping it from you, Mom. Honest. I didn't think to tell you. I wasn't sure you'd even care."

Bella scoffed. "You didn't think I'd care?" She shook her head.

Amarynth wasn't sure what to say to that.

"How are you holding up? It must be awful," Bella said, her voice softer now.

"It's not so bad. I could use a break. I've been out straight with that job for so long, I'm not even sure who I am anymore outside of it. Maybe it won't be so bad. I can…" Amarynth thought for a moment. What *was* she going to do anyway? She'd only been suspended for a few weeks, and up until this point, there had always been something to do, a backlog of tasks from the past that she'd pushed off because she was too busy.

And then there had been helping Penny out, a favor that had sprung up at exactly the right time, at the moment she ran out of other things to do.

What was she going to do next?

"They so mistreat you there," her mother said, snapping her out of her thoughts.

"It's not so bad, Mom," Amarynth said. "It's interesting work making the connections that help the rest of the team solve crime. I feel like I'm making a difference."

"It kills me to have you working there, you know that?" her mother said. "Absolutely kills me. I feel like such a bad mother."

"Aw, Mom, stop. You're not a bad mother at all. I consider myself very lucky in that department," Amarynth replied.

This made Bella Watson smile, but she would not be dissuaded from finishing her line of argument. "I thought you were insane when you wanted to go work there, you know."

Amarynth nodded. "I remember."

"Still do. I still think it's insane," Bella said. "But do you remember what I did? What I did when you wanted to work at PsyOps?"

"Yeah," Amarynth said. "You got them to take me, even though they didn't want to."

"Well, there are *always* exceptions," Bella said, "especially if you know the right people."

Amarynth frowned. Her mother's connections were eternally handy. That much was hard to deny. But it was hard to pretend it was fair that she benefited so much from them. And it frankly had a way of making her feel like she wouldn't be able to make it on her own if she were forced to operate on a level playing field like nearly everyone else.

"Anyway, it's a dumb rule, isn't it? Requiring some silly test to be admitted into PsyOps," her mother said.

"I dunno," Amarynth replied. "Seems to me that the Department of Psychic Operations would want to confirm its psychic detectives are... y'know... actually *psychic*."

"Well, if the Comprehensive Perceptive Battery were a good way to measure that, then maybe you'd have a point." Bella sighed. "As it is, it's a crapshoot. There are so many false negatives on that damn test. It doesn't test for all types of intuitives. It certainly doesn't test for... well, whatever your gift is, honey."

Amarynth bristled uncomfortably.

"But it's not just the CPB, is it? Someone gets lost in every test. That's the trouble with basing everything on standardized testing," Bella continued. "I just wish I could have pulled the strings to send you where your cousins all go."

"Honestly, Mom, I don't mind," Amarynth said. Because she didn't. She wasn't eager to go to work at a research institute or be shuffled off to any of the other places they sent the psychic kids of wealthy people, the ones who largely managed to evade the discrimination and heartbreak that generally met intuitives of lesser means. "At least at PsyOps, I'm making a difference."

"It's what I wanted for you, but you were born out of wedlock," Amarynth's mother continued, as though Am hadn't spoken at all, "and that's a bridge too far for most of these snobs."

"That's the other thing I wanted to talk to you about, Mom," Amarynth said.

Bella pursed her lips together. "Oh?"

"I wanted to talk about Dad," Amarynth replied.

Bella frowned. "Why would you want to talk about him?"

"It came up at work, Mom. That Viv and I have the same father," Amarynth explained.

"Oh," Bella said cringing. "Well, that answers the last question I had."

"What do you mean, Mom?" Amarynth asked.

"Well, I knew who your father was of course. I just didn't know for sure that he was also Viv's father. I had my suspicions. But you knew, didn't you, sweetie?" Bella said.

Amarynth nodded.

"Just like you know everything else. You've always been my little smartie," Bella replied. "I know you get frustrated sometimes, that you can't say everything that's in that head of yours. But one day you will. Those who are the most afraid to speak are the ones with the most powerful voices."

Amarynth blushed, embarrassed. She shook her head. "I don't think that's always true."

"And you would know, wouldn't you?" Bella replied, smiling. "Anyway, it's a slap in the face knowing that Viv is your father's kid, too. And it bothers me that you're having to deal with it at work," Bella admitted. "It makes me angry that people are talking about this at all. I was hoping that no one would ever know. I don't even like to think about that miserable woman."

"Viv?" Amarynth asked.

Bella shook her head. "No, not Viv. Her mother, Tender Lee. She stole him from me, you know. Stole your father, had her way with him, and then discarded him when someone richer came along. I knew she'd had a kid, and if I followed the timing back, it looked an awful lot like the kid could be his. But with Tender, you never knew. She was... popular, you could say."

"Was?" Amarynth said. "You talk about her like she's dead. She's locked up, but the last thing I knew, she was still alive."

Bella shook her head. "Alive's a bit of a stretch. You don't lock up a woman like Tender Lee in the Black Square program and call that living. No, for someone like her, life behind bars isn't a life at all. And anyway, she's dead to me, so what's the difference?"

Companionate Echoes

Amarynth turned the key, and the door to her luxury high-rise apartment swung open.

Her parakeet Tesla squawked to welcome her.

"Yes, yes, Tesla, I'm home. I love you, too," Amarynth called across the apartment to his cage. As her home was largely bare of furnishings, her voice echoed in a familiar way as she spoke.

When Amarynth had first moved in, she had considered purchasing more belongings to deaden the sound, but she'd soon discovered she liked the echo. Even though it was an indicator of emptiness, the echo had a way of accomplishing the opposite, of making it feel momentarily on some deep reptilian level that someone else lived there, aside from an exhausted introvert and a parakeet.

That echo was someone who only spoke when she did. Someone who slept when she did, ate when she did. The echo never hovered over her while she cooked in her tiny kitchen nor did it block whatever drawer she needed to open next.

An echo was like having a roommate but without any of the downsides of having a roommate.

"Is it though?" Amarynth said aloud, shaking her head as the question reverberated back at her.

Tesla was still squawking his greeting, and his tweets bounced off the bare walls and floors, making it sound like an army of birds heralded her arrival.

"In ancient Greece, you could have scared off an invading army that way," Amarynth said to Tesla. "Impersonating a mob of birds."

She walked over to his cage and opened the door. Eagerly, Tesla crawled onto her hand. She strode to the window and looked down at the great view of Cambria Square. The towering apartment complex she stood in bore the name Cambria, as did nearly everything else in this immediate vicinity. She had heard it said that her neighborhood was named after somewhere in New York City, the handiwork of a transplant to Skinner and the Psychic State who wanted to bring a touch of big-city class to what had previously been a frontier outpost. That was of course before Skinner had gotten a boost from new money and a bigger boon in the form of the psychic explosion, which had brought cheap specialized labor found nowhere else in the world — or at least not with this frequency.

It was certainly an anomaly, Cambria Square, a throng of amenities and high-class living arrangements that were completely unaffordable by intuitive residents who lived less than a mile away in the psychic-dense area of the city. Many of the local establishments boasted of their independence of psychic labor, advertising that many of their employees were actually normals, and the prices often reflected that.

Still, Amarynth knew, beyond a doubt, that plenty of intuitives worked in these psychic-free businesses, just in the backrooms where public customers couldn't see them.

Every day that Amarynth took the elevator up to her apartment, she smirked, knowing that they had at least one psychic living in Cambria Towers, imagining the disgust of her psychophobic neighbors were they ever to find out. Not that she saw much of her neighbors. Even though Cambria Towers had hundreds of residents, it was rare that she saw more than a few on any given day and usually only briefly in passing. Whoever had planned the building had designed it in a way that cleverly staggered the entrance and egress points and spaced the units well enough apart that many times it felt to Amarynth like only a few other souls lived in the entire building.

She supposed that was part of the luxury. The illusion that you owned everything instead of only a small piece.

It was supposed to feel like New York City, she thought as Tesla peered at the window and sang a little song to his reflection in the glass. But sometimes the word Cambria made her think of the Cambrian Period, that portion of ancient history when evolution exploded on Earth, when life had gone from tiny single-celled organisms to sea life that was still primitive by modern standards but a far cry from protists.

"What do you think, my little dinosaur?" Amarynth asked Tesla, who was still whistling at himself. "Is this the place where it all happens? Is this where life changes forever?"

Her own voice echoed back at her.

That night she had the dream again. The one she'd had so many times.

Within the dream, she'd wake up and walk through her empty apartment in the dark, but as soon as she got to the window next to the bird cage, the lights would all turn on at once.

And as she looked out the window, she'd see it: A contiguous mass of buildings and platforms connecting them, like a giant city of ropes and bridges threading through a forest. Except the trees were modern edifices, and the platforms were industrial grade, sturdier stuff, reminiscent of the stacked highways that were becoming so popular in Skinner these days, looping over and under each other, reaching a depth of four or even five through the metro.

As Amarynth looked out her window and peered down, she could see several levels of roads and buildings leading all the way to the ground. As she looked out and across, she could see the sprawl reaching, ever-connected, as far as the eye could see.

And she knew, without a doubt, that it reached all over the planet, that everything was now connected, woven together tightly in an urban blanket that covered the Earth.

It was a planetwide city. There was no space anymore between settlements. No space anymore between individuals. Everything was connected.

She and everyone else were finally living in the ecumenopolis.

The sky burned with an angry dusty-pink papaya haze.

When she awoke from her dream, she at first thought someone was in bed with her. But it was only the scent of an oversized shirt she'd fallen asleep wearing.

She knew better than to admit it to anyone else, but she had come up with many tactics to cope with loneliness throughout her life, ones that would sound downright strange to other people.

It had started when she was very young. Her mother Bella Watson was a great many things — bright, vivacious, funny, lively. But there was one thing she was not interested in doing: Going outside and exploring the world.

When Amarynth was very young, she hadn't known anything different. She certainly hadn't yet learned the important word she would learn later — *agoraphobia*. No, when Am was little, she'd assumed everyone's mother was the way her mom was. She thought that other families didn't go outside either.

Slowly but surely, however, she'd figured out differently. Some of it had come from the books she read voraciously. A little came from television. And even more insights were gleaned from her later interrogations of the staff that tended to their estate, who unwittingly showed Amarynth glimpses of lives that didn't involve hiding away from perceived danger that never showed up.

But before all that had happened, Amarynth had assumed that her loneliness and desire to go outside and meet other people were unusual. And she'd worked hard to find ways to make staying away from others more bearable.

The echo was one trick that had served her well. Thrift store clothing was another. Because no matter how many times you washed a used garment, thrift store clothes tended to smell indefinitely, however faintly, like their previous owners.

So as she lay in bed in a giant secondhand shirt, there was a moment when she confused the previous owner with a bed partner as she came to from her nightmare, and her anxiety accordingly dissipated.

However, when she spotted the empty space next to her, her stomach plummeted in response.

It had been a foolish idea to buy such a large bed, she thought bitterly. A moment of lunacy. A decision born of the kind of hope that can get you in trouble when it gets dashed over and over again.

The   Psychic   Phenomenon   &   Proxy Ecumenopolitan Structure

The ecumenopolis is a theoretical construct in which all the world's population centers are essentially connected — if not directly by one municipal government and set of governing bodies, then in spirit.

In the ecumenopolis, no rural, unsettled areas exist. The world is one contiguous settlement.

It will be quite some time before a proper ecumenopolitan structure is upon us, even going by the most aggressive estimates of population growth and presuming that the world can bear that burden.

However, some have argued that a proxy one will emerge soon.

The psychic phenomenon—and the prevalence of telepaths — have eroded the normal interpersonal boundaries that kept humans separated for thousands of years.

We are all connected. Or will be soon enough.

from The Urbane Planner by Ambrogino Boccaccio

Love in the Time of Ennui and Overjustification Effect

Somebody's boring me, I think it's me.

-Dylan Thomas

"I don't drink it myself, but one thing I've learned is you never mess with a person's coffee," the barista said.

Smart young woman, Amarynth noted. Especially today.

This wasn't a normal coffeehouse visit. It was a desperate attempt to have meaning and purpose again.

The barista helped Am wrangle her other supplies to a table by the window on the second floor. Amarynth liked the height since it made her feel like she was the queen of all she surveyed. Well, maybe not the queen. The queen's scribe. Cataloging all her citizens as though they were possessions.

In any event, being on the second floor gave her a terrific view of people that wasn't easy for them to return, due to an architectural outcropping that obscured the street view of elevated customers enjoying their drinks.

Or sipping on them tentatively as they wrote on laptops. Or *tried* to write on their laptops, as Amarynth was doing now.

She'd expected for the going to be tough, going into this writing session.

There were two kinds of people in the world, Amarynth had learned: People who were good with actions and people who were good with words.

She'd learned that someone who expressed themselves well with words likely knew very little.

Even if it were frustrating at times that she could never find the words to explain what she knew to others (and it certainly was), she was an action sort of person. Unquestionably competent.

Most of the time this tendency was quite advantageous. Life posed few challenges for her. She could see what needed to be done as clearly as a skilled player could see the position of pieces on a chessboard.

It came with a cost, however, one that she paid whenever she needed to convince other people she knew what she was doing.

That was how she'd ended up in this coffeehouse in the first place. Cambria. Not Cambria Café, not Cambria Coffeehouse. But Cambria, named for the neighborhood like the rest of the surrounding businesses, but unlike those others, the name didn't expound. Cambria, just Cambria. She'd seen this café many times but had never come in, rushing to work at the Department of Psychic Operations, as a Connections Agent. Amarynth loved her job at PsyOps — mostly. What stress she did have came from her coworkers, from their inability to take what she knew on faith. From their perpetual insistence to be shown the receipts, have a path traced from one fact to another. A process that often wasted valuable time and resources.

How could she explain to them that the right answers frequently popped into her head with no explanation?

"Show me your work," they said, like teachers grading an exam and giving separate credit for the final product and the calculation it took to create it.

What did you do when there was none?

In the early days of her position, Amarynth had manufactured a path there, reversed engineered how someone else might conceivably get there.

But after a few years, and once her caseload reached critical mass, she stopped doing it. She'd discovered that the deception and extrapolation were harder than making the actual deductions.

And it had all come crashing down on her last case, her first brush with beating feet as part of the detective force. Amarynth had left her causality board behind, and she and her colleague Detective Viv Lee had been pursuing a serial arsonist. Mistakes were made. Amarynth was professionally sanctioned as fallout.

And now here she was on involuntary suspension.

Not her ideal picture of funemployment. But hey. It could be worse.

Don't say that, Amarynth thought. *Don't even think it.*

Every time a person says or thinks that it could be worse, it's like holding a door open to fate, inviting things to become worse.

And fate's an awfully good listener.

"That's why you work in a coffeeshop, isn't it?" Amarynth said suddenly to the barista. "Because you don't drink coffee, I mean."

The barista startled. A bit of an overreaction, but it made sense to Amarynth.

"You know," the barista said, "I believe you're the first customer who has ever said that to me. Normally, people are confused that I work in a coffeehouse and don't drink coffee."

Amarynth shook her head. "Doing something for a living has a way of taking the fun out of it. They say to do what you love, but that's the surest way to hate your job and ruin a hobby."

"Overjustification effect," the barista murmured.

"I'm sorry?" Amarynth said.

"Oh, no, I'm sorry," the barista replied. "I'm a psychology major. Been studying really hard. Sometimes I just end up talking about what I'm studying when it comes up in conversation with people. It's almost like responding to flashcards. I really need to stop. I know it's annoying. Sorry."

"Don't be," Amarynth said. "I just didn't quite catch what you said is all."

The barista smiled. "Overjustification effect," she said. "It's a phenomenon they found in research where people who are rewarded for what they do come to enjoy doing it less. So if you start to do something professionally and you're paid money for it, you'll naturally become less passionate about it."

"Huh," Amarynth replied. "It has a name."

"It does."

"Do you?" Amarynth said.

The barista laughed. "Leigh," she said, pointing to her nametag. "Leigh Lines."

Amarynth noted that Leigh pronounced her name like "lay" and not like "Lee." She had heard somewhere that Leigh and Lee were interchangeable but apparently not to Leigh. *Lay, lay, lay,* she rehearsed mentally, for she knew all too well the pain of having people call you by the wrong name. She thought of sharing this information but decided that Leigh was likely far past sick of the stress of having an unusual name and the incessant conversations that seemed to follow it, so she tried a different conversational tack.

"Dr. Lines has a nice ring to it," Amarynth said, surprising herself as she did. She'd never been one to socialize with strangers in public. She usually needed structure, a sort of script to interact with people she didn't know — and even that didn't always work. Even the act of ordering food could sometimes fill her with anxiety, depending on the day and the mood of the person taking her order.

But here she was… making small talk. Highly unusual. Amarynth suspected it was because she hadn't been to PsyOps for a while. She considered herself a cactus socially, able to sustain herself on limited interaction for great stretches of time. But she hadn't factored in how much her day job fulfilled those needs.

Perhaps that was what was plaguing all those people who hounded down strangers in the street, ready to tell their life stories to anyone who seemed even remotely interested.

Maybe they were just lonely.

Amarynth opened her mouth and noted with great alarm that she began to tell this practical stranger everything that had happened recently. The recent arson case at PsyOps, the irregular thoughtography audit, her suspension, and the incredible ennui that came now that she didn't have her day job to go to.

"It sounds like you need a new adventure. You need to get out there. Take a few risks. Make connections with other people," Leigh summarized.

Amarynth frowned. "That sounds like a lot of hassle to me."

"Connection is scary but worth the risk," Leigh said.

Amarynth dismissed the comment with her hand. "Maybe. But I think for now I'll just sit here by this window drinking this incredible coffee and eating pastries and trying to write."

"Oooo, trying to write what?" Leigh asked.

Amarynth eyed her suspiciously. "No one wants to hear about what writers are working on."

"I do," Leigh insisted. "And besides," she added after a beat, "you were kind enough to take an interest in my psych geekery."

"Okay," Amarynth said. "Don't laugh, but… there's a series of poems I've been thinking about writing ever since I was a little girl. I've written them over and over again in my head. Not always in words but more in a blur of abstract concepts. Not exactly images. But more emotions. They've been with me my whole life in one form or another."

"Huh," Leigh said. "That sounds kind of heavy."

Amarynth shrugged. "It's not, but maybe I'm not explaining it well." She frowned. "Goodness knows it wouldn't be the first time."

"Well, try again," Leigh urged her.

"Hm?"

"If it comes out wrong the first time, just try again. It's a writer's prerogative, or so I've heard. There's a guy who comes in here all the time who's always saying it. That writers get infinite tries at getting it right. There are no mess-ups when you're a writer, just rough drafts." Leigh nodded. "The magic, he says, is all in the edit."

"Sounds like quite a guy," Amarynth said.

"He's okay," Leigh said, shrugging. "A little full of himself. But most people are, I guess."

Amarynth thought for a minute. "Okay," she said. "I'll try again." She took a few breaths in, calmed her mind, and then it came to her. "They're letters I've been writing to an imaginary friend."

Leigh smiled. "That sounds pretty neat."

"Thanks," Amarynth said. "I bet it sounds a little crazy."

"Not at all," Leigh said. "You're talking to a psychology major, remember?"

"Who's probably psychoanalyzing me every second."

"Nah," Leigh said, shaking her head. "That's for amateurs. For someone who takes one abnormal psych class and thinks they're an expert. I'm a more serious student than that. The more you learn about psych, the more you realize that a lot of what we experience in our everyday lives isn't objective or unbiased but actively constructed by our minds."

Amarynth nodded.

"Given that, isn't every friendship at least a little imaginary?" Leigh said.

Amarynth laughed. "Can't argue with that."

"Good," Leigh said. "Maybe I should go into law."

Amarynth smiled. "Leigh Lines, Esquire, sounds okay. Maybe not as good as Dr. Lines though."

"Just promise you'll let me read it when you're done," Leigh said, leaving Amarynth to her writing.

Amarynth promised nothing.

```
Gino the Reactionary
by Amarynth Watson

Somewhere along the way,
you understand that there are
a handful of things more
important than money
but that no one
wants to buy them
and all your proselytizing
will only leave you with a bill —

        I don't know how I got here, Gino

Because we get more
rugged as we go along
because every minute
we come closer to bursting into full light
— into brilliance —
because I've learned to look ahead and
behind simultaneously

        because there's no easy way to break
the bad news — because I don't want to give
```

```
up the only good thing that's been granted
me—

Gino,
     Some days I walk through public places
and everyone recognizes me
and I wonder how they came to own that part
of me
       their memory of me
```

As soon as she was done writing that first poem, Amarynth knew for certain that she wouldn't be showing Leigh, or anyone else, what she was working on.

When she'd been writing, it had felt to her like the unfiltered truth. Like everything she'd struggled to say but never quite could.

But as she read the words back, she knew that what was there would never communicate to anyone else what she'd actually felt. And that reality deeply depressed her.

"Well, it's only a first draft," she found herself saying quietly to the lit screen and the neat little café table covered with coffee and pastries. Her voice didn't echo back at her.

She stared out the window.

She could always try again.

Leigh walked behind her, startling her. Amarynth reflexively covered the poem on the screen with her hands.

"I promise I won't peek," Leigh said. "I realized after I went back to the espresso bar that I forgot to give you this."

She handed Amarynth a piece of paper.

Amarynth studied it. "A writers' group?"

"I promised the rough draft guy I'd spread the word," Leigh explained.

"Thank you," Amarynth said, placing the slip of paper in her laptop bag. She half-expected she'd never see it again. Her laptop bag had a mysterious habit of swallowing objects. Amarynth sometimes found herself wondering where they'd wandered off to — but not too hard. She kept track of the objects she cared about, after all.

And a handout advertising a writers' group didn't make the cut.

This was why Amarynth was quite surprised when she later found herself standing at that very address trying to talk herself into going inside.

"You can do it," Amarynth said. "Just walk in and sit in the back of the room like it's no big deal."

The group was practically over, she reminded herself. All the pressure was off. It would be so easy to step inside.

Oh yeah? Her anxiety answered. *That's exactly why you shouldn't go inside.* Because there was no sense of even attending now. She'd missed everything. Better to leave and come back another day.

She had just about surrendered to her anxiety's wish to flee in the other direction when the door swung open and almost hit her.

And just like that, she came face to face with one of the most attractive men she'd ever seen. He had perfect olive skin, dark intense eyes, and something soft and boyish about his face that made her feel safe. She felt as though part of her recognized him, although she was pretty sure she'd never seen him before.

Oh no, Amarynth thought. *I'm doomed.*

All the great tragedies of her life had started the same way — in a harmless conversation with a strictly platonic acquaintance — until the light caught their eye in just the right way.

There's a reason why cartoonists always include the glint in a person's eye. That's the nexus of personal power, the place at which a person's soul can snatch your own.

As soon as she saw him, she knew something very important, with that strange sense of hers that told her what was going to happen but never provided any evidence. She knew that this man was going to change her life forever. And that somehow he'd been with her all along, even if she hadn't realized it.

But at that moment, poetry wasn't what sprang from her lips. "Oh shit," she said aloud.

The man cocked his head, a confused expression spreading across his face.

"I'm sorry," Amarynth said. "You just surprised me."

"Were you coming to the group?" he asked.

"I'm just leaving," Amarynth replied.

"Well, if you're leaving," he said, "then maybe you could leave with me."

Normally, such an offer would raise Amarynth's hackles in an instant. She'd quickly rebuff him. Fabricate an excuse. Run in the other direction.

But she found herself stopping to consider his offer.

"Oh, why not?" she said. "It's been a weird week."

He laughed. "And it's only going to get weirder."

"What do you mean?" Amarynth said.

He shrugged. "I get these hunches sometimes. I know things but don't know how I know them."

Amarynth gasped.

"Right, I'm a freak show. Fine," he said.

"No," Amarynth replied. "Well, if you're a freak show, you're not the only one in it."

She walked alongside him on the sidewalk, and as she did, she found herself sharing again. Oversharing probably.

I have to get back to work before I completely lose it.

She realized suddenly they were standing outside of the Cambria café. "I was thinking we could get coffee," he said.

Amarynth beamed. "I would love that."

They entered and got in line. Leigh wasn't working tonight. Amarynth found herself relieved. If this coffee... date (oh my God, was this a date?) went badly and she struck out, it was probably better to do so without an audience who would remember to console her the next day in a way that was uncomfortable for both of them.

The barista at the register was a younger man with flagrant acne and rather large ears. He looked a little annoyed at everything Amarynth's companion said.

"And what name should I write on the cup?" he prompted.

"Am," Amarynth and her companion said at once.

"Wait," Amarynth said. "My name's Amarynth. What's your name?"

"Ambrogino," the man replied. "Tell you what," he said to the barista, "just write 'Gino' on mine."

Gino? Amarynth thought. It was the same name as her imaginary childhood friend, the one in the poem she'd just been writing. The kind of coincidence that made a meeting feel like destiny.

Oh get a grip, Watson, Amarynth scolded herself mentally. *Stop looking for signs that he's the one.*

Besides, she reminded herself, this could be yet another manifestation of her gifts. Perhaps whatever gave her the accurate hunches she always had was also responsible for this flash of intuition.

It wasn't impossible, was it? Odd perhaps, as she typically never knew things so far into the future. Typically, her intuition was best at grokking the present or the past.

But it's not impossible, she told herself. *And a lot more likely than "destiny."*

"Am and Gino, got it," the male barista said, clearly unimpressed.

"Well," Gino said, "nice to meet another member of the club of people with long names that are impossible to spell or say."

"They're not impossible," Amarynth protested. "People just don't give a shit."

Gino laughed.

"Seriously," Amarynth said. "Do you know how many times people have asked me if Am is short for Amber? Or Amelia? Do you know how many people have called me Amethyst? For *years.*"

"Probably the same number who have called me Amadeus."

Amarynth snorted. "That's awful."

"Oh yeah?" Gino tested her. "What's my name?"

"Oh c'mon," Amarynth said. "I would look like such an asshole for forgetting already."

"Well?" Gino prompted her.

Amarynth pretended to forget. "Hmmm..." she said, scratching her chin.

Gino frowned.

"It's Ambrogino obviously," she said, laughing. "It's a beautiful name. Like I'd forget."

He beamed at her. "Thanks," he said. "It means 'ever-living one.'"

"That's a lot better than being named after a grain, I suppose," Amarynth said. "Although amaranth literally means 'undying flower.'" *But my name is a misspelling of it,* she thought but didn't say aloud. She figured she'd let him find that out later, the first time he saw her full name written out.

Later? She caught herself. It was strange, but part of her fully expected to know Gino for a very long time.

Gino, too, apparently as after they got their orders and retired to their table, he raised his latte cup in a toast and said, "To the start of something long and beautiful."

While love at first sight is treated by many skeptics as something fictional, a pure invention of a romance industry keen to sell products, it turns out that there is a scientific basis to the phenomenon.

However, it's worth noting that what strikes an individual as "love at first sight" is instead a combination that research has demonstrated is the following:

A quick assessment of that person's physical attractiveness (a process which takes a little over a tenth of a second on average), with a particular focus on their face.

A subconscious survey of their reproductive compatibility— based on our perception of that person's health, their facial symmetry, and their waist-to-hip ratio.

The feeling that we have a lot in common with them. This is quite an important consideration for long-term relationship compatibility, in that we tend to have better, longer-lasting, more fulfilling relationships with people when they are similar to us. While opposites may attract our *attention*, it is similarity that drives compatibility. Familiarity plus novelty is an intoxicating combination, to be sure.

And of course, all this boils down to what underscores "love at first sight" — a good first impression of someone else.

These assessments are a subconscious series of comparisons that take place in a split second, well beyond the speed and level of our conscious awareness, so that those processes are largely invisible to the person falling in love.

Instead, the lover walks away from the meeting with the subjective experience of "love at first sight," which as it turns out is not a mystical awakening or the product of destiny but complex math done at breakneck speed by parts of us that do not communicate explicitly with the rest of our brain.

-Dr. Leigh Lines, "The Empirical Basis of Love"

That is how Amarynth knew — in a split second — that Gino was right for her. Very right for her.

She knew it in a place beyond knowing. It would take a lot to change her mind.

When Amarynth awoke the next morning in her giant bed, she thought for a moment that she saw Gino's naked body outstretched, tangled in her sheets.

But no, she was alone.

Perhaps it was scent that had confused her once again. He had insisted on walking her to the lobby of her building, and as he said his goodbye, he had leaned in for a kiss that caused every pleasure neuron in her body to fire at once.

She wasn't sure how long the kiss lasted, but it wasn't long enough. Afterward, he'd simply winked and walked out of the lobby out onto the street. But his scent had stayed behind. Something sweet and spicy and oddly familiar. It reminded her of being a child, of having no worries.

And it lingered. It was there the next morning. And for a moment, she thought he was as well.

But no, she was alone. Just thinking of him.

She picked up her phone and scowled at it. No calls. No texts.

Well, he'd only just left her, after all... but still...

If he felt even a fraction of what she'd felt last night, she would have expected at least a "good morning" text.

It was practically afternoon now, Amarynth noticed with some embarrassment. How had she slept so long? She never slept this late.

Perhaps this was what funemployment did to a person. It had a way of eroding your routines.

Amarynth supposed this was the appeal of it for a lot of people. They liked that you didn't have to set an alarm. You didn't have to get up at any particular time.

Because no one was waiting for you. You had no obligations.

It was a seductive premise, especially when you were stuck in the middle of another frustrating work week, and it seemed like no matter what you did, it was the wrong move. Where circumstances double-bound you, created no-win situations.

It was at those times that she'd fantasized about being free of restrictions. Free of routine.

But now that it was starting to happen, she noted with great alarm that she was beginning not to feel free but unmoored. Drifting. Listless.

She picked up her phone and scrolled through the contacts list, pausing briefly to hover over Gino's entry. No, she couldn't call him yet. It was still too soon.

It was a short list, she realized. Sighing, she selected one of the only other numbers on the list.

"What do you want?" Viv said sharply.

"Hey Viv, can I speak to Penny?" Amarynth asked.

Viv scoffed audibly into the phone. She didn't respond, but the next thing Am knew, she was talking to Penny.

"Hey, Amarynth, everything okay?"

"Oh yeah, everything's great," Am replied. "So… I was wondering… could you meet me at The Afterlife in half an hour?"

"Hey Viv," Penny said, "I'm gonna go out shopping for a bit. Is that okay?"

Amarynth heard Viv say something in a grumbly voice back to Penny, although exactly what she said wasn't intelligible.

"That'll work," Penny said to Am.

As a store, The Afterlife knew it was extra — and that was what made their whole schtick work. They were in on the joke, both telling that joke themselves and exaggerating it even further on each retelling with iterative absurdity.

Whoever owned the place had peppered the décor with visual references to Heaven and Hell: angel wings, halos, horns, fire, and clouds.

Their sales and promotions, too, were similarly appointed. "Heavenly Savings," "A Hell of a Find."

It was tacky, and if they'd done things halfway, it would have been off-putting. The wrong kind of camp. But they'd gone all-in on the kitsch, so it worked like a charm.

The left half of the building's face featured a burning Hellscape populated by demons. The right half was a grand ivory celestial palace mired in clouds, complete with pearly gates and ethereal angels strumming harps. Amarynth waited on the sidewalk in front of the building, standing approximately at the point where the two halves met. *I guess that means I'm hanging out in Purgatory*, she mused. *Typical of me.*

Finally, she spotted Penny, who was power-walking towards her in a form-fitting pink pantsuit. As Penny neared, Amarynth noted that Penny's pants were starting to strain a bit in two places — around the belly and across the seat.

"Have you told them yet?" Amarynth asked.

"Hi to you, too," Penny replied.

"Yes, good morning, isn't it a lovely day, et cetera," Am said. "Do Viv and Karen know you're pregnant?"

Penny shook her head.

"When are you going to tell them?" Am pressed.

Penny shrugged. "I dunno. I keep waiting for the right opportunity. When it comes, I'll know."

"And you've figured out what you want to do," Amarynth said.

It wasn't a question, but Penny nodded in response anyway. "I have. I think I've always known. I had a dream that told me I have to protect the children. I think that means I'm supposed to keep the baby."

"The children?" Amarynth asked. "That's weird."

"What do you mean?"

"Well, if your dream were some sort of prophecy, it'd be a strange one. Because the dream would tell you that you need to protect the child. Singular. Your dream wouldn't tell you to protect the children, plural. That makes me think that the message isn't about your pregnancy."

Penny shrugged. "Well, dreams are approximate, Amarynth. Visions can be hazy. Viv is always telling me that, that visions usually aren't literal. They're analogies, require interpretation. They're more like poetry, less like a news report."

Amarynth nodded.

"Anyway, is *that* why you asked to meet me at my favorite thrift store? To interrogate me about my reproductive choices?"

Amarynth shook her head. "I've known all along you were going to carry to term," she admitted.

"Of course you did," Penny replied, looking annoyed. Because of her gifts, sometimes Amarynth really could be a walking "I told you so."

"That's actually why I asked you here. You're gonna need maternity clothes," Amarynth said.

Penny brightened. Then her face fell. "Well, it was nice of you to think of me, but I can't exactly afford to buy a whole new wardrobe, Amarynth," she said in a small, pained voice.

Amarynth waved her hand in the air dismissively. "Penny, don't worry about that. I've got it."

And besides, she thought, *this gives me an opportunity to gush to someone about Gino.*

"Amarynth," Penny said sternly, "I can't keep taking all this charity."

"Look," Amarynth countered, "I'm gonna be a half aunt. I can't exactly let you walk around naked for nine months."

"Probably more like eight," Penny corrected her, "but thank you."

They strolled around the store together, Penny hard at work hunting for potential outfits. It was only a few minutes before she had what seemed like half a rack draped over one of her arms.

"I don't plan on getting them all," she told Amarynth. "I just want to have a lot of options in the fitting room."

"Penny, it's fine," Amarynth assured her. "I really don't mind."

"It's just that... I don't know what size I am anymore," Penny continued, as though Am had said nothing at all, "and I suppose I should probably get them a bit bigger, leave room to grow. I don't want you to have to do this again for me a few months from now."

Amarynth grinned as Penny continued to carry on. It seemed to Am like Penny was in one of those moods where she just had certain things she had to say to get them out of her system. It didn't much matter what the other person said. It was like this sometimes at work, too, Amarynth thought, when they were working a case together, part of the same team.

Sometimes Penny just needed to talk it out. And when she got that way, she was a truly terrible listener. Scratch that. She wasn't a listener at all.

Well, there was no harm in it. Amarynth waited until the mood passed.

Abruptly, like Penny always did when she got into one of these moods, she caught herself in the act and apologized. "But just listen to me," Penny said. "I've been going on and on about me. I haven't even stopped to ask you how you're doing. How is the Great Funemployment Staycation panning out anyway?'

Amarynth grinned. She couldn't remember the last time she had an answer to a question about her life that she was eager to share with someone else. She hesitated for a few moments, savoring this rare feeling of anticipation.

As she did, she wondered at the rarity. It wasn't like life had been terribly unpleasant to her. Not at all. But without this latest development, without Gino and passion and the promise of what could be coming next — what that small voice within her that never led her astray told her was *surely* coming next—well, it all had been a bit featureless and empty, hadn't it?

Not unpleasant. Certainly not stressful —particularly as she came from a family of means, one of the Four Families that pulled a great many strings in Psychic State society, even if from a disgraced wing.

But empty. So empty that many things echoed in a way that surely would have been unsettling to most people who would visit her life — but echoes that she had grown accustomed to. Companionate echoes that she had, perhaps, mistaken for company.

Finally, Amarynth opened her mouth and replied, "It's absolutely wonderful, Penny. I've met someone. A man."

Penny let out a wild shriek that caused Amarynth to startle.

"Amarynth Watson, are you shitting me?" Penny challenged.

Am shook her head.

"I *have* to know all about him," Penny insisted.

"His name is Gino," Amarynth said.

"Oooo," Penny replied. "Hot name. Very macho."

Amarynth grinned. She eagerly spilled what little she did know about Gino. It didn't take very long.

Penny prompted her for more. Amarynth realized uncomfortably that there was a lot she didn't know about him.

"Well, that's fine," Penny assured her. "That's part of the fun of meeting someone new, isn't it? You get to learn all the things about them you don't know."

Amarynth nodded tentatively.

"I'm so happy for you, Am," Penny beamed, putting her massive haul into the shopping cart that Amarynth had procured and was pushing as they walked through the store. "I really am." She strode over to a rack loaded down with dresses and browsed through them.

"Aha!" Penny declared. She pulled out a low-cut satin royal blue dress trimmed with black lace. "You have to try this one on," she insisted.

"Me?" Amarynth said. "But this trip is for you."

"Well, this dress wouldn't be for you, would it? It'd be for Gino. It'd be criminal to leave here without finding a little something for you to wear for him."

Amarynth blushed. "Penny, I'm not like that. I'm not... seductive."

"Well, you could be," Penny replied. "You never know until you try."

And improbably Amarynth later found herself in an adjacent dressing room staring at her reflection as she wore that very garment, astonished at how well it flattered her. "Penny, are you sure you're not a precog?" Amarynth called to her over the dressing room partition.

"Doesn't take a precog to tell you that you'd look good in clothes that actually suit you," Penny called back.

Amarynth grinned and changed back into her normal clothes. She sat in a chair and waited as Penny paraded out in the outfits she liked, putting on an impromptu early maternity fashion show for her.

Amarynth chuckled at the throw pillow Penny had shoved into position over her belly "for maximum realism," as she put it.

When they arrived at the register, Penny fretted about which clothes to put back. "It's a stupid problem, I know, but there were too many things that look good."

"Not stupid at all," Amarynth said. "It's usually harder to pick between good and good than good and bad." She grinned. "Luckily, you don't have to pick." She put the entire haul up on the counter.

"No, no, I can't let you get all of that," Penny argued.

"Penny," Amarynth said, giving her a stern look, "I know what I'm doing."

"Alright," Penny said, "you can cover this, just so long as you get this, too." She placed the royal blue dress on top of her haul.

Amarynth laughed.

"For Gino," Penny said firmly.

"Okay," Amarynth said, still laughing. "For Gino."

Overcrowding and the Calhoun Studies

Every aspiring urban planner must contend with the risk of behavioral sink. Behavioral sink was first described in a series of experiments performed by ethologist John Calhoun on a population of rats.

These experiments simulated what were essentially "rat utopias," in which all rodent residents were sheltered in enclosed spaces that provided unlimited access to food and water.

Uncontrolled population growth soon followed.

Calhoun found that social pathology followed as well, as the overcrowding set in. This spiral was known as "behavioral sink." In Calhoun's experiments, infant mortality spiked to as high as 96 percent.

Female rats miscarried at higher rates and died more often during childbirth, and rat mothers who did survive childbirth were observed to be worse at caring for their offspring.

Not to be outdone, male rats resorted to cannibalism.

Calhoun later replicated this experiment using mice instead of rats. Results were similar. Societal collapse ensued.

As society moves towards a state of heightened physical and mental connection, overcrowding and behavioral sink remain persistent concerns. The lessons from the Calhoun experiments haunt many an urban planner.

There is much controversy among our ranks as to whether the ecumenopolis is a holy grail or a poisoned chalice. Nonetheless, with population density increasing every

day, continued vigorous birth rates, and mental privacy
a near-impossibility in this age of psychic expansion, it
would seem we are tasked with tackling this inexorable
quest, regardless of our feelings on the matter.

from The Urbane Planner by Ambrogino Boccaccio

Amarynth was tucked away in her empty apartment staring at
her phone screen, which in an act of flagrant betrayal still showed
no notifications, when the eleven o'clock nightly news began.

"We begin tonight's broadcast with troubling reports from
Skinner County Health Department."

Troubling? Amarynth turned up the volume with the remote.

"Earlier reports downplayed the severity of this phenomenon,
but the latest information coming from area hospitals paints a
more troubling picture of a dangerous new illness."

"Troubling, troubling, troubling," Amarynth said, shifting her
weight on the bed. "Someone needs to buy this newsroom a
thesaurus."

A montage played of earlier clips. A quick flurry of headlines
popped onto the screen as Amarynth yawned so hard her eyes
watered. *Flu season numbers unexpectedly high.* And then *Skinner
hospitals showing unusual admission rates.*

No cause for alarm, say health officials.

When the series was shown together in a sequence, it was...
well, troubling. For lack of a better word. But each of the reports
would have seemed harmless in isolation, nothing too out of the
ordinary. "Ah," Amarynth said. "Guess that's how I missed this
until now."

The montage faded. A spokesman from the Health Department
flicked on screen with a chyron below identifying him as such.

"We're seeing an astonishing number of cases of patients being admitted with sensory loss. A number of them have blindness. Others are deaf. Still other patients are reporting anosmia, or loss of smell. The one commonality in all these cases is that the sensory loss is sudden onset. There seems to be no gradual sensory worsening."

"Is that all the patients have in common?" an offscreen voice presumably belonging to a reporter asked.

The spokesman shook his head. "A high number of them are experiencing..." He cleared his throat and looked around him, as though worried he would be overheard.

You're on TV, dude. You have a big audience, Amarynth thought.

"It seems that most of them are developing new psychic powers," the spokesman said.

"Most of them?" the disembodied voice said. "But not all of them?"

"It seems like all of them," the spokesman said. "Although due to psychophobia and general anti-intuitive public sentiment, I wouldn't blame patients for not wanting to admit it."

"Does this mystery condition have a name?" the disembodied voice asked.

"Yes," the spokesman said. "We're calling it psychic-transmitted illness, or PTI for short."

"Psychic-transmitted illness?" the voice said.

The spokesman nodded. "It would seem at this time that everyone who has come down with it had contact with intuitives. Many of the sickest patients were friends with telepaths or worked with them. The disease seems to be spread whenever a psychic connection is formed between two people."

"If that's the case," the off-screen reporter pressed, "then why aren't intuitives sick?"

"That remains to be seen," the health department official said. "I'm sure it's affecting them somehow, but we don't know how yet. For now, it just seems like they're asymptomatic superspreaders of the disease."

Amarynth's stomach fell into her feet.

At that very moment, her phone buzzed. She looked down at a text from Gino.

I just saw the news. Thought of you. Are you okay?

No, Amarynth texted back truthfully.

A mile away on Bell Avenue, Penny sat on the serviceable secondhand couch in the living room of her little house with her two partners, Viv and Karen, on both sides of her, watching the same news report.

"PTI? That's the last thing we need," Viv said. "Another reason for people to hate us."

Karen readjusted her hoodie so that it better covered her face and telescoped her hands back into the sleeves. She crossed her arms and stared at the floor.

Penny rubbed her abdomen reflexively. And though it filled her with dread, she knew it. The time had come. She had to tell them.

"Look," Penny said, "there's no easy way to say this, but I have to tell you something. It's a big something. Actually, it's a couple of big somethings."

Viv sat up straighter. Karen slumped down on the couch.

"Karen, please," Penny said softly. "It's important."

Tentatively, Karen thrust her hands back out and lowered the hood of her sweatshirt. She sighed as she did it. "What is it, Penny?" Karen said. "I'm not sure if I can take more bad news."

"It's not bad news exactly," Penny said. "Although it's gonna mean a lot of things are going to change."

"C'mon, Penny, enough with the hemming and hawing. Out with it," Viv said.

"Okay," Penny said. She nodded resolutely as if to give herself strength. "I'll just say it then."

"Please," Viv urged.

"I'm pregnant," Penny blurted out.

"You're what?!" Karen and Viv both yelled in unison.

"Do not start with that fucking 'jinx, you owe me a Coke' business," Viv warned Karen.

"Wouldn't dream of it," Karen said.

"Penny," Viv said, "how did this happen?"

"It's gonna sound weird," Penny said, "but I don't know."

"We passed weird already. We are somewhere else. Somewhere beyond weird," Karen said.

"I've been trying to let you have your privacy, but honestly, Penny... I don't know if I can just sit here and not ask questions anymore," Viv said. "You ran off without telling us where you were going, and you come back pregnant. You said you went home... but I'm starting to have my doubts. Maybe you went to some clinic where they reversed your sterilization procedure. And then you went and found some guy and... Ugh..."

Penny shook her head. "No, nothing like that."

"Then what happened, Penny? Where the Hell did you run off to?" Viv asked.

"You're not going to believe this," Penny said, "but Hell is right. That's it exactly. I went to Hell."

Viv and Karen sat there, incredulous and slack-jawed, as Penny recounted everything she'd learned about herself and where she came from over the past few months. That she was originally from Hell, a princess of Hell actually, that she'd run away as a child and hidden her memories from herself when she'd plane shifted, wanting a new start on Earth, one where she wasn't the reject daughter who was spoiled rotten for material comforts but starved of respect by emotionally withholding parents.

"Wait," Viv said, once she was finished. "You left something important out."

"Oh?" Penny said, fidgeting nervously, knowing she'd glossed over the part of the tale she was the most embarrassed about, the fact that she'd had to promise to marry the ferryman upon her next return to Hell in order to come back to Earth.

"You didn't say who the father was," Viv said.

"Oh that," Penny said, relieved. "That's because I don't know."

"Penny!" Viv said. "That's ridiculous."

"Only on Earth," Penny said in a small weak voice.

"What's that supposed to mean?" Viv said sharply.

"Life works a little differently in Hell," Penny explained. "In a lot of ways. But particularly when it comes to reproduction." She shook her head. "I wish I'd known before I went there, but I didn't. In Hell, you can become atmospherically pregnant. You don't need to mate like we do here. It's how my mother had me and my twin sister."

Viv and Karen traded confused looks. "You have a twin sister?" Karen said.

Penny nodded. "Although due to planar time dilation, we don't look the same anymore. I appear much older than she does. I grew up, and she's still a little girl." Penny sighed. "I know it all sounds strange, and I honestly don't know if I would believe what I'm telling you unless I'd experienced it myself, but I'm telling you — it's the truth. I don't know why I'm pregnant or how. Just that I am."

Penny rose to her feet. "I'm pregnant, and I'm scared. Because I don't know how I'm going to go to work with a mystery illness all over Skinner, not knowing how it's going to affect my unborn child." Penny walked away from them, stormed up the staircase, and loudly closed the bedroom door.

"What do you think?" Karen asked Viv once Penny had left.

"About what?" Viv replied.

"About Penny's story. Do you think that she's really from Hell and that she went home to see her family, the royal family? Do you think that Hell just knocks people up?"

Viv shrugged. "I dunno," she said. "But the good thing is it doesn't matter."

"It doesn't matter? How do you figure?" Karen asked.

"Well," Viv said, "the way I see it, either Penny is telling the truth, as messed up as it sounds..."

"Or?" Karen prompted.

"Or it isn't true, and she's lying about part or all of it," Viv said. "I know one thing for sure about Penny though."

"What's that?" Karen said.

"If she's lying, it's for a good reason," Viv replied, "so whether it's true or not, I'm choosing to believe her."

"You know, Viv," Karen said, "you can be really gracious sometimes. I underestimate you."

"Most people do," Viv said.

"I guess we'd better start trying to figure out what we're going to do for a nursery," Karen said.

Viv smiled. "Guess so."

"I have a confession to make," Amarynth said. "Something I've never told anyone. The only other person who knows is my mother."

"I'm honored," Gino said. "What's up?"

Amarynth hesitated, swallowed. "I... I don't know my status," she said.

"Really?" Gino replied.

Amarynth nodded.

"But you work at PsyOps, don't you?"

"I do," Amarynth confirmed.

"How is it possible that you don't know if you're psychic? I thought they only let intuitives be PsyOps agents," Gino said.

"Normally, that's the case," Amarynth said. "But my mother... well, she knows people."

"Have you ever been tested?" Gino asked.

Amarynth nodded. "And it said I don't have psychic powers... but for as long as I can remember, I've always been different from other people. I know things they don't. That it's not possible for people to just know."

"But surely you spill psyons," Gino said.

Amarynth shook her head. "No. Negative CPB. No psyons. As far as science is concerned, I'm just like anyone else. It looks like I'm a normal, going by the tests." She frowned. "I know I'm not a normal though."

"Can you keep a secret?" Gino said.

"Better than anyone you know," Amarynth replied.

He laughed. "I don't know my status either."

"What?" Amarynth said.

"I've been tested, sure. Officially, I'm negative, just like you. Which is why I'm not registered, why I don't have a designation." He shrugged. "But I know I'm not a normal either. I can... just tell. Like I can just tell everything else."

"Huh," Amarynth said.

"Although I can't tell one thing, I'll admit," Gino said.

"What's that?" Am replied.

"What I can't work out is why you faked a status to get into PsyOps. Usually, people are faking in the other direction, trying to hide their psychic powers or prevent being registered. Most folks want to escape detection. But you were different. You ran headlong into registration, even if it meant forging the results." Gino shook his head. "Why would you lie to get into a system that's just going to oppress you?"

"Oh, that?" Amarynth said. "That's simple. I know I'm one of them. And I want to make a difference. I don't want to just stand back and watch my people get oppressed."

"Amarynth Watson, you are a better person than I am," Gino observed.

"I-I-I didn't mean—" Amarynth began defensively.

"No, I mean it. You are. Here I am, teaching urban planning at a community college to kids who didn't do the reading and wish I'd just email them the PowerPoints and tell them when to show up for the exam, while you're out there beating the mean streets trying to make life better for people who are suffering," Gino said.

Amarynth shrugged, embarrassed. "Urban planning, huh?" she said, desperate to change the subject.

"That's right."

"What do you think about sprawl?" Amarynth said.

"I think there's plenty of it in Skinner, but you don't need a doctorate to see that. Or to see how it's getting worse. Especially in the Psychic City. There's a secondary kind of sprawl that's inevitable in an age of psychic expansion. A psychic sprawl."

"Psychic sprawl?" Amarynth said.

Gino nodded. "There was a time not too long ago when privacy was available. Sure, not everywhere and not all the time. But so long as you kept certain things to yourself, people never had to know. The information age has brought enough privacy concerns all by itself. There's so much that's in the public realm that's easily accessible, and it's getting worse every day. But that's nothing compared to the lack of privacy that comes with being surrounded by telepaths."

"Like the hive mind in those spooky sci-fi movies?" Amarynth asked.

"Something like that," Gino said, grinning. "But think about it… high population density and a high concentration of individuals who can penetrate that normal barrier, between minds… well… it makes cities dense in a completely new way. In a way, we were due for an epidemic," Gino said.

"How do you figure?"

"A lot of illness is directly linked with population density. The Black Plague, for example, onset at a time when population density, trade, and travel had all exploded. So... if you look at the Psychic Phenomenon as an increase in density of a specific population, then it would follow that you might have a disease arise that takes advantage of it."

"So you see PTI as an inevitability?" Am asked.

Gino nodded. "Not to be alarmist, but while it's the first epidemic predicated on mental connection, it probably won't be the last."

"Boy, Gino," Amarynth said, "you really know how to comfort a girl."

Gino laughed.

"Well, I'm glad that the psychophobes didn't think that far ahead," Am said. "The panic was bad enough in the early years. I can't imagine what they would have done if they'd known something like this was coming — or like, you said, that it was inevitable, given the circumstances. Many normals wanted to preemptively exterminate the psychic population based on gut feels. If they'd had anything concrete to point to, it would have been so much easier to get those gears moving."

Gino considered this. "Sure," he said, but there was something hollow in his tone.

"You don't believe me?"

"Oh, I do," Gino replied. "I'm just uneasy is all."

"Why's that?"

"I think whether the threat is proactive or retroactive that the psychophobes will find a way to argue their point of view. That intuitives don't deserve to exist. That the risk of having them around outweighs the benefits," Gino said. "It's never too late to do something rash out of fear."

Amarynth frowned.

"I saw several signs on the way here. *Know a psychic? Report and register. It's your duty.*" Gino shook his head. "I hadn't seen one of those since the very beginning. Since the early days."

"Back when they were still working out the designations. Before Green Star or Blue River."

Gino nodded. "Or Black Square."

Am shuddered involuntarily at the mere mention of Black Square status. Black Square intuitives were the most restricted class of psychic citizens, deemed too dangerous to society to be part of it and accordingly confined to permanent imprisonment. The Black Square program was quite insular, and even high-level PsyOps agents like Amarynth didn't have access to what went on there, but rumor had it that the State dampened the powers of its residents — except for times when those powers would be useful.

The open secret was the research program, which studied these erratic and dangerous intuitives, with the stated aim of advancing collective knowledge of the Psychic Phenomenon. Some whispered that this was a cover and that the Psychic State was instead developing weapons. This made a lot of sense because the country was young and flanked to the south by Mexico and on all other sides by the United States. Both countries were larger and richer than the Psychic State. The United States bore the additional danger that it still held a grudge against the Psychic State for the War of Independence that had been fought — and narrowly won by the Psychic State —a few decades ago.

Before that, the Psychic State had been just another one of its states, albeit one of its largest.

Officials in the young government feared that any day now the United States would be back to reclaim its former property. And this time they would bring more powerful weapons. These new weapons would be ones that your standard-issue psychic powers, the ones that had enabled them to win the first war, wouldn't be able to defend against.

And just like that, the Psychic State would be reabsorbed into its former sovereign.

But it wouldn't be as neat as that, would it? Surely, the United States would punish the state that had rebelled against them. The Psychic State leaders would be traitors, likely tried and executed in some pseudo-humane way employed by societies that considered themselves civilized — as the United States generally did, able to look the other way about a lot of brutish nonsense they performed without a thought.

And who knew what would happen to the rank-and-file citizens? Even the normal folks were suspect. Sure, they didn't possess psychic powers and because of this hadn't typically fought in the War of Independence themselves, but on the other hand, they hadn't done much to prevent secession in the first place and were, by that logic, akin to traitors themselves.

And of course, the psychic population feared what would happen if the United States government got their hands on them. A great many of them had fought against U.S. troops in the War of Independence. Yes, it wasn't usually done freely, and there was a great deal of coercion involved, especially in the early days — when the Psychic State was new and tentative, little more than a flag and a rallying cry by a few moneyed movers and shakers.

But that didn't matter, did it? American citizens were dead and gone because of what intuitives had done, even if it were mostly done under duress.

Not to mention that there was a second potential threat to the intuitive population if the United States resumed control. There was a possibility that all intuitives would essentially become Black Square. It wouldn't be called that, no. It would have some banal name that was easy to flip past when it was mentioned in governmental budgets. But it would be the same thing. Permanent detention. And this time not just for the most dangerous intuitives — the ones whose powers were inherently destructive — but for everyone who fell outside of the paradigm of normal.

The United States had the infrastructure, the lack of scruples, and frankly the budget to pull it off in a way that nobody noticed.

And it was part of what kept Psychic State intuitives from worrying too much about the Black Square program. Oh, sure, everyone knew someone in it — especially once you worked out past two or three degrees of separation.

But the alternative wasn't good either, was it? Being reabsorbed back into an angry country that would detain all the intuitives and dissect them like aliens, trying to get at their secrets. Anything to fast track the United States to world domination.

Of course, no one knew for sure that this was what would happen if their former sovereign took them back over. But it was something a lot of people feared. And at this point, enough prominent precogs had weighed in on the possibility that no one was taking any chances.

No, it was better to stick with the devil you knew. To tolerate the Black Square program. And just hope that you never had to be part of it. And that no one you loved was ever involved.

"Well, there's always a cost to security, isn't there?" Amarynth said.

Gino frowned. "I suppose there is." He hesitated. "I guess we'll just see what the bill comes to when this is all over, huh?"

Karen peered out the front window. "Why in the world is Martin driving a murder van?" she said.

"A murder van?" Viv joined her at the window. "Karen, that's just a panel van."

"Oh sure," Karen replied. "Then why are serial killers always driving them? Snatching up children. Or college students. Or... whoever."

"Because there are no windows in the back and plenty of storage," Viv replied. "The same reasons they're a popular choice for handymen."

"So Martin's moonlighting as a handyman now, huh?" Karen said.

Viv shrugged. "Guess we'll see."

The van backfired as Martin pulled it to the curb. Martin momentarily felt embarrassed as he exited the dented white panel van, but then he heard a loud commotion coming from behind the house, and all was forgotten.

It sounded to him like raccoons were knocking over trash cans.

But all he found when he went to investigate was Penny bent over next to a small grill that was lying on its side. It was a black kettle-style barbecue, and it looked very much to Martin at that moment like a tiny UFO that had crashed. Penny was frowning... and speaking rapidly in an agitated tone. The cadence reminded Martin of when people curse, but the words were gibberish and punctuated with... growling and hissing?

"Am I interrupting something?" Martin said.

"Oh geez, Martin, I'm sorry," Penny said, clearly startled. "I was trying to set up the grill, but I must have done something wrong."

He walked toward her and helped her right the barbecue, which promptly fell over again. "Our little friend is pretty lopsided," Martin observed. "Where did you get this piece of junk anyway?"

"Now, now, junk's a little harsh, especially right in front of our friend." Penny grinned as Martin laughed. "Across town. It was just sitting on the curb. A real beauty, right?"

"It looks like somebody ran over it maybe."

"Maybe," Penny said. "But then again, so do I most days. I've perfected a look I call roadkill chic."

Martin surveyed the rest of Penny's setup. There was a dented folding table that was only marginally more stable than the wobbly grill. He noted a motley assortment of cuts of meat. They weren't in shrink-wrapped packages, however, but instead piled haphazardly on kitchen plates.

"What are these, Penny?" he asked her.

Penny shrugged. "Scooped them up at the butcher's," she said, her eyes darting around evasively.

"You found them in the dumpster, didn't you?" Martin said. "And the labels were all blurred, so you have no idea what these are."

Penny threw up her hands in the air, clearly exasperated. "Martin! I'm doing my best here! It's hard entertaining on a psychic detective's salary. Or three."

"I know, I know," Martin replied. "Luckily, I came prepared."

"What?" Penny said.

He led her back out front to the panel van. "Ta-dah!" he said, throwing open the back doors.

Penny peered inside. There were a state-of-the-art grill, a folding table, two blue coolers, and several large storage containers.

"Alright, Karen, you know what to do," Viv said from behind them, as they had joined Martin and Penny on the lawn. Together everyone but Penny hauled the contents of the van outside onto the curb and out to their back lawn.

Penny flushed crimson as she pushed the grill and card table to the edge of their lawn, doing her best not to lift too much. She brought the mystery meats back inside and wrapped them up for the freezer. They'd eat them for dinners. No need to waste perfectly good — if mysterious — food, after all.

"Princess Penny's not going to help us with the heavy lifting, huh?" Martin joked.

Karen winced. "We'll get to that in a bit, Martin," she said.

Martin raised an eyebrow but didn't press further.

It didn't take long for the three of them to get set up anyway. "Looks really nice," Viv said. "I probably should be more upset that you had so little faith in us that you came here prepared to throw an entire barbecue yourself. But I gotta say... between being impressed with your head for logistics and absolutely starving, I don't have it in me."

Viv opened a fresh bag of charcoal briquettes Martin had brought with him and filled the bottom of the grill before lighting them with Martin's starter. She grinned at the array of grilling implements he'd packed as well and had arranged on the table behind her. It would be nice to have a long-handled spatula to flip the steaks — actual steaks — he'd brought with him.

This way, she wouldn't have to worry so much about burning her hands using the short dollar store utensils that they normally used for everything.

Martin opened the fresh packages of steaks and salted them liberally on both sides. As he did, Viv marveled that he'd even thought to bring the salt. Again, potentially insulting that he'd come prepared for them to have absolutely nothing done right.

But in this case, accurate and appreciated. So what the hey.

The grill was easy to use — and yes, this one stayed upright without fuss. The steaks smelled magnificent as they cooked when the coals were finally ready.

It was a beautiful day, and everyone seemed in good spirits... well, except for Penny. Viv noticed that she kept mostly to herself, sitting in one of the four folding camping chairs Martin had also packed in his van, staring at the fence.

Karen and Martin chatted companionably.

Finally, the steaks were done. "I'm sorry," Martin said. "I didn't bring any side dishes with me."

"Oh that's fine," Viv replied. "It's pretty much the only thing you *didn't* bring."

"Side dishes," Penny murmured, still staring at the fence.

"Anyway," Martin said, "I suppose there must be a reason that you asked me over. I know you don't entertain often."

"There is," Viv replied. "We have something important to tell you."

"Something we didn't want the monitoring at PsyOps to pick up," Karen blurted out.

"Oh?" Martin said.

Viv frowned. She'd wanted to work up to it a bit more, but Karen had forced her hand, hadn't she? Well then.

"Well, it's kind of Penny's news," Viv said.

Penny sighed. "You know," she said, "this is honestly the weirdest news I've ever had to give *anyone*. And you would think that it would get a little easier each time, but it doesn't. It still feels impossible to me. Like some bizarre dream I just can't seem to wake up from. It just feels ridiculous to expect anyone else to understand it, to believe me, let alone accept it."

Martin considered this. "You've been different since you got back from your trip, Penny," he said. "Did something happen while you were gone?"

Penny nodded. "A lot of things," she said. She squeezed her eyes shut so she wouldn't have to see the expression on his face when she told him and blurted out, "Martin, I'm pregnant!"

Silence. Penny saw only blackness behind her closed eyes. And the only thing she heard was the normal sound of the suburbs, of cars passing, children playing, and the far-off whine of a table saw as someone on the next block was doing some carpentry in their backyard.

When she opened her eyes, she saw Martin was still eating his steak. He hadn't choked on it. It was as though she hadn't spoken at all.

"Okay," Martin said after he'd cleared his mouth of steak, "what you're saying is you need medical leave of about nine months? A year maybe?"

Penny nodded and then she shook her head. "Well, yes," she said, "I do want that. But I am also saying that I'm pregnant. I'm going to have a baby, Martin."

Martin grinned. "It shouldn't be possible. And it's not allowed of course. Completely illegal. But you know all of that. You've put me in a difficult position by telling me. So no matter what you say to me about this, I'm going to hear it as a request for a year-long medical leave. Nothing more, nothing less. It's better that way. Are you seeing a doctor for this... condition?"

Penny nodded. "Amarynth knows someone, a good doctor who doesn't have a problem with my... circumstances. And Amarynth's taking care of everything."

"That's generous of her," Martin said. He felt a pang of guilt at the mere mention of the Connections Agent's name. She was a good employee, and it had been hard to suspend her, even if it was what the situation had required.

Penny felt a wave of panic rise within her. She knew that Amarynth was well off because of her mother's riches, but she'd also promised Amarynth not to tell anyone. She conjured up her best flippant hair wave. "It is."

"This is great steak," Karen said.

"Thanks," Martin and Viv said in unison.

"Appropriate," Karen said. "The chef and the procurer should both get credit."

"Aren't you going to ask how?" Penny said to Martin.

"How what?"

"How I got pregnant?" Penny prompted.

"One, you're going on medical leave for a year for general health reasons. I'm not hearing the P-word, even unofficially, even here, away from PsyOps. And two, I figure it's some psychic mumbo-jumbo that I'll never understand anyway, so why drag you through the indignity of trying to explain it to me?" Martin replied. "Just eat your steak and enjoy the weather, Penny Dreadful, and I'll see you back at work sometime next year. No questions asked."

"Oh Martin," Penny said, putting her plate on the table and throwing her arms around his neck. "You are amazing. I really appreciate it."

"Eat your dinner, Penny," Martin replied, clearly uncomfortable with the praise and the hug. "You need to keep your strength up."

"Sure thing, boss," she replied.

Martin turned to Viv. "The leave will be unpaid of course."

"Of course," Viv replied.

"Fewer questions asked that way," Martin explained.

Viv nodded. "We'll find a way to make it work."

"I know," Martin replied. "You three always do."

Disease-Sniffing Dog

Amarynth heard the gentle knock on her apartment door and recognized it instantly. There was a thoughtfulness, a tentative way that the knuckles touched the door that she had come to know quite well.

It was one of the building staff — she believed his title was package concierge, and she was rather embarrassed she didn't know his first name, only that he always looked rather smart in a navy blue suit and a matching semi-triangular hat that managed to look futuristic, classic, and militaristic all at once.

No small feat, straddling all those styles.

Amarynth would see him often in passing, pushing a large mail cart down the hall or sometimes even a flatbed cart heaped with boxes for heavier deliveries. She nodded familiarly to him whenever they were in the elevator together.

It was embarrassing, not knowing his name. She was reasonably sure he didn't know hers either, but that was hardly fair. There were hundreds of residents in Cambria Towers and maybe… a dozen building staff. Two dozen at most, if there were some tucked away in back offices, ones she never saw.

That was a little embarrassing, too, wasn't it? Not only did she not know the names of the people who made her life possible, but she wasn't even sure exactly how many of them there were. She could only picture a handful of them clearly, although she'd never been good with faces — or visualizing anything that wasn't there.

Amarynth walked to the door and peered out the peephole. Yes, there was a package for her, laid gingerly next to her apartment, in a small brown box. She opened the door and brought it in. When she lifted it, she noted it wasn't very heavy, certainly less than a pound.

He moves fast, she thought as she closed the door, for she had not seen the concierge anywhere in the hallway.

Amarynth Watson, Green Star, Level 3 Connections Agent, #61537, Department of Psychic Operations.

Yes, those were her credentials. And underneath was her address. She glanced at the return address. It was simply a PsyOps seal, but it was standard issue as far as she could discern.

"What do they want from me now?" she grumbled, noting that even a grumble echoed slightly in her apartment.

Tesla shrieked in response.

It must be freeing to be a parakeet, Amarynth mused, always so sure that everything is intended for you. Always trying to flock with whatever is around you, ready to jump right into the fray socially and get lost as quickly as possible. Brave and a little foolish but the good kind of foolish, she supposed.

She rifled through her drawers, found a small knife she didn't care much about, and cut open the package. It was mostly filled with packing peanuts. But there were also a small bracelet and a sheaf of papers folded in half and bound together with a rubber band.

"I wonder if we're on house arrest," Amarynth joked about the bracelet to her parakeet, who faithfully responded in his birdly way. She had suspected that PsyOps might institute some sort of tracking equipment, considering her suspension was a disciplinary measure. Perhaps she'd had her status temporarily demoted from Green Star (No Restrictions, Additional Privileges) to Yellow Circle (Light Monitoring) or Red Cross (Heavy Monitoring). It would only make sense.

But as she opened and unfolded the packet and began to leaf through it, she quickly realized the contents had nothing to do with her suspension. The very first page was an info sheet about PTI — psychic-transmitted illness. Amarynth frowned reflexively at that name. You would think they'd name it something less stigmatizing. *Perhaps they would if they gave a shit about us*, she thought sharply.

She glanced over the information quickly. There were plenty of pictures on these glossy handouts, but the bottom line seemed to be that there was still a lot they didn't know about the illness. Anecdotal reports were indicating that it was transmitted primarily through telepathic links.

Then why don't they call it TTI, telepathic-transmitted illness? Amarynth thought crossly. No, it was better just to call it something that created problems for all intuitives and not just telepaths, who of all the intuitives were generally considered the most obnoxious anyway, since they tended to be very good and accurate at their specific ability but suffered from overconfidence in other areas. Telepathy itself was a strange talent, for it could convey cognitive denotation — i.e., the literal meaning or content of thoughts — but was wildly deficient in cognitive connotation, or context.

This often led to telepaths being certain of the exact wrong thing. They were menaces as coworkers, Amarynth reflected.

I'm not surprised that they're responsible for all of this, she thought and then felt immediately guilty for the ugly thought.

"That's probably the kind of thing the normals say about us," Amarynth said to her parakeet.

Tesla sang back at her. He was whistling a wild improvisation that was likely bits and pieces of multiple songs he'd heard over his lifespan, all chopped up and reassembled.

Amarynth dug further into the packet.

In order to comply with county health officials, all PsyOps agents are required to report to a mandatory PTI testing facility to ascertain current status.

Amarynth looked at the address. She recognized it instantly, although this was hardly unusual for her. Amarynth had a peculiar ability with local addresses her entire life, gifted at producing exact addresses from... memory? She'd say memory, but it was fainter than memory. She had no certainty that she'd even been exposed to the information that she produced. It was more like she was calculating it, although if asked directly, she'd have been hard pressed to explain exactly how she made those calculations or what the "math" was.

It worked in the other direction, too. When presented with an address, she knew what business was there. When it came to private addresses, she was a good deal fuzzier. She was quite good at knowing who lived at a private residence, so long as she knew the person in question in some way, shape, or form.

But she usually didn't know who lived at a private home if the residents were strangers to her.

She didn't know quite why this was, only that it was this way.

"PsyTex," Amarynth said, looking at the address. "One of their satellite campuses."

Tesla chirped happily in response.

"What do you think they're doing working with PsyOps on this?" Am asked Tesla. "They're competitors, and PsyTex is private sector."

Tesla didn't seem to know. He jumped from perch to perch, soaking up the attention from his owner.

"I guess the day has come for the Psychic State to start using contractors," Amarynth said.

Tesla bopped and tweeted.

This government contractor was owned by the Watson Family, precisely the powerful empire that her mother should have been part of, if not for her indiscretion. "If not for me," Amarynth said aloud.

Tesla screeched at her in an ugly way.

"I suppose you're right," Amarynth replied. "It's no good to feel that way."

She leafed through the packet some more.

Due to security concerns, we ask that you wear this bracelet for at least 30 minutes prior to arriving at our facility. It is the latest in dampening-field technology, perfected by administrators of our Black Square program. It will help ensure that no inadvertent telepathic contact is made while you are being evaluated. This measure protects everyone — you and everyone you come in contact with.

Our latest studies show that if everyone were to wear a dampener that PTI would be eradicated in 7 months.

"Simulations," Amarynth grumbled. "Predictions. It's math, not research. Kind of misleading to present it that way."

Tesla squawked his support.

Sighing, Amarynth picked up her phone. She scrolled through the very short contact list and pressed the call button. "I'll need a car in the morning," she said.

The first thing Amarynth noted about the bracelet was that it itched. Well, sorta. Not full-on itching but the kind of minor irritation you might feel if you focused your attention on an area of your body and thought about it itching.

The suggestion of itching rather than an unbearable itch that demanded to be sated with the raking of claws.

This was also the last thing Amarynth noted about the bracelet. She felt quite normal wearing it. She had noted during the entire car ride out to the facility that she still got her normal hunches, uncanny ones that she shouldn't have had.

The dampening fields... left her feeling normal.

Well, maybe they just affect telepathy, she told herself.

But it was a strange feeling as she waited in the car to be told she could come inside. A strange feeling to feel... so normal.

So utterly normal.

Amarynth shook her head. A woman wearing an identical bracelet and a large smile emerged cradling a clipboard against her chest. She waved at Amarynth and beckoned for her to come inside.

"I'll be parked around Post 3, Miss Watson," the driver informed her.

"Thank you," Amarynth replied, feeling silly as she did so that she didn't know his name either. She slipped out of the car and followed the woman carrying the clipboard into the facility, admiring her hair as she did. It was long, limp, stringy, and pale as snow.

She probably gets frustrated with her hair, too. Probably thinks it's boring and she can't do anything with it, Amarynth thought, *but I'd kill to have hair that stayed in place, that always behaved.*

She led Amarynth into a testing room and did an awkward curtsy as she left.

Amarynth spun around to meet her tester and cried out in alarm.

"Oh no," she said. "How is it you? Why are *you* my tester?"

For she knew the person sitting in front of her very well.

Ryan Roscoe. Telepathic boy wunderkind of PsyOps. He was young enough that he couldn't legally drink, but he acted as though he knew everything, smirking underneath his strangely becoming bowl-cut hairdo.

"Nice to see you, too, Amarynth," he said.

I didn't not say it was nice to see you, she thought.

"You didn't have to," Roscoe said. "And can I just say that it's annoying when you think in double negatives?"

"Hey," Amarynth said. "Stop doing that."

"Doing what?" Roscoe replied, smirking.

"Telepathy. Reading my thoughts. You're going to get PTI, or give it to me."

Roscoe shrugged. "You don't know that for sure," he said noncommittally.

"Shouldn't you be wearing a dampening bracelet?" Amarynth challenged him.

"I am," Roscoe said coolly, raising his wrist.

Sure enough, there was a dampening bracelet on it.

"Seriously though," Amarynth said. "How did you get this gig?"

Roscoe smiled. "Funny story about that," he said. "I'm basically like one of those drug-sniffing dogs."

"Oh, c'mon," Amarynth shot back. "Don't be ridiculous."

"No, no," Roscoe said. "I'm not. See, I woke up one morning last week, and I could suddenly smell it."

"Smell what?"

"PTI," Roscoe said.

"What?" Amarynth said.

"It has a distinct odor," Roscoe replied.

"Really?"

"Really," Roscoe said, nodding. "Not to everyone of course. But just to a few of us. I'm one of the lucky ones who can smell this new illness, and I'm telling you, it's just crazy."

"What does it smell like?" Amarynth said.

"Hmmm," Roscoe replied. "It's a little tough to describe."

"Well, try," Amarynth said.

Roscoe smiled. "It's like someone's cooking pancakes next to an open window, and outside that window, someone else is mowing the grass."

"That sounds nice," Amarynth said.

"It's not so bad, and hey, it's coming in handy. I get to be *helpful* today," Roscoe said with a sarcastic eye roll.

"Oh, that's you, isn't it? You're just Mr. Helpful," Amarynth said. She meant to be part of the joke, but it became immediately clear Roscoe was having none of that.

"Hey, I can be helpful if I want to be," Roscoe snapped. "Anyway," he continued, "I figure it could be good for my career. Get ahead at PsyOps."

"By being... how did you put it? By being a drug-sniffing dog?"

"Well, I don't want to be a detective my whole life, that's for damn sure," Roscoe said.

"Better to be a dog?" Amarynth pressed him.

"It can be," Roscoe said. "It's better to be a dog in a good house than the master of a bad one."

"Whatever you say," Amarynth replied, rolling her eyes.

"It helps to be connected," Roscoe said. "You never know what tomorrow will bring. There are lots of rumors going around about what comes next. What PTI might mean. What the State might try. Figure it's best to have the right kind of friends when that happens."

"When what happens?" Amarynth said.

Roscoe shrugged. "You probably know better than I do, the way you are." He paused for effect. "They're discussing interring all the telepaths, putting us on Black Square, until this whole business is cleared up."

Amarynth gasped.

"Who knows if they'll go through with it? But I figure I'll hedge my bets just in case. Anyway, you don't smell like PTI at all," Roscoe said, "which is honestly a little strange."

"Why is that strange?" Amarynth asked.

"Because I should have infected you just then," Roscoe said.

"Ryan Roscoe, what is wrong with you?" Amarynth replied.

"Oh calm down, Am. It's no big deal," Roscoe said.

"Oh, yeah, giving people a debilitating disease is no big deal, I should calm down... no, seriously, Roscoe, what the fuck?"

"Amarynth, PTI is a debilitating disease to *normals*," Roscoe said. "But to intuitives... well, it's an empowering altered state of consciousness."

"You're a creepy bug chaser, that's what you are." Amarynth scowled.

"Not at all!" Roscoe said. "It'll be public knowledge before long. The researchers here all know, but they haven't told the public yet. PTI robs normals of one of their typical five senses, yeah? Well, it gives intuitives an extra one, in addition to the ones they already have. For us, we basically get a seventh sense. Wild, right?"

"Yes," Amarynth said. "*If* it's true." Although as she said it, she had a strong sense it was, that Roscoe was telling her factual information.

"I mean, mine's kind of lame. Not exactly the life-changing extra power I'd be hoping for, the ability to smell PTI," Roscoe griped. "Although, like I said, there's career potential here."

"What? The potential to sniff people out and try to infect them in the process?" Amarynth said. "I can't believe they're letting you take charge of something so important."

"Well, I'm just the screener. If I smell it, you get the more scientific test, the accurate one. It's kind of expensive though, so they go through me first," Roscoe said. "And anyway, would you quit calling it 'infecting' people? I'm really giving them a gift."

"You're like a nasty telepathic vampire, Ryan Roscoe," Amarynth replied.

"Oh, you're just mad because I couldn't give it to you," Roscoe snapped back.

"How did you read my mind with the dampener active?" Amarynth asked.

"Oh, that?" Roscoe laughed. "You know those two buttons on the side?"

"Yeah," Am said.

"If you hold them down together for five seconds, it reprograms the bracelet to a different frequency. Presto, change-o." Roscoe grinned. "I don't know what it's dampening now, but it's not my telepathy."

"Unfortunately," Amarynth said.

"Bah," Roscoe said. "This whole psychic dampening business is suspect as it is, the way I see it. Why should I diminish my gifts to make other people comfortable?"

"To protect people."

"Same thing," Roscoe said. "Just a matter of what you're protecting — their lives, their security, or their ego."

"Well, the good news for me is that your little shenanigans didn't work," Amarynth said.

"Yeah, they didn't, did they?" Roscoe said. "You know, Amarynth Watson, if I didn't know any better, I'd say that you were immune."

"Mark the date," Amarynth said. "Ryan Roscoe finally admits there are some things he doesn't know."

"Well, I wouldn't go that far," Roscoe replied.

On her way out, Amarynth made sure to let site officials know about Roscoe's reprogrammed dampening bracelet.

Dust in the Wind

Between the earth and that sky, I felt erased, blotted out.

-Willa Cather

There was no reason the Skinner-Watson metroplex should exist. None whatsoever. It did not come about because it was located near a body of water, as many other major cities did.

There was significant water there now in its impressive reservoirs, more than enough for its ever-growing population to drink even during the hottest summers. But that water wasn't there when the city started. Those reserves were created. Like nearly everything else in Skinner-Watson, the reservoirs came about because of the efforts of human beings.

In this way — and many others — Skinner-Watson was entirely artificial, a marvel of modern engineering. The urban sprawl connected what could have been disparate municipal entities into one contiguous mass that covered an area the size of the state of Connecticut.

The Skinner-Watson sprawl seemed to range forever when you were moving through it. One could drive for hours through the city feeling as though it would never end only to have the surroundings clear out precipitously when you reached the outer limits of the metroplex.

It was then — and only then — that you realized that this massive city of the future, a paragon of art, culture, and innovation, had been plopped down in the middle of the prairie.

The first time Amarynth had left Skinner-Watson, heading south towards Bosque, she had been amazed to find herself so quickly in wide-open spaces. She found herself wondering what the original settlers must have thought, traversing the open ranges in covered wagons. There were more trees now than back then,

Amarynth knew that much, but even now she found herself struck by how few there were. The ones that had been planted were short and bent. They'd grown adaptively in this stance to help them resist windstorms.

And all around her, she noted whorls of color-shifted grass, bushy and snarled, in tinted hues that struck her as alien.

What must it have been like for city dwellers used to the well-forested cities of the Northeast to strike out under such a large sky and wide-open plains, rolling their tiny wagons over this alien grass?

It must have felt like you were venturing into country that wasn't quite finished. Whoever the creator was had simply forgot to render it. That had to be freeing, in a sense, like you were moving beyond the purview of a wrathful god — into forgotten lands, places where you could remain unseen, unwatched, unknown.

On the other hand, Amarynth thought, it would be terrifying. For you were indeed on your own. No chance of divine intervention here in the land that God forgot to finish.

But the early pioneers had figured it out. Well sorta. They'd forever clashed with the people who had been here first, slaughtered them and their cattle, the bison, before moving in their own herds.

And if that weren't enough, when they settled down and put the wilderness to agrarian purpose, they'd screwed that up, too. In the 1930s, a combination of drought and improper farming methods left the plains open to unprecedented windstorms.

And that's when the dust descended. Or when it rose from the ground.

While the storms centered to the north and west of Skinner-Watson, in American Oklahoma and the 26 northernmost counties of the future Psychic State, there were indeed days during that troubled time when a suffocating black curtain of soil whipped through Skinner-Watson like something possessed, enveloping, dirtying, and even choking anything in its path.

It was long before Amarynth's time of course, but what it had been like to live in the time of dusters had been passed down in her family like a legend.

The reality was that the prairie wasn't a place that God had forgotten. It wasn't unfinished at all. Instead, the prairie was completed already, just differently, in a form that city dwellers didn't recognize. And the worst thing that the pioneers could have done was to treat the prairie as though it were a work-in-progress that simply needed to be turned into something more familiar. A fixer-upper biome that needed the white man's touch to spruce it up into something serviceable. Manifesting their destiny and all that.

Nature pushed back. The storms had been the natural consequences of such hubris.

But on many days, as Amarynth regarded the artificial city complex of Skinner-Watson, a network that spread for so many miles on what was once prairie, she wondered when the natural consequences for this sin, a larger sin to her thinking, would arrive.

It's coming, the text read. *I can smell it.*

Give it a break, Roscoe, Viv had written back, as well as another follow-up text: *Or give us a little of what you're on.*

Amarynth grinned. Good old Viv. As she scrolled through the recipient list of the group text Roscoe had created, Am's eyes widened.

"There has to be half of Level 3 on here," Amarynth said aloud.

"Level 3?" Gino replied. "Is that supposed to mean something to me?"

She cringed. "Oh, it's just work stuff."

"So not your problem then," Gino shot back.

Amarynth sighed and set her phone face down on the nightstand. "I suppose not."

But she had a hard time moving on mentally. *He can smell it?* She wondered. *Smell what?*

She thought of what he'd said before, at the PsyTex testing facility, that he could smell PTI. Was that what he meant?

She still wasn't sure she believed him. And besides, how did a person smell PTI coming towards them? What did that even mean?

"You're still thinking about something," Gino observed.

Amarynth sighed. "Guess I don't hide it well."

"Not at all," Gino agreed.

She handed her phone to him, feeling strangely vulnerable as he held it and looked over the group text conversation. It was such an intimate thing to surrender your phone to someone else, wasn't it? She'd never done that before, she noted in hindsight. And yet it had seemed so natural to her, so easy to trust him that way.

This bodes well for the future, she noted, before swatting the thought like an errant fly. That level of optimism was crazy. She barely knew Gino.

"Does this Roscoe guy have a drug problem?" Gino asked.

Amarynth laughed. "Not as far as I know. It'd make more sense if he did though, now that you mention it." She smirked.

"I smell something else," Gino said.

"Oh?'

"French toast," Gino replied, waggling his eyebrows.

"A vision?" Amarynth prompted.

"More like wishful thinking," Gino said, wrapping her in his arms and giving her a deep kiss.

Amarynth lay frozen afterward, blinking, dazed, as Gino got up and walked away from her. She heard the refrigerator door open, a luxurious pause, and then the door closing.

She heard his big feet plodding back.

"Tell me, Amarynth," Gino said, pausing dramatically. "Do you eat?"

Amarynth laughed. "Of course." A beat. "Why?"

"Because your fridge tells a different story."

Amarynth giggled. "I don't even know what's in there," she confessed.

"I'm not surprised," Gino replied. "Anyway, I'm a little short on what I need to make French toast."

"Well," Amarynth said, "just let me know what you need. I can pop out to the market." After a fire had leveled the corner store, Cambria Market had worked to rebuild quickly. The speed of construction had astounded Amarynth. One day it had been ruins. A few weeks later, the structure was almost done.

To be fair, it was a small storefront, but still, the celerity had surprised her. The market had always seemed to her like an afterthought, not a big priority to the citizens of Cambria Square.

Perhaps there was a prominent place, after all, for an establishment that primarily existed because other people didn't plan. Because people could be generally forgetful.

Well, you couldn't exactly blame folks for being forgetful with all that was going on these days, could you?

"Earth to Amarynth," Gino said.

Amarynth snapped to attention. "I'm sorry," she confessed. "I was thinking about Cambria Market. I haven't been there since the day of the fire. Since they rebuilt."

"I imagine it's a painful memory," Gino validated her.

Amarynth shook her head. "Not at all."

"Really?" Gino said.

"Really."

"Even though that was the case that got you suspended, the whole reason you're slumming around with yours truly?"

Amarynth laughed. "It wasn't the fire that got me suspended," she said. "I mean, it was that case, but..." She thought of how to explain it. "I was protecting a colleague. And it had to be done."

"It had to be done?"

Amarynth nodded. "It was the right thing to do, sticking my neck out like that."

"Amarynth," Gino said, his voice becoming softer and gentler as he spoke, "just because something's the right thing to do, it doesn't mean that's what needs to be done."

"Where do you teach again? Villain college?" Amarynth teased him.

Gino rolled his eyes. "I'm not saying that I wouldn't do the right thing, given the same choice. All I'm saying is that not everyone would. That you deserve credit for doing the right thing."

"You don't always get a cookie for doing the right thing, Gino," Amarynth said. "Better get used to it."

"Oh, I am," Gino said. "I just don't want you to lose sight of how great you are. How kind."

"Oh, sure," Amarynth said, "butter me up right before I'm gonna do you a favor. Okay, handsome, what am I getting at the store? And make sure you tell me everything because I'm not putting on clothes twice today."

Gino grinned. "A dozen eggs, a loaf of bread, a carton of milk," he breathed into the nape of her neck.

Amarynth shuddered at that moment but not from pleasure. That was how her agoraphobic mother's standard grocery order started, too. As the person charged with bringing provisions to her mom, Amarynth had gotten used to the overall shape of the list, which always began this way.

The syllables struck her like an incantation.

She turned her face towards Gino. "Who *are* you?" she asked him, her eyes widening with wonder.

"Only the best lover you'll ever have," Gino replied, before giving her a kiss that completely reset her thoughts.

Amarynth was still smiling as she walked home from Cambria Market, clutching a nondescript brown grocery bag in her hands. She was so giddy from her time with Gino that she had floated through the admittedly brief shopping trip and likely would have cruised through her neighborhood and into her high-rise building on autopilot had she not been brought back to harsh reality by one of the strangest sights she'd ever seen.

The clouds were in the wrong place. They were much too low.

Why have the clouds dropped?

For there they were, far off on the horizon, looking all the world like normal fluffy clouds you might see while sitting in an airplane — except they were low.

It looked like the sky had fallen.

"Chicken little, eat your heart out," she joked, before noting with great alarm that the clouds weren't just too low — they were also coming closer. By the second, really.

She clutched the grocery bag to her chest and began to power walk. The cloud chased her. She picked up the pace. It still pursued.

She began to half-jog to the front door of the high-rise building.

And noted with astonishment that a familiar face was manning the front desk. A different one than normal.

Leigh Lines was the newest front desk concierge. She looked smart in her uniform. A bit historical, like the rest, the puffy pleated shirt under a blazer reminding Amarynth for all the world of early American colonial fashion but topped off with that futuristic hat.

"Leigh Lines!" Amarynth exclaimed. "What are you doing here?"

"The same thing I was doing the last time you saw me," Leigh Lines said. "Working my way through school."

"I thought you'd be at the café," Amarynth said.

Leigh shook her head. "They downsized a lot. Cafés are a hard sell with PTI on the loose. Lots of folks don't want to hang around like sitting ducks in public and risk a telepath rummaging through their thoughts, you know?

"I see," Amarynth said. She felt silly for not connecting those dots. And for bringing up the café.

"But as you can see," Leigh continued, "I've rebounded quite nicely."

"That you have," Amarynth replied.

"I'm glad you're inside," Leigh said. "There's a storm coming soon."

"I saw a low-hanging cloud outside," Amarynth said. "It's coming this way."

Leigh beckoned for Amarynth to follow her into a small back office. The TV was muted but employing closed captions. It was tuned to the weather channel.

UNPRECEDENTED DUST STORMS HIT
SKINNER-WATSON.

"A duster?" Amarynth said. "Like during the Great Depression?"

Leigh nodded. "A big one, too, judging by some of the footage coming in from Watson." The radar on the screen indicated that the storm had started at the far Western edge of Watson and had moved steadily eastward.

"You'd think they would have warned us ahead of time," Amarynth said.

"No one saw this coming," Leigh replied.

"Is that even possible?" Amarynth said.

"What do you mean?"

"Well, they know about hurricanes a while in advance. Snowstorms. Even tornados, they have a sense when there's at least an increased risk," Amarynth replied. "Is it possible for a dust storm to sneak up on meteorologists?"

"If you'd have asked me yesterday if it were possible that no one would see a dust storm coming, I wouldn't have known," Leigh confessed, "but now I'd say that it's gotta be possible. Because it's what's happening."

"No one saw it coming," Amarynth said, shaking her head. "Wow." She considered this for a minute, before adding, "Although maybe someone smelled it."

"Come again?" Leigh asked.

But as Amarynth opened her mouth to speak, a great roaring sound drowned out what she was going to say next. The room went dark as the glassed-in entryway was quickly coated in dirt, blocking out the natural light.

Moving the Mountain One Grain of Sand at a Time

Telekinesis

Telekinesis, also known as psychokinesis, is the ability to move objects without making physical contact.

When the Psychic Phenomenon first emerged, the most common intuitive practitioners were precognitionists and telepaths. However, it was thought by many self-professed experts of parapsychology that other powers would shortly be found in the population *en masse*. The foremost of these theoretical intuitive outcroppings was to be a rash of telekineticists.

Indeed, this possibility was heralded by many sensationalist news network programs that warned of the dangers of widespread telekinesis. It would create fresh opportunities for easy assault and battery, making crimes significantly more difficult for police departments to investigate, as would-be attackers would be much more difficult to identify if they could harm their targets from a distance and without physical proof of their involvement.

Public fear of telekinesis was in fact what prompted the formation of the Department of Psychic Operations, quickly shortened to PsyOps, an agency preemptively established to guard against the anticipated coming psychic onslaught, fears from a time that is now known as the telekinetic panic.

A dramatic increase in telekinetic assault never materialized. True, there have been scattered incidences of telekinesis — some of those acts criminal — but for the most part, telekinesis has remained a relatively rare psychic power, much to the relief of intuitives and psychophobes alike.

In addition, as our collective understanding of telekinesis increases, it's become evident that just as individuals vary in their strength when moving objects physically, telekineticists possess differing levels of strength when moving objects mentally. The size of those objects and the speed at which they can be moved — and therefore the physical impact a moving object can have on anything or anyone it contacts — are quite a bit more limited than was originally theorized. Even the strongest telekineticists can generally move considerably less with their minds than they can using their physical bodies.

However, it has been theorized that with the proper amount of cooperation that telekineticists could combine their powers to be quite strong in aggregate. Or, as the great mononymous demotivational speaker Mallow once put it: "It's possible to move the mountain one grain of sand at a time."

It is worth noting, however, that a relative scarcity of telekineticists among the psychic population as well as a tendency for psychic practitioners to infight and compete amongst one another has rendered this hypothetical scenario highly unlikely, albeit poetic.

Still, as with all fields, taxonomists will be keeping a close eye on this subset of the psychic population and adjust our reports based on any new developments.

However, the initial telekinetic panic was good for something. The PsyOps agency continues to thrive and to aid the Psychic State and the scientific community as first responders and the public's eye into how the Psychic Phenomenon continues to manifest.

from Insecta Psychica: Towards an Intuitive Taxonomy by Cloche Macomber

"Our intrepid reporter Danielle Dawn is first on the scene."

"That's right, Jim."

"Danielle, can you hear me? I imagine there's quite a racket going on behind you."

"That there is, Jim. But I can hear you loud and clear."

"So Danielle, what have meteorologists been saying about this duster? What were the origins? Will it happen again?"

"Well, Jim, I'm here with Professor Din Larabee." Danielle swiveled her mic towards him, leaving nary a crease in her cornflower blue pantsuit as she did. "Dr. Larabee, can you explain to the viewers at home the meteorological point of view regarding this storm?"

"Certainly, Danielle." The professor spoke unnaturally slowly as he did, sounding glacial even against the backdrop of the reporter's slow speech, which had all the hallmarks of diction that's practiced to be as easily understood by as many people as possible. Dr. Larabee peeled back his gums in a wide grin, making a strangely friendly expression at the camera.

"Professor," the reporter urged.

"Right, right," Dr. Larabee said. "The general scientific consensus" (somehow he made this word have four syllables) "is that these dust storms aren't a meteorological event whatsoever."

"I'm sorry, professor. What?" Danielle said. "Are you saying that this giant dust storm...isn't weather?"

The professor shook his head. "Not in the traditional sense, no, in that it's not part of an overall system. It does not appear to be driven by atmospheric changes whatsoever."

"Dr. Larabee," Danielle pressed, "dust doesn't just fly through the sky for no reason."

"I didn't say there wasn't a reason," Dr. Larabee huffed, "just not a meteorological one."

Danielle frowned. "Well, you heard it here first, Jim. Scientific experts are saying that the weather's not to blame on this one."

Jim chuckled back in the studio. "Reminds me of that good old Kentucky Meat Shower."

"Jim, this is a family program!" his co-anchor protested.

"That wasn't a euphemism," Jim said. "Meat fell from the sky in Kentucky, up in the United States, in the nineteenth century. They think it was vultures."

His co-anchor stared at him, her mouth agape in horror.

"Right," Jim said, clearing his throat. "A family program."

Over the next several days, explanations began to emerge. Some pointed the finger at over-cultivation of the fields. This was known as the "horse" explanation after an old saying in medical school teaching: "When you hear hoofbeats, think of horses, not zebras."

Of course, this colorful label might have been a mistake in hindsight. Fringe groups latched onto it literally, claiming that stampedes of wild horses had disturbed the fields to the point where they were easily kicked up by gusts of wind.

Many citizens of the Psychic State began to worry that wild horses would soon overtake the rural homesteads and eventually find their way to city centers. Profiteering groups emerged, establishing shops that specialized in horse protection gear.

In this case, however, horse protection gear simply seemed like deer hunting equipment — only rebranded and marked up at a steep premium, with guarantees that the devices would work well against would-be stampeding equine marauders.

The most lucrative of these ventures was A Horse Of Course (Enterprises). Despite stocking the most low-quality bargain basement hunting gear of the bunch, sourced from the most destitute parts of the Psychic State as well as overseas depots from countries whose human rights were on par with the treatment of Psychic State intuitives, A Horse of Course was nonetheless able to command the highest prices for its wares.

When they were featured in a business segment that Amarynth watched later that week, they were asked what their secret was. Exactly what *was* their ticket to success?

The company rep pondered this question carefully before responding, "At A Horse of Course we make the preparation process something more than a transaction. In our stores, it becomes an *experience*. One for the whole family."

Perhaps he had a point, Amarynth thought as B-reel shot in their stores played on the screen. In the images, tiny children laughed with wild abandon as they rode mechanical horses on the store sidewalk. Then it cut to an in-store shooting gallery — one whose targets were all horses but of wildly improbable sizes, both much too small and too large to represent a normal horse. It appeared to Amarynth as though store ownership had simply converted an existing shooting gallery and had transformed previous non-horse targets to equine ones.

On monitors throughout the stores, footage from the Kentucky Derby played — only it seemed to be poorly edited to cut out just as the winner was reaching the finish line to another lower-production quality film in which a horse was summarily executed.

"Oh yeah, this is really a family program," Amarynth grumbled, turning off her set.

The horse explanation didn't make much sense to her anyway. She was solidly on board with what was being known as the zebra, the unusual explanation that was being treated as the less likely and more fantastic of the two.

Going by the zebra explanation, the dust storms were a direct result of PTI. More specifically, the dust storms weren't natural whatsoever and instead caused by newly minted telekineticists moving the dust all at once.

It did make a bit of intuitive sense, Amarynth mused, smirking at the pun. It did, however, fall apart at one crucial point: The level of coordination needed to transport that much dust at a time had been unprecedented among telekineticists.

So how in the world would neophyte telekineticists manage such a feat?

The level of competence required made most folks dismiss it as a zebra. Yes, even as others could easily accept that herds of stampeding horses were the greatest threat to public safety that the Psychic State had heretofore encountered — with perhaps the only real competition being the emergence of the Psychic Phenomenon and first intuitives themselves — more discerning people were having a hard time making the zebra explanation fit.

Wild as it was, however, Amarynth knew it was true. And strangely, she had an inkling of why — which was more than she usually got.

Everyone was saying that novice intuitives weren't competent enough to accomplish this. That much was true, but it was also beside the point.

Intuitives didn't need to be competent to accomplish this — if it wasn't a purposeful event but an accident.

And that was precisely what the dust storm seemed like to Amarynth. A purely accidental side effect of thousands of new telekineticists coming into their powers at once.

And that's why when the epidemiologists finally traced the origin of that great storm to a hospital ward with an entire wing of PTI-infected telekineticists, Amarynth wasn't a bit surprised.

Still, it was aggravating waiting for the rest of the world to catch up, wasn't it?

It always was. The curse of Cassandra.

When she tried to talk to Gino about it, he agreed with her assessment but had a hard time understanding why it frustrated her so much that their views were a minority.

"I'm tired of being in my own little world all the time, Gino," she said.

"You're not," he insisted. "It's our little world now. I'm here with you."

And as much as that felt good to hear, another part of her rose in response. *Two people can't make an entire world, Amarynth,* the voice said. She thought of her childhood, shut up in the giant house with her mother. If her mom had gotten her way, Amarynth would have stayed there with her permanently. She would have been homeschooled. Kept hidden from the world.

But Amarynth had been very young when she knew that would never be enough for her. That she needed to get out there — into whatever the world looked like — and connect with other people.

As she studied her lover's face, she realized that she'd worked very hard to go out and get into that world and finally connect with someone... only for them to try to force her back inside. Locked away.

"You look like you have something on your mind," Gino observed.

Amarynth tried to think of what to say but came up empty.

"That's my little Amarynth," he said, smoothing her hair. "Always thinking."

In the days that followed, Amarynth went online, searching out like-minded others. Other proponents of the zebra theory. There weren't too many of them, especially not at first, but as she searched out specific corners of the Internet, she found more and more of them hiding in strange groups and subgroups. Often they were named for something else. One of the biggest clutches of zebra believers was stationed in a low-fat slow cooking recipe forum.

From this group, Amarynth learned that the way they signaled each other in public was to wear a zebra pin with a simple but telling modification: One normally white stripe on the animal was to be repainted any color other than black so that the colorful stripe stood out. Some members colored their white stripes with nail markers. Some used fancy artist-grade paints.

Amarynth doctored hers with a bit of purple nail polish.

She clipped it to the cardigan sweater she wore as a light coat this time of year and completely forgot about it until one evening she was in the lobby moving towards the elevator and was called over to the concierge desk by Leigh Lines.

"Yes?" Amarynth said, before glancing down at Leigh's blazer, which sported a zebra with an orange stripe.

"There's a meeting at eight o'clock tonight in Conference Room C," Leigh hissed. "Come alone."

"No Gino?" Amarynth asked.

Leigh shook her head. "He's not one of us."

Amarynth thought of arguing, but she knew Leigh was right. Life with Gino was proving more and more every day that as much as she shared with him, there was an awful lot about him that was different — not just different than her but different than virtually every other person she'd ever known. The way he talked about the world sometimes wasn't simply off-putting or arrogant; it was like he didn't think of himself as belonging here.

Besides, she thought, *I can check out what this group is all about, and if it's something that Gino would be into, maybe I can work it out later.* For all she knew, this would be boring, stupid. Time wasted.

Amarynth waved at Leigh and walked back across the lobby and into the elevator. As the doors closed and she selected her floor, Amarynth realized she had no idea what the meeting was about.

The Web Spinners

Self-Sealing Beliefs and Conspiracy Theories

The establishment of cities has been a vital part of connecting human beings for thousands of years. However, recent innovations have accelerated an already impressively quick-moving process into one whose speed verges on terrifying. And these innovations were well underway even in the years preceding the Psychic Phenomenon — an incident that of course brought a level of uncomfortable connectedness to the populace all on its own.

To wit, telecommunication technology has made it possible for human beings to interact when separated by distances — even great physical distances. Progressive advances in communication media have rolled in over the years, culminating in our most immediate and impressive technological human innovation yet — the Internet. Now, ideas fly from person to person at top speed, not even impeded by cultural or land borders, except in the case of totalitarian regimes or certain governments that engage in extreme censorship.

While censorship is generally considered odious in a democratic society, other schools of thought argue that authoritarian censorship is simply one response to a new problem in civilization — not just the open exchange of ideas, but what is increasingly being considered in many circles as the much-too-open exchange of ideas.

Because, as with all advances, the level of connection possible because of the rise of the Internet has made it incredibly easy not only for conspiracy theories to take root but for secret societies that peddle in rumor, hearsay, and often pure fictive lies to form and become nonstop propaganda engines.

To what end? Well, that depends on the organization of course. In many cases, such cabals are started by a single individual who wants to feel powerful, special, or important — and doesn't much care what they have to do to achieve that. They also grow larger as other core members present with the same basic motivational needs, expanding into a kind of self-esteem pyramid scheme.

However, in the last few years, government groups watching conspiracy theorists have noted that more organized cells are coming into existence. These outfits are less like clubs and more like political splinter factions. They have agendas underscoring their targeted messages.

It's worth noting that not every member of these sophisticated conspiracy groups even knows what they're joining when they do. For some, the moment they realize might simply come too late. This is because it is, generally speaking, much easier to believe conspiracy theories than to disprove them because conspiracy theories are self-sealing.

A self-sealing narrative is an argument that is constructed in such a way that no evidence can be brought against it. Since most conspiracy theories have an air of persecution built into them — the whole world is against us and doesn't want us to know the truth — then even any *attempt* to disprove a conspiracy theory can be taken by its believers as confirmation that the theory is correct — that people are against them and don't want them to know the truth.

In conditions such as these, it's understandable that so many local and larger governments are moving towards discussing censorship in a way that they hadn't even a few years ago.

Cities bring us closer together — that is true — and the Internet is the world's biggest virtual city — but not all connections are healthy or productive.

As fantastic of a possibility as an ecumenopolis presents, a world without boundaries would be one with many problems, some of them potentially insurmountable.

from The Urbane Planner by Ambrogino Boccaccio

Conference Room C was as nondescript as Amarynth had expected it to be. It was simply a fifth of a larger room that it formed with its counterparts, Rooms A, B, D, and E once the dividing wall partitions were moved out of the way.

In the years that Amarynth had lived at Cambria Towers, she realized she'd never been in any of these conference rooms. She supposed she technically knew they were there. Sometimes special occasions were held on-site. Usually weddings or large parties thrown by the residents of the high rise.

Was there an actual conference one time? She thought about it for a moment. Not precisely, although she could faintly recall a job fair perhaps that had taken place here.

Again, all these events were announced on the sign that hung in the lobby. But as the message was never really intended for her, Amarynth hardly even glanced at it anymore. She only read it when the elevator took a long time to return to the ground floor, and she was left waiting with an awkward interval of time that could end at any moment but might not. A waiting interval that was not suited, not really, to whipping out her cell phone and perusing something mindlessly until the lift arrived.

Even then, the contents of the sign at any given time seemed to vanish nigh immediately, as she stepped into the lift, ascended to her floor, and entered her apartment — where she was free to do whatever it was that the moment required.

The happenings of a never-before-seen Conference Room — or Rooms — was no competition when pitted against such thrilling activities as having a conversation with her lovely young parakeet.

Having dinner. Relaxing. Showering. Going to sleep.

As she stepped into Conference Room C for the first time, Amarynth discovered she hadn't been missing a lot. Cheap brown carpets. Beige walls that had a peculiar texture that she imagined was a result of the material used to construct the room, selected not for cosmetic reasons but to deaden sound. No need to disturb tenants with the music and laughter of a lively wedding reception, was there?

Curiously, there was a large Halloween decoration tacked to the center of the back wall. It was a giant black spider that seemed to have been constructed using the longest pipe cleaners known to man. Around this arachnid was a web of pulled white cotton.

Of course. It was a web. Suddenly it all made sense.

Leigh Lines stood in front of this spider and web, arranging handouts on a folding table with her head tilted down.

"I knew you were a zebra, Leigh," Amarynth said. "But a Web Spinner? That I wasn't expecting."

"Really?" Leigh said, looking up from her work. "I thought it was obvious."

Amarynth shook her head. "Not at all."

"You're early," Leigh said.

"I know," Amarynth said. "Didn't have far to travel."

"I suppose not," Leigh replied.

Amarynth walked over and picked up one of the handouts. This one had a drawing of a cartoon web and spider. The spider was labeled "PTI." At the far corners of the complex web, which took up most of the page, bits of the web were labeled "dusters," "monsoon," "talking animals," "strange disappearances," and "mass comas."

"That's odd," Amarynth said.

"Hm?" Leigh replied as she corralled a collection of pens into a presentable arrangement.

"Well, PTI has happened. Dusters, check. But there haven't been monsoons, disappearances, and mass comas," Am said.

"Not that you know of," Leigh said. "Not yet."

Amarynth frowned.

"Look, I'm not used to convincing people about what we do here," Leigh said. "Typically, they come here willingly and ready to dig in — or not at all. I'm not an evangelist. I'm a seeker."

"You're a conspiracy theorist," Am said.

Leigh winced. "And you're a coward," she shot back.

Am flinched. "Excuse me?"

"Anyone who needs firm evidence before they take any kind of stand, even an informal one, is a coward. Especially if waiting until the point that everything becomes clear in hindsight costs human lives. Which this will," Leigh said.

Amarynth frowned.

"I'd love to have better evidence available to sort through all of this. I really would. But by the time the scientists catch up to what's going on, it will be too late," Leigh replied.

"How do you know all of this?" Amarynth asked.

"We have our processes," Leigh said. "Some of our intel comes in through precogs, ones who have been vetted by our organization, whose predictions have been qualified. Ones who tend to be right more often than not."

Amarynth said nothing. This was a sound strategy, if not watertight.

"The rest is a lot like what you do in your line of work," Leigh said.

"Connections?" said Am.

Leigh nodded. "We take the facts as we know them and then set them out visually and work through it together, noting any connections that seem evident. As a thinktank."

"Just facts?" Am pressed her, as this description was at odds with what she'd heard about the Web Spinners through the grapevine. The group had quite the reputation for playing fast and loose with the truth.

Leigh sighed. "Well, no. We also... act on other sources. Not exactly facts but leads."

"What do these leads look like?" Am pressed her. "In lay terms?"

Leigh grimaced. "You have to understand, Amarynth, that when we're starting at zero, when we're starting with nothing, that anything could be a good place to begin. Like a thread you can pull loose to start to unravel the whole knotted structure."

"Or like the first strand that begins to weave a web. Flimsy by itself but foundational," Am offered.

"Exactly," Leigh replied.

"Tell me about the threads," Am pressed again.

"Look, it's nothing impressive. Myths, legends, stories, rumors, and sometimes... member dreams. Whatever elements are buried in our individual or collective subconscious," Leigh said.

Am groaned.

"This was a mistake. I should never have invited you," Leigh said.

Amarynth opened her mouth, hoping to reassure Leigh somehow, to say something that would make her feel better. But nothing came out.

The small voice in her head was silent. Not even a small tingle of activity.

Wasn't that how it always went? The more you wanted to say something, the less able you were to actually say it. It was easier to do things by accident, to stumble into them without realizing where you were going.

Going anywhere on purpose could be hopeless.

Well for me, Amarynth added. Because other people had always seemed a lot more straightforward. But she had been born backward somehow. Sometimes this reversal came in handy, but, boy, was it inconvenient most of the time, trying to navigate a world that seemed like it was built for people who were her exact opposite.

"Am," Leigh was saying.

Amarynth snapped to, realizing she'd been frozen in place and didn't know how long she'd been that way. She made a grunting noise. No actual words.

"The meeting's about to start. Take a seat," Leigh said, gently. Her eyes were wide with worry.

"Oh yeah," Am said. "Of course."

Her first impulse was to run, to head back up to her apartment, but she decided she didn't want to do that to Leigh. Instead, Amarynth slunk off to a seat in the back row, at the end of it, which put her in the far corner of the room.

She adopted a less-than-affable facial expression, hoping to look unapproachable and scare off anyone who might think of coming close — or worse yet, striking up idle conversation.

However, no sooner had she sat down than a tall slight man sat next to her, despite the plethora of open seats to choose from. His medium-long ginger hair was styled into a bold updo, not quite a pompadour but close. It seemed to Amarynth like his hair was asking her a question.

As she pondered what question that would be, the man spoke. "I was hoping you'd be here."

Amarynth's unapproachable expression bloomed into a frown. "Do I know you?"

"You know *of* me," the man offered.

Amarynth studied his face for a moment. She had never seen it before. Never in her life.

Although… there was a little something around the eyes, wasn't there? Something that was so familiar but she had a hard time placing.

She was sure she'd passed him on crowded streets. That this wasn't the first time she'd ever seen those eyes. She had seen them many times.

And every time those eyes were on a face that looked completely different.

One night she had even seen those eyes on a stray cat, she was positive. The voice within her agreed. And it provided even more context. The voice within her told her why that made sense, that these particular eyes kept appearing everywhere.

"You're the shapeshifter," Am said. "Change." She hesitated for a moment, before pointedly adding. "Change *Peterson*."

"Patterson," Change corrected huffily. "Amarynth, you knew that. You knew my last name. You're just doing that thing."

"What thing?" Am said.

"That thing that people do when they get people's names wrong on purpose. Saying the wrong name just to be mean," Change challenged her.

"People do that?" Am said coyly.

"You're bad at acting," Change stated.

"And you're bad at eyes," Am said.

Change bristled. "Did Viv tell you that?"

Amarynth shook her head. "You know that Viv barely gives me the time of day. No, anyone can see that you're bad at eyes. Why else would you only ever do them one way?"

Change groused unintelligibly before regaining his composure. "You did, too, do it on purpose. I'm sure you've had it done to you."

"Had what done to me?" Am said. She was liking this. It was fun drawing it out, making Change work for it.

"You've had people say your name wrong before. No matter how careful you are to tell them what your name is. Even if you spell it for them — aloud and in writing. A as in Alpha. M as in Mike. They still get it wrong. You know how annoying it gets when people call you... what do they call you?"

Amarynth stayed silent.

"Amy," Change ventured.

Amarynth bit her lip.

"Amethyst," Change pressed.

Amarynth's leg bounced.

"Amber," Change continued.

Amarynth twitched and screwed up her face. "You've made your point."

"You knew exactly what you were doing when you called me by the wrong last name," Change said. "You were sending a message."

"And what message was that?" Amarynth asked.

"When people get your name wrong, they either didn't think you were important enough to remember, or..."

"Or?"

"Oh, you're listening now, are you?" Change said.

Amarynth shrugged.

"Or," Change continued, "they assume when you tell them how to spell your name aloud or even when you write it down for them, that you've gotten your own name wrong. That you don't even know your own name. And that *they*, a complete stranger, would certainly know it better than you do."

Amarynth didn't say anything.

"People are jerks, Amarynth. They don't mean to be. But they are," Change said. "But you don't have to be, at least not in the same way. So don't drag yourself down to their level."

"You say that like I'm not a person," Amarynth said.

Change shrugged but didn't say anything.

"Is that why you came to this meeting?" Amarynth said. "To give me life tips?"

"No," Change said. "I'm here to help."

"You have a funny way of helping," Am said.

"Thank you," Change said.

"It wasn't a compliment," Am said. "Just an observation."

Change's question mark hair gleamed under the fluorescent lights as his strangely familiar eyes regarded her.

"So what's your take, Mr. Shapeshifter?" Amarynth said. "What do you think is going on? Why do you think psychic powers are transmitting a mystery illness?'

"I'm not sure that they are," Change said.

"Come again?"

"Things are not as they appear," Change said. "They may call it PTI, but early names don't mean much. It doesn't mean that it actually comes from psychic activity. No one knows at this point where it comes from. It's all guesses."

"Well, what's wrong with that?" Amarynth challenged him. "Isn't that the way it always is with a new illness? It takes a bit for the scientists to catch up to what's really happening. You can't expect them to be experts on something that only just began existing."

"Sure, it's the way things usually happen. The scientists always take a little while to catch up," Change conceded. "But just because it's the normal way that it happens, it doesn't mean that there aren't costs to it. To that lag."

"What do you mean?" Amarynth asked.

"People are used to thinking that scientists have all the answers. Not that they arrive there by trial and error, hypothesis and rejection of hypothesis. So when an expert tells them their best guess one day and revises it later when research doesn't bear out, they can't see that as the scientific method. They can't see that as trustworthy. Instead, they internalize the message that no one knows anything. And that there's no sense in staying informed because the information is just going to change. When in fact the opposite is true. When the new information, the contradictory information is usually closer to the truth — even if it hasn't quite arrived there yet. Even if there's more study to be done," Change said.

"I think I get what you mean," Amarynth said. "I'm still not sure whether it's a bad or a good idea to eat eggs. Too many studies."

"Precisely," Change said.

"Well, if it's not transmitted psychically, then what's your best guess? What do you think is causing PTI?" Am asked.

Change considered this for a moment, before responding, "I suspect one of my own, frankly."

"Your own?" Amarynth said.

"The shapeshifters," Change replied.

"There are more of you?" Amarynth asked.

"Ah, I guess you've finally run into something you don't just know," Change shot back.

Amarynth frowned.

"Of course there are more shapeshifters," Change said. "There are more of you, aren't there?" He paused for a moment. A doubtful expression passed over his face as he seemed to reconsider. "Well, maybe not more of *you*. You seem to be one of a kind."

"What do you mean by that?" Amarynth pressed.

"What would you say if I told you that I know but can't explain?" Change replied.

Amarynth sighed.

"It's frustrating being on the other side of it, isn't it?" Change said.

Am felt as though she'd been jabbed between the ribs.

"You are just as infuriating as I expected you to be," she replied.

"I know," Change said. "I'm infuriating because I don't need anyone. That really gets under people's skin."

"No," Amarynth replied. "That's not why. It's because you're annoying."

"Six of one," Change said.

"There's a difference between not needing other people and being annoying," Amarynth shot back.

"Is there?" Change challenged her.

"Of course there is," Amarynth said.

"I wonder," Change said. "I wonder how many people would become insufferable if they needed nothing from other people. I wonder how many people are simply considerate of others because they have to in order to survive."

"Not all of them, that's for sure," Amarynth said. But as she thought about her mother's upper-class connections, the people she had personally known who needed the least from others, she had a sinking feeling. The best among them had irritating quirks, and most of them trended towards the insufferable. Wealth and virtue were often at odds, something she worried about a lot due to her uncomfortable proximity to those social circles.

"There's this myth about rugged individualism and how it makes you better than other people," Change said. "We're told that the strongest people don't care what other people think of them. That worrying about what others think of you is a form of weakness. It's an especially popular myth in the Psychic State. The flag with that dumb lone star that's supposed to be an inspiring symbol. Talk about upward mobility porn. Blech." He shook his head and scrunched up his nose as though he had smelled something disgusting.

"The truth is," Change continued, "it's the most reprehensible people who don't care what anyone else thinks of them. The real assholes. Oh, true, you shouldn't let randos be the judge of whether you're living your life right. That's taking it too far in the other direction. Just like you wouldn't judge your beauty in a cracked mirror, you shouldn't let any old jackass determine whether what you're doing is right or wrong."

"You like to hear yourself talk, don't you?" Amarynth said.

Change nodded. "Anyway, Amarynth, it's important to learn to look to the right mirrors. You gotta care what someone thinks about you, or else you turn into a real creep. And that's my whole problem. I don't have a mirror. I'm on my own. I don't need anyone." He shrugged. "That's why I'm annoying. There's no getting around it."

"When you put it that way," Amarynth replied, "I almost feel sorry for you."

"Some might," Change replied. "There's nothing like being in constant flux to make you feel like you're stuck in a rut."

Amarynth frowned. "That's paradoxical. I'd think that the constant change would be quite stimulating."

Change shook his head. "Nah. It's true what they say. The more things change, the more they stay the same. I'm so bored."

Amarynth considered this silently.

"Just promise me you'll choose the right mirrors," Change said.

"Why would I promise you anything?" Amarynth scoffed.

"Because I might be annoying," Change said, "but I'm on your side. And if you knew everything I know, you'd be worried about what's going to happen to you."

"I wish you'd just tell me what's going on," Amarynth said.

"I can't," Change replied. "But not for the same reason you can't explain."

"Then why? Why not tell me then?"

"Professional conflict of interest," Change said.

Amarynth rolled her eyes. "Whatever," she said.

But even as the meeting began, and the group started to reason out potential links between the known information, Amarynth couldn't get what Change said out of her head.

He left right before the meeting officially adjourned. Amarynth rose to follow him but was blocked by Leigh, who approached with an apology.

And before Amarynth could even spin back around to call after him, Change was gone.

When Amarynth returned to her apartment, she was greeted by a wary-looking Gino. His arms were crossed. "Where were you?" he asked.

"Am I not allowed to have a life?" Amarynth challenged him, and the strength of what she said took her off guard. It had sounded so much more like light joking in her head.

Gino frowned. "Of course you're allowed to have a life," he said. He sighed. "I just want to be part of that life. An important part of that life. One you always remember to check in with."

Amarynth's heart sank. "You're right. I should have let you know I was going out."

Gino nodded. "I was so worried."

"Can you forgive me?"

"Well, I don't know..." Gino said, drawing out the words. "I could probably be convinced." He planted a kiss on her that nearly knocked her over.

"That's one way around resentment," Amarynth replied breathlessly once they had finished kissing.

"What's that?"

"Amnesia," she replied.

Gino laughed.

"When you kiss me like that, I forget who I am, let alone what either of us has done." She smiled.

"Well," Gino said, kissing her forehead. "I'll have to keep that in mind." He trailed kisses down her face with each word until he was kissing her lips. "That and nothing else," he added. "Because the kisses will have emptied our minds of the rest."

Amarynth smiled.

"Where were you anyway?" Gino asked.

Amarynth felt a jolt of panic. "Hanging out with Leigh," she said quickly, before feeling a little guilty. It was true of course. Leigh had been the one to invite her to the Web Spinners meeting. And Leigh was the one leading the group, after all.

But there was a lot she left out. A lot she wasn't telling Gino.

"Leigh at the concierge desk?" Gino said. "The girl who used to be a barista at the coffeehouse?"

Amarynth nodded.

"I didn't know you two were friends," Gino said. He looked at Amarynth with a peculiar intensity, and she felt uncomfortable, as though she were being scrutinized. As though he could see through her and see that there was a lot she wasn't telling him.

How do you lie to someone with intuition as uncanny as mine? Amarynth felt herself wondering. Not easily, that was for sure. And certainly not comfortably. It was better to speak truthfully, if evasively.

"I didn't know we were friends either until recently," Amarynth said. And that was true, too. A lot of friendships started that way, as two people who simply knew each other and not well. And then gradually over time, one or the other would take more social risks, and those risks would pay off, maybe by revealing something personal about themselves or by asking to spend more time together, and eventually, there would come a point where they were friends.

Often that exact point wasn't entirely clear. Friendships were allowed to be significantly fuzzier by society than romantic relationships — which had people asking for clarification as soon as possible and rushing towards the "are we exclusive?" talk.

As Amarynth wound this through her brain, she realized uncomfortably that even though Gino spent every night here and his belongings were starting to creep in one by one and not leave with him the following day, that they had not had The Talk. The "so what are we?" talk.

They hadn't said, "Let's be exclusive."

She hadn't asked, "Will you be my boyfriend?"

A chill traveled up her spine. As curious as she was to know where things stood, talking about it was all too awkward to contemplate. Even thinking about having that conversation filled her with dread.

Aloud, she said, "Friendships just sort of sneak up on you, don't they?"

Gino grinned. "Lots of things do," he said, before kissing her again.

Like me? Did I sneak up on you? Amarynth found herself thinking as they kissed. But by the time the kiss ended, the thought was forgotten. That glorious amnesia again.

"Well," Gino said, "the next time you go out with Leigh, just let me know your plans."

"Okay," Amarynth said.

"You're used to being single and so am I. Don't get me wrong. I don't want to keep you on a tight leash. And I don't want you to keep me on one either," Gino said.

"Good," said Amarynth.

"I just want to know where my girlfriend is. That's all I'm asking," Gino replied.

Girlfriend. He'd said it. Amarynth's lips curled involuntarily into a smile. She liked the sound of it.

And she delighted in the fact that she'd gotten her answer without the awkwardness of having to ask the question. Still, she couldn't help herself. "Girlfriend?" she teased him. "This is the first I'm hearing of this. Didn't you think it was important enough to ask me first?"

Gino cringed. "I was nervous," he confessed.

"Me, too," Amarynth replied, causing Gino to grin. "And I have another confession to make."

"Oh?" he said.

"You still make me nervous. I think you always will," Amarynth said.

"I know the feeling," Gino replied.

"The answer is yes by the way," Amarynth said.

"The answer?"

"I'll be your girlfriend," Amarynth said.

"So, you want to be exclusive?" said Gino.

Amarynth nodded.

"Great," Gino said. "Me, too."

"You're half living here already," Amarynth said.

"Was it that obvious?" Gino asked.

"Painfully," said Amarynth. "Although it's not the first time I've seen someone try to move in one item at a time, so I had a leg up, I think."

"Ohhh," Gino said. "Storytime."

Amarynth laughed. "There's not much to tell. It was back in college when I lived in the dorms. There was a boy I befriended because he was even more awkward than I was. He seemed like he needed a friend, and I never really gave any thought to what he must have thought of me."

"Oh boy," Gino said. "He fell for you, didn't he?"

Amarynth nodded. "Hard. But I was oblivious to it for a long while." She stared into the distance. "Just like I am to a lot of things."

"You've always seemed really perceptive to me," Gino reassured her.

"Oh sure," Amarynth said, laughing. "I'm really good at knowing things that no one else will believe. Things that I can't explain. What a paragon of perception." She shook her head. "Sorry. I know you were trying to be nice."

"Nah," Gino said. "Just telling it like I see it."

"Well, at least you're not used to being believed either, so it'll sting less when I dismiss you, huh?"

Gino frowned. "Amarynth..."

"Hm?"

"You're feeling too far ahead again. Making assumptions about you and me. Just finish the story," Gino prompted her.

"There's not much of a story," Am said. "I warned you."

"Well, what happened when this guy fell for you?"

"He kept leaving this huge book he said I had to read in my dorm room. It was by his favorite fantasy author. He kept raving about it. I tried to start it, but it was so dull. I'd stop by when his roommate was around and he was out and drop the book off, but I'd turn around and the book would be back in my room again. Finally, my roommate pointed out what was happening... that he was just leaving it with me to have an excuse to talk to me, to have a reason to meet up again, and something for us to talk about. She said he'd clearly fallen for me. It was apparently obvious to everyone who knew me, just in the way he looked at me. I never saw it though," Amarynth said.

"And then what did you do? Once you realized he had feelings for you."

"I stopped by his dorm room when I knew he'd be there, and I brought the book with me. I told him that I didn't want to read the book. That he should stop bringing it by," Amarynth said. "It was hard. He was so hurt. I never rejected him romantically... he never approached me directly about becoming involved that way. But in that one conversation with the book, there was so much subtext. We both knew. And he was so brokenhearted."

"Did you stay friends?" Gino said.

Amarynth shook her head. "He avoided me after that. And I let him have his space. We drifted apart."

Gino nodded. "One of those unspoken things?"

Amarynth nodded. "I picked up a copy of that same book a few years back," she confessed.

"Oh?" Gino said. "Decide to give it another shot?"

"Yes," Amarynth said. "I thought I'd see what I think of it now, several years later and without all the subtext and pressure from him."

"What did you think?" Gino asked.

Amarynth grimaced. "It was terrible."

Gino laughed. "Blunt."

"I don't pull punches when it comes to literary criticism," Am said.

"Great," Gino said. "Now I'm nervous to have you read my book when it's finished."

"Look on the bright side," Amarynth said. "At least you'll know if I say I like it, I'm not bullshitting you."

"I suppose that's something," Gino replied, "although there's always the surefire route of never finishing the damn thing."

"You're probably right," Amarynth said. "They do say that the surest way to avoid criticism is by never doing anything. Everything else is a gamble."

Water, Water Everywhere

Sustainable Urban Water Management

Many of my students are surprised to learn how much effective urban planning hinges on the proper management of water. While the development of large cities has undoubtedly been a boon to civilization, moving so many people into densely populated city centers has presented many challenges.

A city population needs to have enough clean water for its citizens to drink, and it also must purify and deal with a large quantity of wastewater produced by its residents. This purview of course includes sewage treatment facilities to deal with the natural byproducts of dense population:

Blackwater: toilet water and excrement.

Greywater: runoff from sinks, tubs, showers, dishwashers, and laundry machines.

Soaps and detergents.

Toilet paper.

It is said that you can learn a lot about how urbane a culture is by looking at what they do with their waste, far more than you can learn by looking at their achievements.

However, there is much more wastewater than these sources that must be managed. Heavy rains carry a risk of flooding our cities because of the increased amount of paved area, which prevents the ground from absorbing rainfall, as well as the way that rooftops tend to funnel rainfall and encourage flooding.

If left unchecked, flooding can easily wreak havoc on densely populated city areas, causing great damage to buildings and other important infrastructure.

Thankfully, urban planners have taken great pains to address the issue of flooding — so while it remains a threat, there is much that can be done.

Since natural drainage is less available in paved areas, alternative methods must be used. Streets are typically the first line of drainage, allowing excess rainfall to route into gutters. Unlike other forms of water, this excess rainfall is diverted into a storm sewer system that does not pass through wastewater treatment facilities, as these systems would be easily overwhelmed by the large amounts of water that unexpected rainfall can bring.

The MS4, or Municipal Separate Storm Sewer System, is crucial here. The MS4 offloads the burden on the system by gathering stormwater and diverting it to streams and rivers.

Another technique that was used more historically but has fallen out of fashion is known as channelization, in which existing urban streams are widened to increase flow rate and cause water to move as quickly away from an area as possible. While the method does bear results, it carries a few downsides. Channelization is not only ugly, but it also doesn't exactly mitigate the problem of flooding and instead simply seems to force effluent away, making it worse for whoever is downstream.

Given the interdependency of not only the modern city but of civilization, this is hardly a desirable solution.

Cities are now working with developers to encourage water-responsible development as cities continue to urbanize, requiring developers to build in detention and retention ponds that offset the effect of their constructions.

However, the most urbane of these modern urban planners never forget that rain isn't strictly a waste product. Instead, it is also a valuable resource. The most forward-thinking cities are now moving towards urbanized watersheds and other alternative methods such as rain gardens, vegetative rooftops, and permeable pavement.

from The Urbane Planner by Ambrogino Boccaccio

It rained for four days straight. Let up for a few hours. And then began to rain again for another three days.

This was no polite rain. Not a drizzle. Certainly not a trickle.

This was a violent downpour as entire blankets of water fell from the sky.

After a local meteorologist had to be hospitalized for trying to capture some footage on the ground, most residents of Skinner-Watson had the good sense to limit their outdoor activity time. The traffic situation became impossible as flooded roads and low visibility rendered the journey anywhere perilous.

Gino inexplicably still left for work at the community college, leaving Amarynth to wonder how he managed. Was he walking? Taking public transit?

She'd assumed at first that he had a car, but since he had moved in, it had become apparent that he didn't need a parking space. She couldn't imagine any rideshare operator making a profit in this clusterfuck.

When she asked Gino, he'd smirked mischievously and said, "I have my ways."

"Oh really?" Amarynth had said.

Gino had nodded.

"Are you riding a broomstick? Swinging from building to building like Spiderman?" Am had said.

Gino had grinned. "Amarynth, a little mystery goes a long way toward keeping a relationship fresh."

And she'd groaned but let him keep her in the dark.

What was important was that he came back safely every night, which he invariably did.

Strangely, he never seemed worse for wear, as one would expect anyone having to deal with this awful storm would be. In fact, he didn't even seem wet.

It wasn't something she told many people, but Amarynth had several routines that guided her throughout the day. There was enough in life you couldn't control, and that was puzzling enough. Might as well nail down the pieces that you could.

That way you had more room for the chaos that couldn't be helped. The stuff that would be forced on her from the outside world.

Repetition anchored her. Having whatever structure she could was calming. It helped a lot.

When she had been suspended from PsyOps, the emotional impact was immediate. Because reporting to PsyOps for work was an important part of her daily routine.

And now that she no longer needed to go to PsyOps, there was a void where that routine had been.

At first, it had been almost too much, but new routines crept into that open space. Gino was a huge help in that department. Dating him — and having him live with her — had been such a major development that it normally would have upset her routine in an unsettling way.

But not this time. There was an open space that he was able to inhabit.

The timing couldn't have been any better, Amarynth found herself thinking as she fell asleep with his arms wrapped around her.

A little too good? Something within her asked. But she chose to ignore it. A great many things were changing. Her professional life was in peril. She was living in sin with the world's most handsome urban planning instructor. The world was unsettled with both the emergence of a new disease and bizarre dust storms.

There was plenty to fill her with anxiety. To throw her off keel.

And besides, she thought, *perhaps these doubts are just fear of success.* Because she'd never been this successful, at least not in a social sense.

Oh, sure, she was suspended from work. Her entire career now consisted of canoodling with Gino, playing house, going to weird conspiracy theory meetings, and writing the odd obscurantist poem.

But she was happy. She was starting to feel like maybe she belonged somewhere.

If this kept up, she wouldn't want to go back to PsyOps when the suspension was over. *If it's ever over*, she reminded herself. Martin hadn't sent word about her employment status, and she hadn't asked for it.

He probably had his hands full, poor thing, with Penny's pregnancy. Amarynth knew that Penny had finally told them — Viv, Karen, and yes, Martin.

She didn't know exactly when or how but was sure that it had happened.

And Amarynth also knew that Martin would reach out when he was ready to talk to her about the next steps. But not a moment sooner.

And until then, she found her way through her new normal. Thankfully, the new normal still contained a lot of the old normal within it. Her shower routine was a great example of one of her standard anchoring practices that still did the job.

She had it all calibrated and timed. There was a certain distance she moved the hot and cold knobs to create the perfect eventual water temperature. And then there was an exact amount of time that the water needed to run until it was ready.

She had it figured out to the millisecond by now, how long to wait to step into the shower so she wouldn't waste any water but also didn't have to cringe away from water that was too cold and not quite ready for her.

While that time elapsed, she gingerly stripped off her clothes and placed them in the hamper. She smiled at her reflection in the bathroom mirror and then frowned, just to get a range of expressions.

Yeah, she looked the same as she had yesterday. Of course. Aging wasn't something you really saw, was it? Especially if you were paying attention, as she often did. It happened too slowly to detect on a day-to-day basis. People who never looked at themselves were more at risk of finding aging sudden, weren't they? Amarynth thought so.

I might not be able to stop myself from aging, she thought. *But I'll be damned if I let it sneak up on me.*

It was a bit like keeping regular tabs on what you spent and earned, she thought. Budgeting was easier if you were acquainted with the day-to-day reality of it. It didn't sneak up on you the same way that it did if you tried to play it fast and loose and rarely checked. Not only did you risk racking up overdraft fees this way, checking what was going on with your finances became something you dreaded — because you had no clue what you were going to see when you looked.

"Shit," Amarynth said.

She had gotten lost in her thoughts and broken her routine. She was late for her shower. Wasting water.

She hurried over to the shower and pulled back the curtain and... almost stepped right onto a lizard.

"You kiss your mother with that mouth?" the lizard said.

Amarynth shrieked and jumped backward, nearly falling over as she did. She grabbed a bathrobe off the back of the door.

"Oh, tell me how you really feel," the lizard in her shower said. "I'm not so bad, you know. And the water is warm. The perfect temperature. You're a real wizard that way, lady."

Amarynth stared at the talking lizard. She blinked several times in luxurious slow motion. Each time she opened her eyes, the lizard was still there. Improbably.

"Take a picture. It'll last longer," the lizard said to her.

Amarynth sat down on the toilet. "I'm losing my mind," she said to herself.

The lizard crawled out of the shower and onto the bathroom floor, leaving wet footprints on the tile as he did.

"If you're really worried about wasting water, you should probably do something about it. I'd get the dials for you, but I'm not equipped for it, as you can see," the lizard offered, glancing at his tiny feet.

Amarynth nodded. Her whole body was shaking. She closed her eyes and turned off the water. When she opened her eyes, the lizard was still there.

"Hey, could you do me a favor?" the lizard said.

"What?" Amarynth asked.

"Oh good, you're talking to me now," the lizard replied. "I was starting to think it was the silent treatment for me forever."

Amarynth involuntarily groaned.

"I'll pretend I didn't hear that," the lizard said. "Anyway, could you be a doll and get me a hand towel or something? The fluffier, the better. I have a hard time retaining my body heat on my own. It's my metabolism. A lizard thing. And if I stay wet, it's *no bueno* for me. *Adios.* Lights out. I haven't gotten the hang of shivering. I hear some reptiles can do it. The bigger ones, I guess. But not me."

Amarynth realized then that the lizard's mouth wasn't moving.

"You're communicating with me telepathically," Amarynth said.

"Very good," the lizard replied. "Welcome to reality. I was getting a bit lonely here."

Amarynth laughed and shook her head. "Am I communicating back telepathically?"

"Well, your lips are moving, so what do you think?" the lizard said.

"Good point," Am said.

"You're making sounds, like you normally do. The only difference is that I can understand them now. *That* I think is telepathy. But what do I know? I'm just a lizard. Nobody's calling me for expert advice," the lizard said. The lizard then telepathically laughed at his own joke, while his physical mouth stayed drawn in a tight line.

"You know," Amarynth said, "when I woke up this morning, I didn't realize I was going to get to experience a lizard laughing at his own joke."

"And I didn't realize I was going to come *this close* to showering with a real babe, only to be denied," the lizard said.

Amarynth laughed.

"Oh good, you laughed," the lizard said. "I was obviously joking about the babe thing. You're a bit… smooth for my liking. Not nearly scaly enough."

"Uhh… thanks," Amarynth said. "I think."

"Thanks that you're not my type?"

Amarynth nodded. "I don't know if I can deal with a world in which lizards find me sexy."

"Lady, you would hate my life then," the lizard said.

Amarynth laughed again. "Well," she said, "I have to say that you are the funniest talking lizard that I've ever found in my bathroom."

"Thanks," the lizard replied. "You're not so bad yourself."

At that moment, Amarynth heard keys jostling in the lock of the apartment door. She strode quickly to the front of her apartment.

"Gino," she called, "you'll never guess what I found."

"A talking animal?" he said, as the door swung open.

Amarynth gasped. "How did you —"

"I made a friend myself on campus today. A stray cat who decided it was his duty to lecture me about my wardrobe choices. You?"

"A lizard I almost showered with."

Gino threw his head back and exploded with laughter.

"I have feelings, you know," the lizard said. He had gingerly waddled out into the living room, not wanting to be excluded from the goings-on. He turned his scaly head to the birdcage. "Do they pull this shit with you? Talking about you like you're not even there?" he asked Tesla.

Tesla squawked a litany in response.

"Oh, I see," the lizard replied. "Very interesting. Very interesting indeed."

"What is he saying?" Amarynth asked.

"Oh, wouldn't you like to know?" the lizard snapped back.

Am frowned.

"It's not nice to be excluded, is it?" the lizard challenged her.

"You've made your point," Gino said.

Tesla raised a racket.

"I feel the same way," the lizard commiserated.

Amarynth groaned.

"Well," the lizard said, "I can tell when I'm not wanted." He waddled over to the apartment door. "If you'd be so kind," he said to Amarynth tipping up his head and bobbing it in a way that looked very much to her like a nod.

She opened the door, and the lizard slinked out into the hallway. Amarynth closed the door. "Do you think he'll come back?" she asked Gino.

"No idea," Gino said. "For once. He does seem the type to leave to make a point and come back for attention afterward. Just to see how much we've missed him."

Amarynth laughed. She peered out the peephole. Their reptilian friend had disappeared down the hall.

"So, little mister," Amarynth said to Tesla, who peeped and cheeped in response. "What do you have to say for yourself?"

Tesla was silent at this question. He puffed up his feathers and shook a little before closing his eyes.

"Looks like the little guy is worn out," Gino observed.

"You know, the silent treatment is rude," Am said to Tesla.

His avian eyes remained closed.

The words *talking animals* flashed before Amarynth's face. It was just as the Web Spinners had predicted. And *monsoon.*

The interminable driving rains.

It was coming to pass. Uncannily. Next would be *strange disappearances* and *mass coma.*

Amarynth picked up her cell phone and selected Leigh from the contact list.

"Hey Leigh," she said.

"You had a talker, too, didn't you?" Leigh replied.

"Yeah," Amarynth said.

"I take it you're finally on board. Finally convinced," Leigh said.

"You could say that," Am replied.

"It's about time," Leigh said.

Am laughed.

And with that, Leigh said an address.

"That's where you live, isn't it?" Amarynth said.

"How did you know that?" Leigh replied, her voice trembling.

"I'm good with addresses," Am said. "Always have been."

"I see," Leigh said. "Never heard of that before. That could come in handy."

They worked out a time to meet up and Amarynth hung up the phone.

"What was that all about?" Gino asked her after the call was over.

"She had a talking visitor, too, I guess," Am said. "She invited me over to her place to hang out."

Another misleading truth.

Gino flashed her a smile that made her feel guilty.

Amarynth found Leigh's place easily. She had expected it to be modest, and it was. But Leigh had made good use of the space.

"Is it just us?" Am said.

"This time, yes," Leigh said. "This is where all the private meetings take place."

"Private meetings? So the one I went to before was public?" Am said.

"Yes, I don't have people here until they're part of the inner circle. Until I know I can trust them," Leigh explained.

"I feel honored," Am said.

"You should," Leigh replied. "This is some kind of record. I don't usually trust people this fast. But things are rapidly moving towards crisis, even if most of the world hasn't figured it out yet, and I have a good feeling about you, so full speed ahead, I say."

Amarynth smiled.

"I wanted to meet with you one on one and get your professional opinion. As a Connections Agent," Leigh said.

"A suspended Connections Agent," Am corrected.

"That's just office politics," Leigh shot back. "Getting suspended doesn't mean you can't do your damn job."

Or does it? Amarynth found herself wondering, as Leigh led her to a large board that was standing in the living room of her cramped apartment.

"We have our own causality board here," Leigh offered. "I'm sure it's not at all what you're used to working with in Connections, but…"

"It's lovely," Amarynth assured her, swallowing the rest of her thoughts. Leigh didn't need to know her entire background with causality boards, how much she stuck out in the Connections program at the Department of Psychic Operations. Leigh didn't need to know about all the times that Amarynth had seriously doubted that she was even a Connector.

It wasn't just her suspiciously negative test results. And it wasn't just the strange feeling she always had, like no matter who she was surrounded with that she was truly alone.

No, it had persisted in more tangible, objective ways. Ways that Amarynth always worried were obvious to other people.

Her first attempts at using a causality board had been one of those times. There had been another Connector in her orientation class of new PsyOps hires named Sophia.

When the normal HR gobbledygook about company policy was out of the way, Amarynth and Sophia were transferred to Connections to undergo their actual job training.

Their trainer had demonstrated proper use of a causality board by posting various known clues in a roughly equidistant manner across the board. Then he walked precisely six feet back from the board, closed his eyes, and rubbed his temples.

And he waited.

Finally, he opened his eyes again and casually traced a series of neon lines between the clues. Quickly he copied the same pattern formed on his board into a small handheld computer, which turned the input into numerical data.

This output was then cross-referenced against a key that produced still more outputs, these ones considered final. Amarynth had studied the outputs of this final key with great amusement, as they reminded her very much of a Magic 8-Ball.

You may rely on it.

Don't count on it.

Outlook good.

Amarynth had snickered. *I suppose next they'll be training us on how to employ pet rocks*, she had thought and almost said aloud but noted that everyone around her approached this method with deadly seriousness.

Well, groovy. So be it.

"It helps if you have a specific question in mind," their trainer reiterated.

Amarynth and Sophia had nodded in unison.

"Who wants to go first?" the trainer asked.

Sophia volunteered, and Amarynth felt a wave of relief. Someone else was going to embarrass themselves doing this strange procedure.

But to her complete amazement, Amarynth noted that Sophia executed the movements flawlessly. Amarynth could even see the light tracers hanging in the air.

"You're a natural," the trainer had told Sophia.

Sophia blushed. "Oh, it's nothing," Sophia said modestly. "It's very close to what I do for myself at home, that's all."

"Okay, Amarynth," their trainer said. "You're up."

Amarynth nodded and stepped forward tentatively. She pinned the clues to the board, doing her best to make sure everything was evenly spaced. She faithfully copied the movements of both the trainer and Sophia, but when she went to trace between the clue points, no light came from her fingers.

No path was visible to her.

She turned around to see her instructor frowning at her.

Amarynth threw her hands in the air. "The answer is 'Signs point to yes,'" Amarynth said.

The instructor furrowed his brow. Quickly he did the path himself and checked the answer.

"That's right," he said, confused, "but how did you know?"

Amarynth shrugged. "I just know," she admitted. "I can't explain it. I can't show how I know, but I do."

The trainer was skeptical, but after he ran her through six different scenarios, he was satisfied. "I don't know how you're doing it, but I don't have much choice. You can't use a causality board worth a damn, but I'm passing you."

"Thanks," Amarynth said, feeling quite embarrassed, as Sophia stared at her.

"Just be warned," the instructor continued, and Amarynth felt whatever blood was left in her face drain completely away, "that if you're cheating, it's going to catch up with you eventually."

"I didn't cheat," Amarynth protested.

"Well, you won't be able to cheat on the job is all I'm saying," the instructor insisted.

"I didn't cheat," Amarynth repeated, but she could tell by the look on his face that he didn't believe her.

And where Sophia had once been friendly and even chummed around with her in orientation, Amarynth found that suddenly Sophia wanted nothing to do with her. It was the same way with the other Connections Agents.

"I think they hate me, Mom," Amarynth had said to her mother at her first visit after joining the department.

"They're just jealous of you," her mother had said. She meant it to be comforting, but it didn't help Amarynth.

"Jealous?" Amarynth said. "That's just stupid."

"Is it?" her mother replied.

"Yes," Amarynth said. "I'm an outcast. What is there to be jealous of?"

"Honey," her mother had said, "being good at things and being an outcast aren't mutually exclusive. It's possible to be so good at things that it makes you an outcast. In fact, it's really common."

"Well, whatever," Amarynth said. "Whatever reason they have for shutting me out, I'm an outcast, which is saying something because all the math nerds work in Connections. It's why I thought I'd fit in there in the first place. Guess I'm not as much of a math nerd as I thought I was."

"You are," her mother said. "You're just doing a different kind of math than they are. That's all."

Amarynth smiled at Leigh Lines. "Don't worry about the causality board," she said. "It's perfect."

Leigh knew the board wasn't perfect but appreciated Am saying so. She appreciated it so much that she didn't say a single word about it when Amarynth simply studied what had been pinned to the board instead of performing a typical causality ritual.

"The dust knows everything we need to know," Amarynth said aloud suddenly.

"I'm sorry?" Leigh replied.

Amarynth turned to her. "Do you know any abacomancers?"

Leigh nodded. "D. B. Mathers," she said. "He was my art instructor."

"Of course he was," Amarynth said. It was a familiar story to her, the artist with psychic powers. There was Viv of course, although she was more of an ex-artist since she hadn't painted for years, not as long as Amarynth had known her. The research institute had recently published a study about it, too, the link between certain intuitive powers and artistic ability. This link was particularly strong among practitioners of avant-garde art, those who worked in analog, the obscurantist, the weird. A love of abstraction was believed to be the common link.

While Amarynth wasn't gifted herself with visual arts, finding she visualized absolutely nothing whenever she closed her eyes, she felt that same link within her manifested in different, less visual ways.

"Here's the address," Leigh said, leaning over to write it down on a slip of paper.

Amarynth waved her hand in the air. "No need. I already know."

Leigh cocked her head and studied her quizzically.

"I'm good with addresses," Amarynth explained. Addresses were generally more fixed than other people, more finite.

"Sometimes I feel like you know everything," Leigh confessed.

Amarynth shook her head. "A lot of things. But not everything," she admitted.

"Well," Leigh said, "it's a good thing then that the dust will tell us the rest."

Throw It Against the Wall, See What Sticks

Abacomancy

When it comes to explaining the Psychic Phenomenon, some psychic theorists take an evolutionary biopsychological approach. This school of thought posits that human culture and society as we know them are only possible due to leaps in logic, sloppy heuristics we use to understand our world.

These theorists point to the mechanisms of spoken language as an indicator. Surely, they say, somewhere in our history someone leaped between sign and signifier, sound and meaning, particularly as we moved away from living solely in terrain where communicating via gesture would always be convenient.

And it was probably not simply one individual but many that began to link sign and signifier and start the painstaking leaps of logic that would be required to form shared spoken language.

All around us, these theorists argue, new beings continue to make logical leaps as they are born, observe the world around them, listen to these strangely ambiguous sounds and guess at their meaning.

Human society wouldn't exist as it is without our ability to guess at ambiguity.

Therefore, these psychic theorists argue, perhaps the Psychic Phenomenon isn't a new process in and of itself, and perhaps it is only a continuation of our current evolution, whereby we are making larger leaps of logic and intuiting more in a way that was previously considered beyond our perceptive abilities.

Indeed, some subtypes do seem to depend on external factors to make predictions. One notable example is that of the abacomancer. Sometimes alternatively known as amanthomancy by the taxonomic heterodoxy (derived from the Greek word for sand, "amanthos"), abacomancy is the art of divination using dust. Abacomancers are similar to precognitionists — intuitive types who can make predictions about the future, albeit not always accurately and particularly poorly in matters in which a precog is directly involved and would be biased.

Thus far, abacomancers don't seem to be quite as vulnerable to the effects of bias. However, they are exceedingly rare. Further, their abilities do depend on the external aid of dust — and curiously so far it seems that the predictive capacity of abacomancers is directly affected by the nature of dust used to make the prediction.

Empirical confirmation is needed, but anecdotal reports have shown a rather bizarre pattern: The farther the dust has recently traveled, the better the material performs in abacomancy.

Enterprising psychic investors tried to capitalize upon this by shipping dust around the world for this purpose, only to find that artificial means of travel do not seem to imbue the particles with any extra predictive oomph.

This has caused some taxonomers to argue that abacomancers derive their true power not from the earth but the wind.

In the next edition of this work, this author hopes to provide substantive updates regarding this exciting area of intuitive research.

from Insecta Psychica: Towards an Intuitive Taxonomy
by Cloche Macomber

If art reflects life, it does so with special mirrors.

-Bertolt Brecht

D. B. Mathers, the mailbox nameplate read.

"Well," Amarynth mumbled to herself, "I've come to the right place."

She hadn't been sure until she saw the nameplate. Well, she knew it was the right address. She was good with addresses of course. But what she saw when she got there really threw her. This home wasn't at all what she expected when she thought of an abacomancer. The driveway was paved. Quickly surveying the front yard, Amarynth didn't spot a single speck of dirt. Everything looked immaculate. Artificial.

Definitely not earthy.

She steeled herself and rapped on the front door.

"Come in," a voice called to her. "It's open."

So she did. As she opened the door, she found herself standing directly across from an elderly man sitting in a recliner. In his hands, he held a red plastic rectangle.

As Amarynth stepped closer, she realized it was an Etch A Sketch. Because of the angle, she couldn't see what he was drawing on it.

"You live in an awfully clean home," Amarynth observed. The settings she found herself in were indeed spotless. And admittedly not at all what she'd expected to find when visiting an abacomancer.

"And just what do you mean by that?" the abacomancer challenged her.

Amarynth cringed. "Oh, sorry. I didn't mean..."

"Of course you meant it," the abacomancer snapped back. "It's a vicious stereotype, but it's a popular one. Stop backpedaling this instant, or I *really* won't trust you. You're on thin ice already, missy."

Missy? Amarynth stifled a giggle. She'd never had anyone call her that in her life. As far as she knew, that sort of thing only happened in cartoons, where it was inevitably said by a toothless old codger brandishing *something* menacingly.

The abacomancer who sat before her was elderly, but he appeared to have all his teeth. If anything, he was urbane, cosmopolitan. The button-down and trousers he wore looked expensive — and pristine. Just as pristine as his home. And he wasn't brandishing the Etch A Sketch, just holding it.

"And before you ask," he continued, "D. doesn't stand for Dusty. Or Dustin. It's D.B. or Dr. Mathers to you."

"I wasn't going to —"

Mathers shook his right index finger sternly in the air. Amarynth shushed.

"I don't do this for too many people, you know," Mathers said. "If you weren't a friend of Leigh's, then I would throw you out on the curb. That I would."

"Understood," Amarynth replied.

"Well, time's a-wasting," Mathers said. He set the Etch A Sketch onto the coffee table but with its face down so that she couldn't see what he had been drawing. He rose and motioned for her to follow.

Amarynth did. She walked behind him through a well-appointed house. She noted that artwork adorned every wall. Towards the front of the house, the paintings were largely photorealistic, and as they moved through the dwelling, they seemed to graduate into more impressionistic work that was still based on representation but less literally. However, as they reached his studio, there were nothing but abstracts.

"I used to teach at the Art Institute," Mathers offered. "Before I broke through as an artist. These days I can live quite comfortably off commissions alone. But that's relatively new."

"You painted all of these?" Amarynth asked.

"Of course," Mathers replied. "It'd cost a fortune to buy them nowadays, now that my work is finally selling for what it's been worth all along."

"But they're so different from each other," Amarynth observed.

"It's called range," Mathers huffed. "Anyway, a person is allowed to evolve, aren't they?"

"Of course," Am replied sheepishly.

"It's how I ended up playing with dirt in the first place," he explained. "Evolution."

"Oh?"

Mathers nodded. He led her through the door into the back room.

Ah, Amarynth thought, *this is where all the dirt is.*

In the middle of this room was what appeared to be a giant sandbox filled to the brim with a variety of different colored sands. Several large blank canvases were tipped against the back wall. The floor and wall were both splattered and stained with a rainbow of hues. Amarynth couldn't tell if it was paint or dirt but suspected it was probably both.

"My studio," Mathers said.

"It's lovely," Amarynth said.

"And more what you suspected, I imagine, from an abacomancer," Mathers said.

Amarynth nodded. Denying it now would only make him more guarded.

"I try to keep the mess all confined to one room," Mathers explained. He walked over to a locker that was tucked into a side corner. "I keep extra clothes in here. And here," he said motioning towards the other corner, "is my shower."

"No door?" Amarynth commented, for it was just a bit of tile with a drain in the floor underneath a showerhead and a few plain knobs jutting out from the wall.

"Well, I don't get a lot of visitors," Mathers replied, "and besides, after you've bared your soul with your art, what's the big deal about showing a little skin?"

Amarynth grinned. Maybe there was a little bit of hippie in this old guy, after all.

"I used to try to paint very literally. To capture the world just as my eyes saw it, but free of any biases, free of any interpretation or emotion. Photorealism. That's because I was a cocky young thing. Thought I was a rock star. It's how you get the most compliments, you know? If you can paint like a photograph." He stared off in the distance. "It's a strange thing… how people always look up to folks who can behave like a machine. I mean, what's the point of that? That's what machines are for, to act like machines. You'd think that human beings were meant to be something else. That that's what would impress people." He shook his head.

"I think," Amarynth said, choosing her words very carefully, "that people like to pretend we can escape being human if we only try a little harder. Someone who can do things as well as a machine… well, that feeds into the fantasy. It leaves a little hope for the rest of us."

"Sure," Mathers said. "Sure." He sighed. "Anyway, after a while, I got bored of trying to act like a machine. And I started to sink into my own bias. Sink into my heuristics, my process. And that's when I started painting abstracts." He smiled at the memory. "I don't know exactly when I switched over to dirt. But when I did, it was like going home. But going home a bigger, better man." He swung his arms out expansively to the sides. "And now here I am."

"Well, I suppose you didn't come here just to learn all about me, did you?" he said.

Amarynth didn't respond.

"That's an unfair question, I guess," Mathers replied. "Of course you didn't, but who would want to admit to that?"

Still no response. Amarynth felt profoundly uncomfortable but had no idea what to say. Mathers pulled a scarf out of his pants pocket.

Curious the scarf was in there the whole time and she had no idea, Amarynth reflected. It reminded her of magic shows, where an entire line of flags could be extracted from a normal-looking pair of dress pants, the magician grinning askance the entire time.

"I'll need your help for this part," Mathers said.

"Sure," Am said. "What do I do?"

"I need you to secure this around my eyes so that I can't see," Mathers said, indicating the scarf.

"You want me to blindfold you?" Amarynth confirmed.

Mathers nodded. "Yes, please. It's part of my process."

"Okay," Am said. She stepped forward and tied the scarf tightly around his head so that it obscured his vision. "How's that?" she said.

"Great," he replied. "Can't see a thing."

"Alright, I'm stepping away," she narrated as she did.

"I know," Mathers replied.

Amarynth didn't ask how. Instead, she watched in rapt fascination as Mathers effortlessly found his way to the sandbox and scooped up sand in both hands. He spun in place until he faced one of the canvases.

He moved his right arm in slow, wide circles in a way that reminded Amarynth very much of a baseball pitcher warming up, but on a later cycle, he sped up the motion and flung the rainbow dust at the canvas. The dust spread out in five distinct directions from the point of impact. It reminded Amarynth of a star.

Mathers then did the same with his left arm, working it through gentle circles until eventually winding up the speed and letting that handful of dust hit the canvas. This throw hit higher up on the target, and instead of spreading out evenly in all directions, it slumped down with gravity, like a thrown tomato might slink down a wall. As it slumped, the dust left multicolored trails over the vaguely stellate under-pattern that the right hand had established.

How does he do it with both arms? Amarynth wondered idly.

"I'm ambidextrous," Mathers said aloud.

"Are you a telepath?" Amarynth said.

"No, just good at guessing. People wonder the same things over and over again. It used to depress me how similar even the most unusual person was to everyone else. But these days I find it comforting," Mathers explained.

Amarynth, however, did not. She felt very uncomfortable.

"And before you ask, I know when I'm done throwing sand because I feel it. There's nothing more to it than that. The same sense that guides me in creating these works tells me when to stop," Mathers said.

Amarynth flushed, embarrassed. Perhaps there was something to this man's philosophy of predictability, for he had answered a question that her mind was just beginning to ask before she even had time to phrase it.

This would be much too fast for normal telepathy.

Mathers grinned, looking quite strange as he did so with his eyes concealed under the scarf. He moved back to the sandbox and picked up two new handfuls of dirt.

Suddenly, he shook his head and returned the dirt to the box. He took off his blindfold.

"Unusually soon, but we're done," he told Amarynth.

"What's it mean?" Amarynth asked him. Before them on the canvas was a large star with the strange multicolored streaks appearing to claw through it.

Mathers studied the image for a moment before nodding sagely. "Tell Leigh," he said, his eyes shining eerily, "that the answer is in the mirror."

"The answer is in the mirror?" Amarynth confirmed.

"Yes," Mathers said.

"And she'll know what that means?" Amarynth asked.

Mathers nodded. "Maybe not right away. But eventually. The answer is in the mirror. I know it for certain."

"Okay," Amarynth said, feeling quite uncertain.

"I'd like to wash up now," Mathers said, "so if you wouldn't mind…"

"I should show myself out?" Amarynth said.

"Please," Mathers said. "I can't stand being dirty."

Amarynth nodded. She had barely left the room when she heard the water start to run. She imagined he had shed his clothes already, so she kept her gaze fixed ahead of her and walked towards the front room.

When she got to the coffee table and saw the Etch A Sketch lying there facedown, she hesitated. It was wrong to go through someone else's things, she knew it, but curiosity was killing her. And if it were truly intended to be private, surely, Mathers would have put it safely away. There was ample time to secure it after all.

These justifications felt like a stretch, so she did feel a strong wave of guilt surge through her as she picked up the Etch A Sketch and turned it over.

On its face was a very detailed drawing of what appeared to be a small bird — very much like her parakeet Tesla in fact — sitting on a perch in its birdcage and singing to its reflection in the mirror.

"The answer is in the mirror," Amarynth repeated softly to herself before she returned the Etch A Sketch to its original position and left the Mathers residence.

Was there something to his predictability philosophy or did Mathers have new powers secondary to a case of PTI? Amarynth wondered this the entire time she rode back to her apartment.

Normally she'd have some kind of hunch. One that was easy to trust and reassuring. But this time it was different. Her normal gut feel was eerily absent.

When Amarynth returned home, she called out, "Honey, I'm home." Only Tesla answered. No Gino.

A cursory search of the apartment confirmed this.

"For someone so adamant about being told what my plans are, you think he'd return the favor," Amarynth said to Tesla, who whistled a little tune in response.

Sighing, she dialed Gino's number. No response. Straight to voicemail. "Hey Gino, not sure where you are. Call me back when you get this message."

As soon as she hung up the call, she had another thought. Maybe he was at work. She remembered his saying he had a lot to catch up on. And it did seem like lately he'd been going out at strange hours to do it.

"Why don't you just grade papers here?" Amarynth had pressed him.

He'd shrugged and said, "I'm a creature of habit, I guess. I'm used to working on campus."

Amarynth had considered dropping by to visit him many times. But whenever she'd raised the subject, Gino had swiftly waved it away with one hand. "Parking's a disaster on campus. And there's nothing to see. All those offices look the same," Gino had said.

"Well yes," Amarynth had said, "but wouldn't your workday be a lot brighter if you got to see me?"

"My days are bright already because of you," Gino had replied.

And then Amarynth had started to feel like an asshole being so pushy about the whole thing and had dropped it.

But now, Gino's whereabouts were unknown, and her heart was pounding hard and fast in her chest as her mind conjured up all the terrifying things that could be happening — could he have been hit by a car? Shot? Stabbed?

Was he off somewhere having an affair?

She swatted away the last thought. It was silly. And yet... it would explain a lot. She often had a hard time accepting that someone so handsome and accomplished would want anything to do with *her*. Perhaps he had several mousy little nothings scattered around the city.

She took a few deep breaths to compose herself. After she stopped shaking, she brought up the college website on her cell phone and found the staff directory.

Yes, *A. Boccaccio* was listed there, in the Department of Urban Studies. There were only three people listed in Urban Studies. A small department.

Amarynth dialed the number listed in the directory. She frowned as it went to voicemail.

Even more disturbingly, the voice that said to leave a message didn't sound like Gino's at all. Instead, the man's voice was a higher one than Gino's, and whoever had recorded this message had a thick Italian accent.

Stunned, Amarynth hung up without leaving a message.

Tesla began to squawk.

Amarynth turned and saw Gino emerging from the bedroom. He was rubbing his eyes.

"Ah, you're home," he said. "I was taking a nap. You look beautiful."

Amarynth glowered at him.

"What?"

"I checked that bed," she said. "You weren't in it."

Gino laughed. "Okay," he said, shaking his head, "like that makes sense."

Amarynth frowned. "I know what I saw."

"Do you?" Gino said.

"Don't pull that shit with me," Amarynth said.

"What shit?" Gino said.

"I'm so used to having people question me. I don't need you to start," Amarynth said.

"Well, I'm sorry, Amarynth, but I've been here the whole time," Gino said.

No, you haven't, Amarynth thought. But the words wouldn't come out.

"I called your office, too, on campus," Amarynth said.

"Oh?" Gino said. Amarynth thought he looked a little nervous.

"I got your voicemail," Amarynth continued.

"Well of course you did," Gino said. "Because I wasn't there. I was here."

"Half of that is right," Amarynth said.

"Am," Gino said, "what's gotten into you?"

"It wasn't your voice on the recording, Gino!" Amarynth exploded. "You must think I'm an idiot. Do you even work at the college? Is Gino even your real name?"

"The last one's a philosophical question," Gino joked.

"It's not funny," Amarynth said.

"Am," Gino said, his voice sinking into sotto voce, "that's my teaching assistant on the voicemail. Giuseppe. He's studying abroad. Actually, that's the funny thing about him... we got thrown together even though he has no interest in urban planning."

"How did that happen?" Amarynth said, her voice sulky, as she reserved judgment. This explanation had better be good.

"The dean thought a couple of guys with super Italian names would get on famously. Never mind that I don't speak a word of Italian. Have never been to Italy. And poor Giuseppe doesn't give a flying fig about cities. He takes them for granted like most people," Gino said.

"That doesn't explain why his voice is on your voicemail," Amarynth insisted.

"Oh, that? That's easy. He was so depressed about being assigned to my department that I've had to give him a lot of busywork tasks to keep him out of my hair. Yes, he's on my voicemail. He also types my letters. Gets me coffee," Gino said. "I basically have a secretary now, somehow."

"You expect me to believe that?" Amarynth challenged him.

"Well, I don't know what I expect from you, but you should believe me," Gino replied. "Because it's the truth."

Amarynth studied his face for signs of deception. He was either a very good liar or it was true.

"Okay, Gino," Amarynth said, her face softening.

Gino wrapped his arms around her and guided her into the bedroom. What happened next was so glorious that Amarynth forgot all about what had set her off in the first place: That Gino had seemingly materialized from nowhere and claimed to have been there the whole time.

"Oh Martin, it's too much," Penny gushed. "Really too much."

Martin waved this statement away with one hand. "None of us knows how long any of this is going to last, and taking care of you right now is taking care of my whole team."

"But… a new computer?" Penny said.

"New *to you*," Martin emphasized. "This is an older model, Penny. I was due for an upgrade anyway. My wife has been complaining about this one for a while."

"Well, thank her for me anyway," Penny said.

Martin smiled. "I will." *Not*, he added mentally, feeling a bit immature all the while. But the last thing he needed was his wife griping at him for talking about his team of intuitives. Hell, if she knew that he'd been over here at the little house on Bell not once, not twice, but three times — for a barbecue, to set up a prefabricated insulated back yard shed and porta potty, and to bring a hand-me-down computer — well, he'd never hear the end of it.

She'd probably think he was having an affair or something, with all three of his employees.

In his wife's mind, men and women couldn't be friends, and a boss shouldn't care about those he supervised — especially not when they were tueys. Or "tuey low lives," as his wife liked to say.

"So you're *sure* you can manage the wi-fi situation?" Martin asked Penny, desperate to draw himself out of his thoughts.

Penny nodded enthusiastically. "It's all set." The little shed had been wired for electricity, so after they plugged in and fired up the system, Penny demonstrated network connectivity for him.

"Wow," he said, "I'm impressed. I didn't know you three had an Internet connection."

"We didn't," Penny grinned. "I managed to get us onto a shared one. Half the block is on it, so it'll probably be a little wonky sometimes, but I imagine I'll be able to do what I need to do, particularly if I do it at strange hours."

"Which is probably when you'd do a seance anyway, isn't it?" Martin asked.

"Ideally," Penny replied, grinning. "Anyway, I've got a sense that people will be a bit forgiving. These are strange times, and most intuitives don't exactly have the best infrastructure, so any competitors would have the same issues."

Martin nodded.

"Viv's been putting out ads for me for a while, using the phone to get online. I could probably use the phone to conduct seances if I had to, but since I'm going to be living out back here, it didn't make a whole lot of sense to try to share the phone," Penny said.

Martin nodded again, more polite than anything. He knew all this of course. It didn't have to be said, but when Penny got nervous, she tended to state the obvious, like a lot of other people. And then state it again. And again. He could almost see it if he closed his eyes — a flashing sign over Penny's head that read "EXPOSITION MODE."

"Are you falling asleep?" Penny snapped.

"No, just resting my eyes," Martin said, stifling a laugh as he opened his eyes again. "Sorry."

"We have a whole system worked out for how I'm going to live back here. Karen's going to bring my meals for me. I'm still going to scavenge as long as I can, in places where I can avoid others. Drop the supplies on the porch for Viv and Karen. Won't be able to do as much bartering as I'd like for a while, I'm afraid. But scavenging is a go for sure... until I get too big to do it. I'm not sure what we'll do then. Maybe Amarynth will help out."

"I bet she will," Martin said. "She's a strange one, but she does seem to care in her own way."

"We figured she'd be the best person to be helping me out, seeing as she's going to probably be at home for a while herself. Lower risk of catching PTI. Less risk to the baby. She'll be the one taking me to see my doctor, Dr. Klaxon Clark. Dr. Clark is amazing. She just gets it. Really gets what I'm going through. And she doesn't judge, which is the best thing. That's really what I need right now. To be surrounded by people who don't judge me. Guess it's a good thing I'll be spending most of my time alone then."

Martin nodded. Exposition Mode Penny was a whole mood.

But at least the computer worked. It recognized the network. Martin began to set up some video conferencing software.

Behind him, Exposition Mode Penny chatted on companionably. Martin did his best to coordinate knowing nods and nonverbal signs of active listening with the rhythm of her chatter. He wasn't listening, but hopefully, there wouldn't be a test afterward. If there were, he could just act indignant that she would insult him so by doubting him, he decided, as he focused on the computer and continued to mime comprehension.

Thankfully, no test ever came.

"If you need to talk to me, you can message me," he told her once he was done configuring everything. "I added myself as a contact."

"Thanks, Martin," Penny said, beaming.

"Well," he said, getting up, "I guess my work here is done." He walked out of the shed.

When he'd gotten to the far edge of the backyard, where it met their driveway, Penny popped out of the shed. "Hey Martin," she called to him.

He turned and faced her.

"You left your phone!" Penny cried.

Martin waved his hand dismissively at her. "Keep it. It's your phone now. Your own number. I have another."

"*Martin!*" Penny said. "You gotta quit doing that. There's no way I'll ever be able to pay you back."

"It's only stuff, Penny," Martin replied.

"Thanks," Penny said.

When she had gone back inside the shed and closed the door, Penny muttered to herself, "Only stuff, huh? Easy for a normal to say."

Mirror, Mirror on the Wall

The whole purpose of education is to turn mirrors into windows.

-Sydney J. Harris

Like they do with a lot of commonplace items, people generally take it for granted *that* mirrors work.

Mirrors reflect images back to the viewer. That's what they do. It's part of our understanding of what a mirror does, what makes a mirror a mirror.

But if you ask most people, unless they have a comprehensive background in physics, they're at a loss to explain *how* mirrors actually work.

To understand this, it's important to know how light interacts with things that aren't mirrors. For the most part, non-mirrors scatter light. Why is this? Well, on the most basic level, it's because those objects are rough.

Mirrors, conversely, reflect back almost all the light that hits them — and they do so because they are smooth.

However, not all smooth surfaces are mirrors, which further complicates things. Indeed, light isn't just scattered or reflected. It can also be absorbed.

Non-photo-absorptive and smooth, got it... then you have yourself a mirror. Dark, still water has been used in natural settings as a mirror for as long as human history — and likely even longer, as many animals have also been known to study their reflections.

These days mirrors are typically made of transparent glass that is coated on one side with a thin layer of metal such as aluminum or silver. The mirror that you typically find in your bathroom, one with a flat surface that reflects an image of the same shape, size, and vertical orientation, is also known as a plane mirror.

There are other types of mirrors, of course, ones that do not present an exact representation of what is on the other side, only in reverse. These concave or convex mirrors purposefully distort the size of the reflection, making their reflections either smaller or larger than the original object they're depicting. These kinds of mirrors are used sometimes to create the illusion of depth in homes — and also commonly in fun houses, where a single mirror might have both convex and concave regions, causing the reflected image to bear little resemblance to the person standing before it.

Sometimes convex mirrors can even be found in fitting rooms in clothing stores, where their tendency to display smaller reflections gives the shopper the illusion of being slimmer themselves, potentially causing them to be more likely to buy whatever they try on.

"The question," Leigh Lines said, "is how to convert a plane mirror into a planar mirror."

"Excuse me?" Amarynth said.

"There are so many reports of travel using mirrors," Leigh explained.

"Reports?" Amarynth said. "Don't you mean myths? Legends?"

Leigh screwed up her face. "Am, you don't need to be nasty. Just because evidence doesn't meet your specific standards of what evidence should be, it doesn't mean that the evidence is worthless. And it doesn't mean that there's nothing there."

"But just because someone says something weird happened, it doesn't mean it actually did," Amarynth countered.

"I know what you're thinking. I'm a conspiracy theorist. Not to be trusted. I'm sure that's because you've been dismissed so many times yourself. For your gifts."

Amarynth cringed.

"I'm sure people wanted you to be able to explain it, too, how you know things. And I know you couldn't."

Am didn't know what to say to this.

"You're just as big of a conspiracy theorist as I am, Amarynth Watson. You have even less to base these hunches of yours on, and you know it. But it doesn't mean you're wrong." Leigh frowned. "And just because I don't have empirical, peer-reviewed stuff to point to, it doesn't mean I'm wrong either."

Amarynth nodded. "I guess you're right. It's just…"

"Just?"

"The world gets confusing, really chaotic without some sort of confirmation, some sort of test, some sort of standard. I know your heart is in the right place, that you're just trying to push through and figure out what the heck is going on, but other people do the same thing but for more selfish reasons. It becomes easy for people to spread flat-out lies, ones that would suit their own agendas. Before you know it, there's a power grab, and people are oppressing others based on lies. It's such an easy leap. Speculation can become misinformation so quickly. It's been a real problem lately," Amarynth said.

"The State has real expertise at it," Leigh conceded. "Well, Amarynth…"

"Yeah?" Am said.

"I need you to trust me, not in the same way you trust science, of course. That would be too much to ask. But you need to trust me just as much, in a different way. Trust my intentions. Trust what

I'm doing here. Even if it looks more like madness than method to you," Leigh said.

"That I can do," Am said. "I'm not sure why, but I can."

"Well, lucky for you, I'm not going to require scientific evidence or a geometric proof for your trust."

Amarynth chuckled. "I deserved that."

Leigh smiled. "Time to hit the books, I guess."

"What are we looking for?" Amarynth asked.

"Anything about mirrors," Leigh said.

"Anything?" Amarynth said.

"Literally anything," Leigh said, handing her a book that loosed a cloud of dust as it hit Amarynth's lap.

Together Leigh and Amarynth stood before their makeshift causality board. Amarynth carefully studied the clues they had pinned on it, each one referencing a different legend or apocryphal lead. It had been a strange notion to her to use a causality board this way. She was much more used to seeing legal evidence constellated in such a manner, but she had to admit that once it was all arranged, the overall effect was astonishingly similar to what she usually saw at work, except this arrangement was markedly less sloppy than her causality board at PsyOps, since Leigh was involved, and Ms. Lines seemed to be fairly organized. Amarynth had noted as they arranged the clues upon the board that not only was Leigh a great deal tidier than Amarynth normally was, Am herself felt compelled to be less haphazard and more painstaking in her own placement of clues, not wishing to embarrass herself in front of present company.

Seven years bad luck, one clue read. This referenced the superstition that breaking a mirror would damage something vital within your soul. Conversely, if you drop a mirror, and it doesn't shatter, that is supposed to imply that good luck is coming your way.

Cover mirrors after death until the body is buried. This was once a common practice because it was believed that mirrors were portals between this world and the next. It was also believed that if the ghost of the newly departed who inhabited the house happened to see their reflection that they wouldn't be able to ever leave the house and would become trapped in the mirror for eternity. This made it very important to cover the mirrors in the house, at least until the spirit had ample time to settle into their grave.

Don't sleep next to a mirror. It's believed that if you sleep next to a mirror that it leaves you vulnerable to spirits from the other side of your mirror reaching out and extracting your soul while you're fast asleep and defenseless.

Scare away spirits. Interestingly, other beliefs consider mirrors to serve as protection against spirits, rather than vulnerabilities to them. For example, in China, they hung brass mirrors above idols, believing that if evil spirits saw their reflections as they entered a temple that they'd become scared and run away. Indeed, in modern times, some people do hang mirrors on their front doors as a way of reflecting negative energy away from their home.

Bloody Mary, another clue read. Summoning beings via mirrors was a popular practice, one that Amarynth and Leigh encountered many times in their research. A mirror was thought to be a convenient home for ghosts. In all these tales, if a person stood before a mirror staring at their reflection and performing an incantation, then that trapped ghost would be set free.

It had once been in vogue for young girls to attempt a simple divination in which they conjured the image of their future husbands by chanting in front of a mirror. However, when doing so, there was also a chance they would see a skull instead. This was the face of Death, and its appearance meant they would die before they were married.

As time wore on, this traditional divination ritual became even more sinister. This is how the Bloody Mary game, played avidly by teenagers, came to be. There is little agreement on who Bloody Mary is supposed to be. Some say she is a witch who was put to death long ago. Others contend she is a victim of a fatal car crash. Still others claim she is a vengeful British royal who murdered girls so that she could bathe in the blood of virgins and remain forever young.

She may have been all these things — or none of them.

The evil woman in the mirror is also sometimes known as Hell Mary or Mary Worth.

Regardless, the basic ritual remains the same: A person stands in a darkened room in front of a mirror, chanting Mary's name over and over again until her face appears in the glass.

To date, there have been no credible reports of Mary successfully being summoned and wreaking havoc on the mortal world, but her very appearance is enough to get a good jolt. And this particular ritual is a staple of many a Truth or Dare game.

As Amarynth read about this phenomenon, she found herself driven to read more about why it seemed to be happening. Apparently, it was due to something called the Caputo Effect, or the strange-face illusion. Essentially, minor hallucinations result when staring into a mirror in a darkened room for a prolonged period. The mind's facial recognition system malfunctions in this setting, the sensory deprivation leading to a bolt of imagination that superimposes a strange face or facial features onto something visually boring.

"Or there could be something to it," Leigh had insisted as Amarynth had shown her the scientific explanations.

Sighing, Amarynth had written *Bloody Mary* on a piece of paper and tacked it to the causality board.

Blue Baby, the next clue read. This was another one of those mirror games played at slumber parties. In this one, however, you didn't simply stare into a darkened mirror at your face while intoning a name. Instead, you pretended to rock a baby in your arms and said "blue baby" thirteen times. At that point, it was said that the baby would materialize in your arms and scratch you, causing you to drop them and run away before their mother could come after you. If for some reason you continued to hold the baby, the mother would scream loud enough to shatter your mirror, and if you held your ground, she would kill you and reclaim her baby.

Catoptromancy. The act of divination via mirror. "Just like in Snow White," Leigh had exclaimed when they'd found this one. "Mirror, mirror on the wall. Who's the fairest of them all?"

"Just like Snow White," Amarynth had agreed. "Although it's been a practice since the time of the ancient Greeks." It had been used particularly when people got sick. They would pray to a god or goddess, and then their reflection would be studied to help ascertain whether they would get better or not, depending on whether what they saw within the glass was healthy or deathly.

"Occultists consider it a specialized form of crystal-gazing," Amarynth had continued.

"Oh great, that's the last thing we need," Leigh had protested. "Having to add crystal-gazing into this, too."

"Well, let's leave it out for now," Amarynth had advised. "If we come up empty on this first pass with mirrors, then maybe we can throw it in later. But for now, let's keep this simple."

Vampires have no reflection and shatter mirrors. Although the idea that vampires cannot be seen in mirrors has become a very common belief due to Bram Stoker's popularization in *Dracula*, it wasn't a universal feature of the creatures until he wrote about it in his novel.

This is not to say that Bram Stoker made it up out of thin air. It seems he didn't. The idea is found in certain cultures but not others.

Sometimes powerful vampires are believed to shatter mirrors as well. A little competition for the mother of Blue Baby.

"You know," Leigh said, "the reason it was thought that vampires didn't show reflections was because of the silver in mirrors."

"Oh?" Amarynth said.

Leigh nodded. "Silver was thought to ward off evil."

"Well," Amarynth said, "that would mean that modern vampires would have reflections then, wouldn't it? Since these days most mirrors are backed with aluminum."

"Guess so," Leigh replied. "I bet that's why there are so many hunky vampires in movies these days. Do you think they're looking like that without a mirror at their disposal? I don't think so. Looks that good don't just magically happen."

Amarynth laughed. "Yes, I'm sure *that's* why there are so many people thirsting after vampires."

Mirroring — Psychology. Phenomenon in which one person begins to unconsciously imitate the mannerisms of another. Common in social environments. Believed to be both a sign of and a causative factor towards building strong social bonds with others. Linked to mirror neurons in the brain.

"Are you sure this belongs on the board?" Amarynth said.

"Of course I am," Leigh said. "Otherwise, I wouldn't have suggested it."

"But it's not a myth," Am said.

"I said *anything* that has to do with mirrors, didn't I?" Leigh countered.

Am frowned.

 "I know there's this thick, uncrossable line in your mind between scientific and unscientific —" Leigh began.

"Supported by empirical research and a community of experts," Amarynth interrupted.

"However it's supported," Leigh resumed, "it's not necessarily the same line that reality has in mind. It might be indelible and clear to you, but when we don't know what we're dealing with, well… we have to cover all our bases."

Amarynth sighed. "Fine, fine. It goes on the board."

Mirror world, mirror universe. Many believe that there is another world on the other side of the mirror that is very much like ours but different enough to be highly unsettling and dangerous.

"I guess that's where ghosts come from," Leigh suggested.

Amarynth nodded. "Or demons or whatever," she replied, pointing to other legends.

"It goes on the board," Leigh said.

Smoke and mirrors. Common phrase that refers to the act of obscuring the truth using irrelevant or misleading info. Its origins come from a classic technique used by illusionists whereby smoke and mirrors are used to make it appear as though some kind of ghostly apparition is hovering in space.

"Like spirit conjuring but even more illusory and easily explained," Leigh pointed out, her voice taking on a hint of resignation.

"Well," Amarynth said, "sometimes a fake is a copy of something real, so you never know."

Leigh grinned at this bit of encouragement. Maybe there was hope for their budding friendship, after all.

When all the clues were hung, Amarynth stood in front of the board. She thought about moving through the motions of a ritual that resembled what a standard Connections Agent would do.

"Don't worry about me. Pretend I'm not here," Leigh said at just that moment.

Amarynth nodded. She studied the clues and closed her eyes. She listened to the sound of the room for a moment, the whirring of the HVAC, the creaking of boards, the street noises outside of the building muted somewhat by the walls and insulation but still semi-audible.

Amarynth walked to the board with her right index finger extended. When it touched the board, she opened her eyes.

She was pointing to Bloody Mary.

Amarynth looked at Leigh. "Well, that settles it," Amarynth said. "Let everyone know. We're going to be trying to summon a vengeful spirit using mirrors."

Leigh nodded. She pulled out her phone and started to text furiously.

Amarynth noted with great appreciation that Leigh didn't question her conclusion and certainly hadn't asked her why or how she'd arrived there. It was a strange feeling to be trusted, especially when saying something that seemed so absurd.

Maybe that was one of the perks of having a conspiracy theorist as a friend, Amarynth thought. Being trusted even when you didn't make sense.

No, that wasn't it, Amarynth realized, as Leigh continued to text. Leigh wasn't gullible. She wasn't all-trusting or loyal to a fault. Amarynth had managed to say something that made sense to Leigh, as absurd of a premise as it seemed on a basic level, summoning spirits with mirrors. It was just that simple.

Leigh trusted the conclusion even if it strained credulity. She didn't necessarily trust Amarynth. Not the way that she trusted her conspiracies.

Well, no matter, Amarynth decided. It was nice to not be interrogated about her conclusions. Leigh was two for two on that front.

"Hey Am?" Leigh said at that moment.

"Yeah?"

"Change brings up a good point. Group summoning or one on one?" Leigh said.

"You're texting Change Patterson?"

"He's in the core thinktank," Leigh said. "Group summoning or one on one?"

Amarynth stared at the causality board again for a few moments. "One on one," Am said, "and if that doesn't work, we meet as a group and attempt a collective summoning effort."

"Thanks," Leigh said, communicating that news via text.

A few seconds later, she frowned. "Am, Change says that's fine but not you."

"I'm sorry?" Amarynth said.

"He doesn't want you doing the mirror ritual," Leigh said.

"That's not my problem," Am said.

Leigh's fingers flew into action. "He says that it's not your problem now but that it will be shortly."

"Leigh!" Am protested. "You texted him that? That was rhetorical."

Leigh shrugged. "Is it anything you wouldn't say to his face if he were here?"

"Well, no," Am admitted.

"To the mirrors, we go!" Leigh said. "Well, except for you."

Amarynth stared at the board for a few moments. "I don't take orders from Change Patterson."

"He's a lot like you, you know," Leigh said.

Amarynth groaned. "Take that back."

"He's an outsider, too. He's usually right, but people don't listen to him because they naturally dislike him. Change is unsettling, but you can't escape him. You can't escape what he says," Leigh said.

Studying the board, Amarynth could see that Change was on to something perhaps. As she pondered performing a mirror ritual herself, she didn't see doom *per se*. No inevitable ruin. Nothing that dire. But she did see difficulty. Hardship.

He probably had a point. *Ugh.*

"Do you see it, too?" Leigh asked.

"Well, sort of," Amarynth said. She totally saw it but didn't want to admit it. "I think he's exaggerating," she said. *And that I'm understating it*, she added silently.

The truth was likely somewhere in the middle. Somewhere in between them.

And it called out to her, like a belligerent drunk shouting curses at her and trying to start a bar fight. She knew it was a bad idea to engage, but part of her brain wondered what would happen if she did.

Mirrors Are Not Your Friends

As Amarynth watched Gino sleeping peacefully next to her, the guilt was starting to build up. It had been so easy to keep things from him, by substituting a blander truth, one that kept him from the actual weirdness that was slowly creeping into her life bit by bit.

Once he wakes up, she told herself. *Once he wakes up, I will tell him everything. I will come clean.*

But as she thought this, her breath caught in her throat. She recognized it immediately as not true. She knew it was self-delusion.

This is why you can't connect with other people, she thought. *You find a way to keep them at arm's length even when they're reaching out to you and trying to pull you in.*

It was an annoying thought but one that hit her as infinitely more true than the promise she had made to herself mentally only seconds before.

She rose and walked into the bathroom, closing the door behind her as quietly as she could. She turned on the fan.

"You're thinking about this too much," she muttered to herself. Her voice was quiet enough that the fan would swallow the sound. She'd learned from careful experimentation with Gino living there what that volume was. The one place where she could remain relatively undetected was in the bathroom. This was the one place where she could credibly close the door and Gino would at least knock before entering.

"Yes, you're keeping some things to yourself, but that doesn't mean you can't connect," she muttered. "After all, how can you be sure of what connection is if you've never had it? Maybe this is what people are talking about when they talk about connecting with someone. Maybe it was never about melding entirely. Being swallowed by a person spiritually. Maybe it's about living side by side with someone else, peacefully, but remaining individuals. Individuals who are allowed to have a few secrets."

And with that, she turned to the bathroom mirror.

It's curious how popular mirror toys remain for birds because a mirror is one of the most dangerous things you can give a bird who has no cage mates.

Many pet owners are well intentioned when they buy mirror toys. Birds are social creatures and are hardwired to want to be around other birds and participate in many flocking behaviors.

Getting a mirror seems like a simple solution for people who only own one bird, particularly a bird that they worry they won't be able to pay much attention to. A mirror provides the illusion of social interaction to a bird.

These same folks would never dream of raising a child in isolation, buying a mirror, and expecting the child to play with its reflection instead of finding other children for them to play with. But when it's a bird, it doesn't strike them as odd.

The first disservice you do to a pet bird when you present it with a mirror is calibrating them to socially interact with "others" unrealistically. The "other" bird, the reflection, will always engage in reciprocity. They will never react in a dissimilar manner.

This is *wildly* unrealistic.

This means that a bird who has had a mirror as company will significantly struggle when they finally have a real cage mate. They will have learned all sorts of unhelpful social behavior and be completely puzzled when a real bird reacts to them nothing like their reflection did.

This is like sending your mirror-raised child to public high school.

One solution, perhaps, is to never introduce your mirror-addicted bird to real-life animals. This is fine, although you're resigning them to a perpetually solitary existence. But things do happen. Circumstances change. And if your bird needs to be fostered by someone else who has other birds, you may find that they must integrate into a social setting regardless of your original plans.

And those aren't the only dangers. Some owners have found their mirror-addicted parakeets will incessantly attempt to feed their reflections, thinking the reflection is their mate. Since feeding another bird involves regurgitating food they've already consumed, particularly zealous reflection feeders run the risk of starving to death.

Mirrors can be incredibly dangerous, particularly to those who live alone.

Amarynth knew this of course — and yet something had still possessed her to hang a tiny mirror in Tesla's cage. On the bright side, he seemed to be doing fine with the toy, hadn't exhibited any of the troublesome signs that plagued other birds.

If anything, Amarynth mused, I spend more time staring at that little toy mirror than he does.

Amarynth thought about this phenomenon and Tesla's tiny mirror as she began to perform the ritual that the Web Spinners had settled on.

"Mirrors are dangerous *for birds,*" she reminded herself. "And besides, I don't live alone anymore."

As she said this, she watched her reflection say it along with her.

And then her reflection unexpectedly said something else. "Mirrors are not your friends."

Amarynth gasped. Her reflection did not. She felt herself lurch forward until her forehead touched the glass. Her reflection grinned and pulled her into the mirror.

There is another form of mirror in addition to the plane mirror that we are quite accustomed to seeing, but many of us don't necessarily recognize this other mirror as such.

Retroreflectors surround us but are not the first thing people think of when they think of a mirror. Sometimes also known as cataphotes, these objects also reflect light with minimal scattering. However, they do so at a variety of angles of incidence, whereas a plane mirror only functions perpendicularly.

Cat's eyes are natural retroreflectors, glowing brightly in dark environments when even the smallest bit of light hits them. Artificial retroreflectors work much the same way. The gear that runners wear to jog at night produces a similar effect, allowing passing cars to spot the night joggers easily and avoid hitting them. Reflective strips are also found on bicycles and cycling gear — as well as the roadways themselves.

Such mirrors are fairly ubiquitous — although not often identified as mirrors as such. Humankind even put retroflectors on the moon during the Apollo mission.

Like many other people, Amarynth had given little thought to retroreflectors as she researched mirrors. She had forgotten to recognize the myriad of reflective materials that surrounded her that didn't resemble a traditional looking glass.

And she had certainly not realized that her cell phone camera also functioned as a mirror — in fact, it was the standard way she checked her appearance, not the sheet of glass that hung on her bathroom wall.

She had given little thought to her cell phone as she had set it down on the bathroom counter and even less thought to the reflective material that lined her shoes as she stood before the mirror doing the incantation.

But as all three elements wound into close proximity, she had inadvertently created a mirroring system that intensified as she stood.

And before she knew it, she was trapped by retroreflection that she had taken for granted.

The Phylactery

A procession of the damned.

By the damned, I mean the excluded.

We shall have a procession of data that Science has excluded.

-Charles Fort, *The Book of the Damned*

Amarynth had seen the hands first, as they jutted out of the glass and reached towards her. They were about the same size and color as her own, but more wrinkled, as though they belonged to someone older than her.

As the hands telescoped forward, the forearms became visible, bare at first but quickly transitioning to black fabric, leather by the look of it or a very convincing imitation.

Once the hands had her, Amarynth lurched forward and everything melted into silver, a pervasive thick silver that she was dragged through for quite a distance. This silver journey spanned seconds perhaps — or maybe minutes — it was tough to tell time as she was pulled through scintillation with such violence that Amarynth wasn't sure she would make it all the way. The farther she got, the more the image spun, reminding her of a kaleidoscope.

Finally, the coruscation exploded, and a figure melted into place before her. Amarynth recognized the hands immediately. They were the ones that had pulled her into the glass. The ones who had pulled her here.

They belonged to a tall curvaceous but fit woman wearing a black leather catsuit. Her blond hair was scraped primly into a severe updo. There was a single streak of gray hair running through it. The coloring reminded Amarynth of the Bride of Frankenstein.

The face was familiar, too — though not from old movies. No, Amarynth had seen this face in her mother's photo albums.

There were so many packed away in the giant house, hulking leatherbound tomes that expelled clouds of dust the moment you threw open their massive covers. And under those covers, reams and reams of paper studded with tiny photos.

Amarynth could remember sitting on her mother's lap, awestruck as Bella turned the pages, wondering how her mother might have known so many people once upon a time. How did a woman who was that connected go from living as a social force to shutting herself behind heavy doors and doing everything humanly possible to keep the world from coming in?

Whatever the case, the photo albums were now a way that her mother told stories — and showed Amarynth a small slice of the world — without ever going anywhere.

"There," her mother had said, pointing to a lovely woman with a symmetrical heart-shaped face, eyes that were perhaps a little small but a clear crystal blue, and a tiny wisp of a nose.

"Espoir Macomber," Amarynth said to the same face that appeared before her now, although the face was slightly more lined and cynical from the years that had passed since it had been captured in that photograph.

"Miss Watson," Espoir acknowledged her. "I'm surprised you know my name. I don't believe we've ever met."

Espoir focused on Amarynth's face for a few moments. And then a few moments more.

She's reading my thoughts, Amarynth thought. *Of course, she's reading my thoughts. She's a telepath, don't be silly. You can't expect her to not read your thoughts. It'd be like someone expecting you to walk around with your eyes closed.*

Espoir smirked. "A bit," she said. She combed Amarynth's mind some more.

Amarynth waited, feeling uncomfortable all the while. "You were cruel to my mother once upon a time," Amarynth said finally.

"I see the Watsons have long memories," Espoir replied.

"We remember what matters," said Amarynth. "Who to trust. Who to be wary around."

"And I'm in the second category, am I?" Espoir asked.

Amarynth didn't answer. "Where am I?" she said instead. "In the Coterie?" The Macombers considered the Coterie to be a haven of sorts for their Family. Amarynth thought of it more as their evil lair. A place where they held prisoners and conducted experiments that would have been banned anywhere else, outside of the private bubble they'd constructed to keep the larger world from interfering.

Espoir shook her head. "No, this isn't the Coterie. We're in the phylactery."

"The what?" Amarynth said.

"Surely, you've heard of the Macomber lich," Espoir replied.

Amarynth screwed up her face. The lich was rumored to be one of the many ill-advised experiments going on in the Macomber Coterie. The Macomber Family was matriarchal, with all leadership roles filled by prominent, powerful women. In the Coterie, men were generally servants if permitted to be present at all.

According to gossip, one unlucky man had been selected as a guinea pig, however, imbued with such powerful magic that he expired during the transfusion. However, the undead being that rose the next day was filled with that same magic, and now he had no pesky needs that a living person might. They had created an all-powerful lich.

Rumor had it that if the lich's power could be appropriately directed that he was strong enough to wipe out the three other rival Families, if not the whole plane. However, there had been some problems controlling him. Which was why no one had seen him yet. He was said to be imprisoned in a phylactery, a large repository designed to hold the lich's life force in one place until the time he could be effectively deployed as the Macombers' most devastating weapon. No one knew where the phylactery was of course — it was rumored to be somewhere no one would ever find it. "Perhaps even stuck between worlds," Amarynth's mother had joked, winking, as she relayed this wild gossip.

"I thought the Macomber lich was a fairy tale, something the Coterie was saying to intimidate the other Families," Amarynth said now to Espoir.

"Well, you thought wrong," Espoir said. "We leaked that information, yes. But we weren't bluffing. It's all true."

"I'm standing in a place that shouldn't exist," Amarynth said.

Espoir shrugged. "You picked an incredible time to muck around with mirrors. Great for us, terrible for you."

"Sounds like the Macomber dream," Amarynth replied. "Gaining the advantage by screwing the Watsons."

"Something like that," Espoir said breezily. "If you hadn't come here soon, we were about to come looking for you."

"Looking for me?" Amarynth said. "Why?"

"We are very interested in PTI," Espoir said.

"Who isn't?" Amarynth said.

Espoir frowned.

"You sure you didn't start the plague yourself?" Amarynth challenged her.

Espoir laughed. "No, we're working on too many important projects to be risking anything on something frivolous like a psychic plague. We were hoping you'd know why it was happening. And how to get it to go away."

"Me?" Amarynth said. "Why me?"

"You know everything," Espoir said in an unnervingly level tone.

"I really don't," Amarynth replied.

"You'd be surprised," Espoir said.

Amarynth frowned.

"It's not just the things you know that you know," Espoir continued. "There's a lot that you know… but beneath the surface."

"That doesn't make any sense," Amarynth said, but as she spoke the words, they felt wrong to her. That subliminal voice inside of her writhed, causing her mental pain. If she closed her eyes, Amarynth could almost see the voice as an image. It was a dark cetacean shadow that changed shape as it thrashed. The shadow moaned, and a loud deep wave — like a whale song — vibrated through her body.

When Amarynth opened her eyes, Espoir was staring at her.

"You're lying," Espoir said. "You saw something just then. I saw it, too. Normally, you hear it. You've never seen it before, and it terrifies you. Good. It should."

Amarynth bristled.

"Anyway," Espoir continued, "there's something in you… there's even more to you than you know — more than any of us thought. And we're going to get to the bottom of it once and for all. Because this plague is too costly. The Coterie has too much to accomplish."

"But why the phylactery?" Amarynth said.

"I'm sorry?" said Espoir.

"Why did you bring me to the phylactery?" Amarynth said. "The Coterie would have been just as suitable if you wanted to talk to me. I don't know why I have to be interrogated within the prison of a lich's soul. Seems a bit dire if you ask me."

"Ah, that's just it," Espoir said. "We didn't bring you here. You brought yourself."

"By performing the incantation in front of the mirror?" Am said.

"Precisely," Espoir said. "You see, Amarynth, you weren't captured. If anything, you infiltrated our lair."

"Then I'm free to leave then, I suppose," Am said.

Espoir laughed. "No."

"Well, why not? You just said yourself. You didn't capture me," Am said. "That means I'm not a prisoner."

"You're not leaving, Amarynth," Espoir said firmly. "Not until you tell us why this disease is here. Why any of this is happening. Then, maybe you can go free."

"Maybe?" Am said.

"Well, you've seen a lot. Not many people know this place even exists. It's not up to me whether you're allowed to leave with that bit of knowledge."

"But you've been spreading knowledge of it yourself. Leaking it to the outside world. You just said…" Am cast her eyes down.

"Yes, but when we did that, we had control of the message. There's no knowing what you'd say if you were allowed to just leave." Espoir paused. "But again, it's not up to me. I don't make the big decisions. That's above my position. I am just a person who follows orders."

"Why is it that the worst acts of evil are always committed by people who were just following orders?" Am asked.

Espoir smirked. "I don't know," she confessed. "That, too, is above my station. The answers to questions like that."

Am frowned.

"Anyway," Espoir continued, "if you'll follow me, it's time to see him for yourself."

"Who?" Am said.

"Why, the Macomber lich of course," Espoir replied.

Karen felt her stomach plummet as the elevator to the Department of Psychic Operations began its descent.

It was funny. This was a trip she had made thousands of times, but in another light, it was the very first time.

Because this was the first time she'd ever reported to work with the full intention of working for any length of time without both Viv and Penny present. And this meant that her empathy powers would be fully active for the entire day.

Karen had noticed a drastic shift as soon as she and Viv had pulled away from the curb in their work car. Penny's separate living space in the backyard was just within her zone of comfort, and even though Karen couldn't see Penny — and wouldn't know she was even back there if not for the glow that her computer monitor cast out through the windows of the shed — Penny was still close enough to serve as a psychic security blanket.

But once Viv pulled the car out into the street, that sense of security fell away. Karen was alone. And she was instantly bathed in Viv's emotions.

Viv's face held no expression, but beneath the surface, Karen noted her partner was a ball of anxiety. Worry roiled through Viv — and also through Karen, who caught the emotions, and instantly wished she hadn't.

Not only was this anxiety uncomfortable — but Karen also felt suddenly invasive, like she was going through Viv's possessions without permission.

If Viv realized, she didn't say anything. Which was fine with Karen. She preferred it that way.

And now standing in the elevator, Viv's stomach dropped with the lift — and it took Karen's along with hers.

Does she feel like this every morning? Karen wondered. *Or is it just because it's our first day back?* And after a beat, she added, *or is it because she's working without Penny?*

No, that couldn't be it. She mentally swatted the last question away as nonsense. A mistake to even think. It wasn't a rational question, after all. Viv had spent the last few months working with Amarynth after Penny and Karen absconded, both working on their own versions of soul-searching. Leaving Viv holding the bag.

Or holding the bill because, as Viv had put it when they'd asked her why she had continued to go to work without them, "Someone had to pay the mortgage, loves."

Viv had been working without Penny for a while. *Why did I zero in on that then?* Karen wondered. Why had she thought Viv's sadness had been about missing Penny?

And then it hit her. Of course. Insecurity. That old pain. Despite all the years together — and the beautiful life that the three of them had built — part of Karen always worried that she was an outsider, guesting in Penny and Viv's life. Not really adored but tolerated. An annex.

Part of Karen knew that this was a foolish thing to think. People did not fake the commitment or the devotion that both Viv and Penny had shown her over the years. The more logical conclusion was that they really cherished her. That her relationships with each of them meant as much as the relationship they had with each other.

But it was an easy place for her to go whenever things suddenly changed. This was going to be one of those times.

But she'd figure it out. She knew that much.

Because she wasn't the first person who had to contend with balancing their workload with a sudden change in emotional reality. Certainly not the first person who'd had to puzzle out a new way of working.

Heck, she wasn't even the first person at *PsyOps* who had ever had this problem.

Her situation reminded her of the time Tom Steelman, one of the PsyOps agents who worked in the gaslighting division, went off his antidepressants. If it had gone smoothly, Karen would never have heard about it. But it didn't.

It was a spectacular mess. One that culminated eventually in Steelman passing out in the cafeteria at PsyOps — so immobile with his face plastered to the floor and shellacked there with drool that employees took to decorating him like a Christmas tree. Karen herself guiltily remembered stringing popcorn onto a piece of wire and snaking it around his head like a crown.

King Orville Redenbacher.

Yes, it had been a colorful embarrassment. For Steelman, for the gaslighting division, for all of PsyOps once the merrymaking crashed down to the floor and people began to be disciplined for their mishandling of the situation.

Gaslighting in particular was heavily targeted — and became the focus of a rather thorough investigation, but as predicted, the gaslighting division dealt with it as they did with all controversy: They swore it had never happened.

It worked to a certain extent. While the memories of the incident remained, as did all the records attesting to it, many of the key players simply lost the will to pursue matters further, plagued by nagging doubts.

And Tom Steelman recovered. These days he was a department superstar. Some credited him with singlehandedly turning the gaslighting division around.

If Steelman figured it out, Karen assured herself, *then you'll be fine.*

She grinned at Viv as the elevator doors opened, and they stepped into PsyOps. Viv said nothing as they walked down the series of twists and turns that led to Martin's office. But Karen could feel calm rolling off Viv like a wave.

That's interesting, Karen thought, for one thing was very clear: The Department of Psychic Operations was home to Viv, even more so than their little house on Bell Avenue.

"You're a workaholic," Karen ventured.

Viv laughed. "Is it that obvious?"

"Crystal clear," Karen confirmed.

Viv stopped in place. "You know... I don't know how to do my job with that power of yours trained on me. I don't know how to function with your empathy active all the time, looking at me, with you being able to feel exactly what I feel. I've told you before. I feel very much like I'm under a microscope when you can sense my feelings the way you can."

"You have told me that before, yes," Karen said, nodding.

"But I've been thinking about it," Viv continued, "and I have decided that if you can learn to deal with juggling other people's feelings all the time, then I can certainly adjust to being a little more known. A little more seen."

Karen broke into a huge smile. "Oh, Viv. That means a lot."

Viv cleared her throat. "Don't let it go to your head or anything."

Karen forced her smile down in response to this backpedaling but felt the happiness still coursing through her anyway. "I won't," she said. But in truth, she didn't know if she could stop herself. It did mean a lot. It probably would go to her head. No stopping it.

And as they finished the walk to Martin's office, Karen was grateful that her empathy only went one way and that Viv couldn't feel the warm glow that had taken over her entire chest.

"Alright, I know he's an important cultural leader. You've made that much clear. Crystal clear. But what does he do exactly? What sort of powers does he have?" Amarynth challenged her captor.

Espoir studied her face, seemingly at a loss. This wasn't at all how she'd expected her captive to act. This wasn't what Moche had prepared her for. Nothing she'd experienced during her long tenure working as a guard for the involuntary guests of the Macomber Family had prepared her for this kind of prisoner.

One who, frankly, seemed to see right through the show pony veneer. The bells and whistles.

The waggling finger "magic" that was so easy to stun others with.

Finally, Espoir said, "He has powers that are too great for you to comprehend. Certainly too great for a lowly guard like me to speak of them."

Sitting atop the carved throne, the lich's lips peeled back into a toothy smile. At least Amarynth thought it was intended to be a smile. Perhaps it was a threat all its own, the way that certain primates bare their teeth not as a show of submission or friendliness but as a warning.

Although in those cases, the primates' teeth were always held apart — positioned so that they could bite at any minute. When the teeth were together, *that* was a lot like a human smile.

And it appeared to Amarynth that the lich didn't look particularly bitey. So there was that.

No, she wasn't afraid. She could feel it deep down in her gut. This lich was no one to bow to, even though Espoir was acting as though she should and to the casual observer, it would appear that her captors had the upper hand.

"You're not the one with the real power," Amarynth said aloud. "You're like the Queen of England. You're just a figurehead." She thought about it. "Except you don't even appear on money, do you?"

Something she could swear was sadness passed across the lich's face. It was only there for a moment before the lich sat up straighter and channeled a resolute expression upon his bony visage, but Amarynth detected the fleeting emotion before it passed.

Yup, this was the family pet. And the dog's bark was certainly a lot worse than his bite.

She wondered how many people had been intimidated by his presence. *If I didn't have my intuition, I certainly would have been*, she concluded.

Espoir was staring at her with her eyes bulging open.

"You *are* a telepath, aren't you?" Amarynth said.

Still stunned, Espoir nodded.

"Well, that's good," Am said. "Saves me a lot of hassle, frankly."

Espoir continued to stare at her.

"As I'm sure you're aware — or will be, given enough time to rummage around my thoughts, or at least overhear the ones I have often — I'm terrible at expressing myself. What's in my head is always bigger, clearer, more impressive than what comes out of my mouth," Amarynth explained. "So being around someone like you? It can be a welcome change."

Especially since you're not an obnoxious young man who thinks he knows everything, Amarynth thought. *Not like Roscoe.* She found herself thinking of him for a few moments. The way he'd smelled the dust storm. His insistence on infecting as many people with PTI as possible. The way he smirked. That stupid haircut of his.

Suddenly Amarynth remembered she was being monitored and glanced at Espoir, who seemed particularly interested in these thoughts of Roscoe.

"You know him, don't you?" Amarynth asked suddenly. But she didn't really have to ask. Her intuition already knew the answer. Espoir's facial expression, however, served as welcome confirmation.

Espoir looked quite uncomfortable. "I suppose there's no point lying about it, is there?" she said.

Amarynth shook her head.

"I'm not at liberty to discuss everything that goes on in the Macomber Coterie," Espoir said, "however, I will say that Roscoe is a deeply political animal. Very ambitious."

"That he is," Am said.

"That said, is it any wonder that we're aware of him? You'd expect that anyone that power-hungry would have approached the Families. Multiple Families, multiple times," Espoir said.

"Yes, but which Families, I wonder?" Amarynth said. "And how successful was he?"

Espoir shrugged. "I don't know what Roscoe does with the other Families."

"But with the Macombers?" Amarynth pressed.

"Amarynth Watson," Espoir said, "do you think that if I did know that information that I would be permitted to share that with a prisoner? Especially a Watson?"

"I'm not really a Watson though," Amarynth said. "Mom and I are outcasts. Black sheep."

"Maybe you're not enough of a Watson for your own liking," Espoir said, "but you're enough of a Watson to be a threat to us."

"Is that why I'm still here?" Amarynth asked.

"That's one reason," Espoir said.

"And the others?" Amarynth said.

"Well, for starters," Espoir said, "you're also an opportunity. Most threats are."

"And beyond that?"

Espoir didn't respond.

"If you knew, you couldn't tell me," Amarynth said.

Espoir nodded. "You're very talkative," she said. "Much more talkative than I expected."

"Oh?" Amarynth asked. "What did you expect?"

"Well, you're someone who knows all the answers. I'm someone who can read your thoughts. I came into this assignment expecting that you'd just sit there knowing everything, and I'd sit here listening to you knowing everything."

Amarynth laughed. "And you'd get what you wanted to know out of me? You'd learn how to end the plague?"

"You're very noisy for someone who says she can't express herself," Espoir observed.

"Well, I've been going through some big life changes lately," Amarynth said.

Atop the throne, the lich spontaneously groaned.

"He sounds like a haunted house," Amarynth said.

"I'm sorry?"

"He sounds like one of those tracks people buy with spooky noises that they play at haunted houses. Or that they play at their Halloween party. Groaning undead. Squeaky doors. Feet on floorboards. Insidious laughter." Amarynth grinned. "Those are meant to be scary, but they're so comical that they rarely are. Your lich is the same way. He's trying too hard to be fierce. There's a point where fierce becomes farce."

Espoir frowned.

Same Mind, Separate Bodies

"They're not epidemiologists. They're barely detectives," Martin grumbled to himself as he stared down at his desk.

His office door creaked as it swung open.

"Hey Martin," Viv called as she strode in, a harried Karen following close behind.

"Hay is for horses," Martin said.

Viv snorted. She pulled out the chair in front of his desk, spun it around so that it was backward, and straddled it with her arms folded across the top.

There was something distinctly teenaged about Viv sometimes, Martin mused. Probably because she had to practically raise herself, what with that mother of hers. You only got so far on your own, didn't you? Especially since Viv had become a protector of sorts of her own family. The fighter.

"Well?" Viv prompted.

"Well?" Martin mimicked.

"You called us in for a reason, didn't you? I presume something happened. I can't imagine you're making work for us out of the goodness of your heart," Viv said.

"I can," Karen said suddenly. Her legs buckled.

Viv threw a quick glance back over her shoulder to a supremely unsteady-looking Karen. "Oh geez," Viv said. She rose from the chair, spun it back around, and guided Karen towards it. "You need this more than I do."

Karen gave her a faint smile before collapsing.

Viv cocked her thumb in Martin's direction. "Is he really feeling all of that?"

Karen nodded. "But it's almost normal to him. He feels it all the time. He's upset, but this isn't much different than his normal."

Martin's eyes grew wide.

"I'm sorry," Karen said. "I know empathy feels invasive. It's overwhelming to me, too. I wasn't going to say anything."

"But your body said it for you," Martin finished.

Karen nodded.

"You should be on medication or something, Martin," Viv said.

Martin laughed. "Tell that to my wife. She thinks I'm exaggerating. That it couldn't be that bad."

Viv shook her head. "I don't get it, Martin."

"Get what?"

"Why you're married to someone you don't even seem to like. She doesn't even seem to like you. What's the point of a marriage like that? Why do you put yourself through that? Why does she put herself through it?" Viv asked.

Martin shrugged. "Not all of us are as lucky as you, Viv."

"Lucky?" Viv said. She laughed. "Oh sure, I'm lucky. I'd trade bank accounts with you in a heartbeat."

I wouldn't be so sure about that, Martin thought. He almost said it. Yes, his paychecks were bigger than a PsyOps agent's. And yes, normals didn't have the same taxes levied on them by the State. But the well was dry for him, too. His wife saw to that.

No matter how much he made — and truth be told, his pay wasn't a lot of money for a non-psychic citizen — it would never be enough for his wife. And certainly not enough for his wife's parents. His in-laws constantly put him down any time they happened to be around him — and behind his back even more often, judging by the conversations his wife seemed to be having with her mother on the phone.

He was a disappointing son-in-law to them. He couldn't escape it. They had wanted him to be a better provider for their daughter than he was, no matter how soulless he had to be to earn that money, no matter how much pain he had to ignore, how many little people he had to step on. Their other daughters all had husbands like that, who worked in the ivory towers of Downtown Skinner doing improbable arcane things with money they never saw or touched. Shuffling numbers slightly, watching them tick up.

Not presiding over a team of reckless mutants in a subterranean lair. A poorly decorated lair at that.

No, his wife's family thought he was a loser. And it hurt.

It should have been enough that his own parents seemed proud of him. That they supported him and his decision to work at this weird, often thankless job because he thought it was where he belonged, where he could do the most good.

But Martin watched the way they blindly supported his older sister Darian, who was always getting into legal trouble and whose frequent need for bail money threatened what little savings his parents had left.

His parents were sweet but doddering. Blinded by love.

They would have supported any of their children, no matter what they were like. Their approval didn't mean much.

That left just one family to fit into. And that was his PsyOps team.

"You know, Martin," Karen said. "It's okay. You don't have anything to be ashamed of."

The timing struck him hard. Martin felt his eyes water. He quickly shot his gaze down to his desktop and scooped up a random manilla folder sitting on the corner. He riffled through the pages, hoping to distract both his own emotions and the two detectives watching him.

Karen suppressed a grin. She knew exactly what he was doing. *Well, that's just fine. Let him have a little emotional privacy.*

Martin cleared his throat. "Anyway, yes, you're right, Viv, I do have something to talk to you about today. A new work assignment."

"Finally!" Viv exclaimed. "Getting to the damn point!"

Martin furrowed his brow.

"I mean, thanks," Viv corrected herself. "What's going on?"

"I don't know how to tell you two this because I don't agree at all with the assignment," Martin confessed.

Viv groaned. "Not another one of those."

"Another one?" Karen said.

"The last time Martin said something like that, Amarynth and I had a camera crew following us around."

Karen made a sour lemon face.

"No camera crew this time," Martin said.

"Well, that's a relief," Viv said.

"You say that now," Martin said.

Viv sighed. "Martin, just tell us what's going on already."

Martin stared out his "window," a piece of art that simulated the Downtown skyline almost perfectly, giving the strangely convincing illusion that his office was in a high rise — if you ignored the long journey down by elevator or the fact that the sun never moved in this artwork.

"Psychic State Government has given Skinner County Health Department the power to recruit as many public officials into the effort to combat PTI as they deem necessary," Martin said.

"So?" Viv said. "What's that have to do with us?"

Karen's mouth hung open. She knew.

"They've asked for PsyOps agents to look into what's going on. See what they can find out about the illness. Who has it. How it seems to spread," Martin said.

"Wait," Viv said. "We're supposed to investigate... an illness?"

Martin nodded.

"Martin, that's ridiculous. What the Hell are they thinking?" Viv said.

He didn't say anything.

"We're investigators, but we're not scientists. How are we supposed to even..." Viv shook her head. The situation was overwhelmingly absurd. It was "getting hard for her to word," as Karen would put it.

"Did they give us any details at least?" Karen asked.

"Oh sure," Martin said. "If there's one thing County Health is good at, it's being detailed."

He opened a drawer in his desk and took out a stack of papers that was about as thick as an old-school phonebook. He placed it on the desk evenhandedly. It made a surprising thwomp even so, due to its heft.

Viv narrowed her eyes. "There *is* a thing as too much detail, you know."

"Tell that to County Health," Martin said.

"Too bad Amarynth isn't here right now. She probably knows why this is all happening. We could just ask her," Viv grumbled.

Martin held his right index finger in the air, scooping up his phone with his left hand. He dialed the phone quickly. Everyone waited.

Finally, he set the phone down. "Amarynth's not answering," he said. "That's not like her. You know how she normally is."

"She answers it before it rings most of the time," Karen said.

"It's true. She's always been a wiseass when it comes to phone calls. Sometimes she even calls me first, just when I'm thinking of her," Viv said.

"Well, we know where she lives, don't we?" Karen offered.

Viv grumbled. "Great. First, I find out that I'm investigating an invisible illness — with no medical training — and then my first task is doing a wellness check on one of my least favorite people ever."

"Viv," Karen said, "she *is* your sister."

"Half-sister," Viv corrected. She scowled. "Well, whatever, it pays the bills, doesn't it?"

Karen grinned.

Viv tossed her the car keys. "I've got a headache. You're driving, kiddo."

"Really?" Karen said. Viv never let her drive. The eideticist griped enough when Penny drove — and Penny was an immaculate driver. Excellent at just about every aspect of it.

Karen had never gotten into an accident, but she was... an acquired taste behind the wheel. There was defensive driving — and then there was being a paranoid granny. Karen liked to think of herself as the former, but everyone else considered her the latter.

"Sure," Viv said. "It's not like we're in much of a hurry anyway. It's just Amarynth. She's probably fine. We can take things turtle speed."

They shuffled out of Martin's office, Karen looking a good deal steadier than she had on the way in. They were both chattering, a cascade of private jokes.

Once they were gone, Martin shook his head. "I hope I haven't sent them into great danger," he said to the empty office. "I couldn't live with myself."

The office didn't reply, much to Martin's chagrin. There were days he would kill for whatever inner power seemed to guide Amarynth. The answers that came from nowhere.

Whatever it was, he could really use it right now.

"Amarynth! Don't tell me they got you, too."

Amarynth heard his voice first. It took her eyes a few seconds to adjust to the darkness of the room Espoir had led her to for the evening.

Cell, Amarynth mentally corrected, for calling this space a "room" was giving it way too much credit.

Or so she assumed. It was still difficult to make out many details in the low light, basically a scattered stray beam that was filtering into the dark space from a crack under the door that led to the lit hallway outside.

But slowly her eyes adjusted, and she saw his face. "Hey, Gino."

He smiled at her, moved forward, and wrapped her in his arms.

Amarynth pulled away. "Wait. How did *you* get here?"

"W-w-what do you mean?" Gino said.

"I shouldn't be here. I traveled here somehow using a mirror, casting a magic spell. How the heck did *you* get here?" Amarynth asked.

"I woke up here," Gino replied.

"What do you mean you woke up here?" Am asked.

"I mean… I was sleeping, and then I opened my eyes, and I was here," Gino said.

"So you have no idea how you got here?" Am asked.

"No," Gino said. "None whatsoever."

Amarynth shook her head. "Nothing is making sense," she said.

"Aww honey," Gino said, stroking her back.

"I shouldn't be here. They think I know why PTI is happening. That I know how to fix it. I don't. Don't you think that if I did, I'd have fixed it already?" Am said.

"Shhh," Gino said, smoothing her hair.

"What do they want with you?" Amarynth asked him.

"Hm?" he said.

"They want me to tell them why the plague is happening. To fix it somehow. What do they want from you?" Amarynth said.

"Oh," Gino said. "They haven't told me."

Amarynth's eyes widened. "They haven't told you?"

"No," Gino replied. "I just woke up here. Then you came in. I don't know why I'm here. I have no idea what they want from me. To be honest, I don't even know who *they* are yet."

"The Macombers," Am said. "Bunch of Neo-Freudian wackos. Always performing experiments, pushing the limits of reality, never giving two craps how it affects everything else. Like I told Espoir —"

"Espoir?" Gino said.

"She's one of them. More muscle than anything, although she's a moderately skilled telepath. Helps with guarding prisoners, don't you know," Am explained. "Anyway, like I told Espoir, I wouldn't be surprised if the Macomber Family caused this somehow, with all the unethical risks they take. The way they play God or…"

"Something worse?" Gino offered.

"Something worse," Am concurred. "Something much worse."

"Like the lower-g-gods in mythology that were more like department heads. So and so, the patron of farming and wind sailing. Whosawhatsit, the avatar of admitting when you're wrong. Pieces and parts of deities that are capable of causing more mischief than peace," Gino continued.

"Exactly," Amarynth said. "That's exactly it." She smiled at him. "Honestly, Gino, sometimes it's like you're in my mind. You just get me that well. It's why I love you."

"Are you sure it's not this?" Gino replied, giving her a kiss that almost made her pass out on the spartan stone floor.

"Well, that doesn't hurt," Am admitted after the kiss ended.

"You say you love me because we're of the same mind, but maybe the really exciting part is that I'm in a separate body," Gino said.

"Is that a bed I see?" Amarynth asked, partly to be coy and partly because it was still tough to see. The back regions of the cell where she thought she saw the outline of something vaguely bedlike were still quite dark and murky.

Gino grinned. "I thought you'd never ask."

A Wellness Check at Cambria Towers

"Oh hey, uh…" Viv said, reading the nametag. "Lee."

"It's pronounced Lay," Leigh said.

"Like ley lines?" Viv said.

"My mother had notions of mysticism," Leigh explained.

"You could say that again," Viv replied.

"Viv," Karen said. "Be nice. And if you can't be nice, at least be professional."

Viv twitched. She hated to be corrected by Karen — at all and especially while on the job — but her empath partner had a point. She presented her identification. "Detective Viv Lee. Green Star. Level 3 Investigator, Department of Psychic Operations."

"I see," Leigh said. "And you're a detective as well?" She gestured towards Karen.

Karen nodded. "Yup, ditto. Detective Karen Cross. Same credentials."

"Well, detectives," said Leigh. "What can I do for you?"

"We're doing a wellness check on a resident of your building," Viv said.

"Ah," Leigh said. "And which resident would that be?"

"Amarynth Watson," Viv said.

Leigh startled.

"I take it you know Amarynth," Viv said.

"You could say that," Leigh said.

"You're scared," Karen said. "Why are you scared?"

Leigh took a step back. "How did you...?"

"I'm an empath," Karen said. "You can't hide it from me."

Leigh sighed. "Look, Amarynth and I... we were becoming friends. I met her at the coffee shop where I used to work. And once PTI shut the place down, I got a job here at the front desk."

"So you could keep tabs on Amarynth?" Viv pressed, taking cues from Karen that there was something very suspicious about this situation.

"No," Leigh said. "Well, I don't think so."

"You don't think so?" Viv said. "What's that supposed to mean?"

Leigh sighed. "It's gonna sound stupid."

"We work for PsyOps. Trust me. We've heard everything," Karen said. "We've heard stupid and impossible and absurd. All we want is the truth, no matter how weird it is."

"Okay," Leigh said. "I took the job because it seemed like the right thing to do."

"Why?" Viv said.

"I don't know," Leigh said. "It was... like hearing a voice. A voice that told me things that I could believe with absolute certainty. But I didn't know why. I just knew that it was right."

Viv and Karen exchanged glances.

"I know," Leigh said. "It sounds just like Amarynth. The way she works."

"It does," said Viv.

"I don't have powers like hers. I don't. But... after I spent time with her at the café, something happened. It was like part of her left her and attached to me. A tiny part. Not enough so she'd miss it. But just enough that even after she left, I kept thinking about her. And I always knew where she was." Leigh shook her head. "This sounds so dumb. I sound crazy."

"Viv," Karen said. "No deception. Lots of insecurity. Some disbelief. She's telling the truth. At least what she thinks the truth is."

"What was Amarynth doing at the café?" Viv asked.

"What do you mean?" Leigh said. "She was drinking coffee. Hanging out. Like anyone does at a café."

"Was that it though?" Viv pressed.

Leigh considered this for a moment. "I don't know if it matters, but..."

"It might," Karen urged her.

"She was writing poetry. Trying to find herself. She was on suspension from work and seemed kind of lost, and — oh shit, she worked with you, didn't she? She was a PsyOps agent before her leave," Leigh said.

Viv nodded.

"Did you happen to read this writing?" Karen asked.

Leigh shook her head. "She wouldn't let me. Seemed like she was too embarrassed. That she wasn't at the stage where she was comfortable with other people reading what she wrote. I told her about a writing group another regular customer ran. I never did get to read her work."

"Okay," Viv said. "Any way you could get her to buzz us in or anything?"

"Oh sure," Leigh said. She pressed a bunch of buttons on the remote entry console. "That's strange," she said.

"Hm?" Viv said.

"She's not responding. Maybe the speaker in her unit is busted or something. Just a second. I'll call up," Leigh said.

"We tried calling her already on her cell," Viv said. "She didn't answer."

"Her unit has a hard-wired landline in it, too," Leigh explained. "Just for situations like this."

"Fancy fancy," Viv said.

"How do you think Cambria Towers got its reputation?" Leigh shot back, grinning. She placed a call, stood frozen for several moments, and then hung up. She shook her head. "I don't understand. She's not answering. You know how Amarynth is. She grabs it right away. Sometimes she calls you first."

"Why do you think we came down here?" Viv said. It came out a little harsher than she expected it to. "Sorry, it's just..." Viv looked at her feet. "I'm worried."

Karen smiled. Under all the grousing Viv did about Amarynth, there was genuine affection, after all.

"Understandably," Leigh said. "Marcus," she called to a coworker, "can you cover the front? I've got to check on something."

Her coworker slid into Leigh's place behind the front desk.

She motioned for Karen and Viv to follow her into the lift. As the lift rose, her stomach plummeted. It was more than normal worry. It had the incontrovertible feeling of truth of that voice that did not belong to her. One that knew more than she ever had any hope of knowing.

And yet, with all this certainty — with this knowledge, there was very little she could do to change the situation.

Leigh led Karen and Viv into the apartment. It was strikingly empty. Spare of furniture — and spare of any human occupants.

The only living thing still in attendance was Amarynth's tiny parakeet, who was squawking up a storm.

Viv approached the cage and peered in. The bird was out of food. Another bad sign. "Amarynth wouldn't leave without feeding her parakeet," Viv said aloud to her companions.

Leigh fought the sick, pounding feeling in her chest and bolted for the cupboards. After opening nearly every one, she finally located a bag of birdseed and filled Tesla's food dish. He affably tipped over and began to dine.

Karen clutched her chest, nearly bowled over by Leigh's rising feelings of dread.

They walked in silence, combing over each room. It didn't take long. It was an open layout apartment, after all — considered the height of luxury at the time that Cambria Towers was built.

And Amarynth had done them all a favor by leaving her home so bare. An easy search.

"Looks like she had company," Viv said, pointing to a set of man's clothes that were on the bedroom floor, in that familiar pattern when someone undresses in place and doesn't bring the discarded items to the hamper.

"Gino," said Leigh. "Her boyfriend."

"Amarynth has a boyfriend?" Viv said.

"Yeah. Nice guy. I used to wait on him at the café all the time. He's the one who ran the writing group."

"Does Gino have a last name?" Viv asked.

Leigh concentrated. "It's long and begins with B. Italian. Very Italian."

"Italian and begins with B?" Viv said

Leigh nodded.

"This isn't a game show, Ms. Lines. Amarynth, the most reliable person I know — the most reliable person I've ever known — a woman who is so reliable she's annoying... is..."

Missing.

Viv felt her epiglottis start to swell. What the Hell was happening to her? Was she about to cry over Amarynth, of all people?

A well-timed interruption came from Karen, who had crept into the bathroom in the interim. "You guys have to come see this," she called to them from the bedroom.

"Oh yeah?" Viv cracked. "Is there men's shower gel in there, too? Condoms? Toys?"

"Viv, this is serious," Karen called again.

Viv and Leigh came into the bathroom. Karen pointed to the mirror.

In almost every aspect, it was a perfectly normal bathroom mirror. There were likely hundreds of this identical model all through Cambria Towers, a tool for each resident to regard their reflection and adjust their grooming accordingly.

Except Amarynth's mirror was now special. One of a kind.

For now, it wasn't simply a single contiguous piece of reflective glass. No, now there was a central portion that no longer reflected light. Within this segment was a deep dark void. When you stepped back even a slight distance, it looked as though the glass had either been burned with flame somehow (could that even happen? Viv wondered) or painted a deep dark black skillfully enough that it didn't look artificial at all.

However, when you stood close, it seemed like neither of those things. It seemed like a great darkness was present. This black portion seemed almost like a hole you could fall into if you weren't careful.

The shape reminded Viv of how a torso would look if someone had pitched forward and fallen into the glass. An impossible idea of course. But the shape was quite striking.

Viv donned a glove, silently feeling thankful that she had remembered to put a few pairs into the pocket of her paint-flecked overalls before they'd set out. She brought her hand to the glass and hesitated a moment before touching the blackened portion, taking a few deep breaths, steeling herself, half-expecting the mirror to swallow her hand as she touched it — as irrational as it was.

This didn't happen. It was just a sheet of glass. Blackened somehow.

But nothing to worry about. Viv removed the glove and stuffed it into another pocket. *My trash pocket, for the time being*, she thought.

"Have you ever seen anything like it?" Leigh asked.

"Never," Viv answered.

Karen sighed.

"Thank you for your help, Ms. Lines," Viv said. She handed her a business card with her number on it. "If you think of anything else or this Gino shows up, don't hesitate to call. We can lock up after we're done here if you don't mind. We know the way out."

"Sure," Leigh said. She turned and went to leave and was at the apartment door before something occurred to her.

"Detective Lee?" Leigh said, walking back to where the detectives were now taking a closer look in the bedroom, going through some papers that Amarynth had tucked under what appeared to be her side of the bed.

"Yes?" Viv said.

"I just remembered something that might be helpful. Gino works at the community college. Teaches city planning students," Leigh offered.

Viv grinned. "Excellent. That's quite helpful. Thank you, Ms. Lines."

"And Detective Lee?"

"Yes, Ms. Lines?"

"Thank you for looking for Amarynth. I don't know what I'll do if we can't find her," Leigh said.

"Sure," Viv said. "You're welcome. It's literally my job."

After Leigh had left the apartment, Karen said, "She feels guilty about something, Viv."

"Is it big?" Viv asked.

"It's big to her. That's all I can tell from reading her," Karen said.

"Should we bring her back in?" Viv asked. "Did we let her go too soon?"

Karen shook her head. "She'll tell us when it's time."

Not-Paul-Bunyan, Close to Death

Penny sighed as she drew a pentacle in mustard on her slice of bologna.

It was a sad lunch. Yes. But it wasn't nearly as sad as the isolation.

Going into this arrangement, she hadn't anticipated the sadness. Generally a private person — someone who needed her freedom, who craved flexibility and space — she hadn't had any concerns about moving into the ramshackle mother-in-law house at the back of their property.

Especially considering how much care and concern Martin had taken to ensure she'd have what she would logistically need while she was here... on "medical leave."

It still didn't feel real, did it?

Pregnant. She found herself saying it sometimes while sitting in the tiny shed. She tried to think of it as a cottage, but inevitably she'd notice some small detail that reminded her of how austere it was, how utilitarian. It didn't take much to break the illusion. There was a gap in the insulation that might have been as gaping as the chasms in the outer limits of Hell, the plane she'd grown up on.

Well, that's not true, Penny thought. *Hell is where I was born. Earth is really where I grew up.*

And ever since returning from her recent trip to Hell, Penny wasn't sure which place was harsher.

Not that it mattered. She wasn't welcome at home anymore.

"I'm pregnant," Penny said again to no one, hoping that this time it would seem real.

Of course, it didn't.

She glared suspiciously at the yellow pentacle she'd drawn on her sandwich. "You're supposed to be magic," she scolded it. She picked up a second piece of white bread to cover it, before raising the sandwich to her mouth and taking a bite.

"You were supposed to be a lot of things, Rhea Stygius," a voice from behind her said.

She spat out the bite of sandwich.

"Is that you, Change?" she called behind her. She turned around to see a stocky man, shorter in stature. He wore a red and black checked shirt under a pair of denim overalls. He had black hair and a beard to match. This visitor reminded Penny of a miniature Paul Bunyan. "No," she said. "You're not Change. The eyes... the eyes are wrong."

"Very good, Rhea," the visitor said. "You're correct. I'm not Change. Change is an impersonator. That's all he's ever been. All he'll ever be. No, I'm the real deal."

"The genuine article?" Penny said in a mocking tone of voice, shaking her head.

The visitor frowned while Penny took another bite of her sandwich.

"Anyway, you're dead, right?" Penny said, her tone flat.

"Yes, I suppose you could call me dead," he said.

"Well, are you dead?" Penny pressed. "I could call you a lot of things. That's not the point." She nibbled on her bologna sandwich, wishing she'd had mayonnaise as well. It was a luxury that she sorely missed. However, the mustard had been a pleasant surprise. No need to get greedy.

"I'm in the place between life and death," her visitor said. "Close enough for me to be able to reach you."

Penny shook her head, taking a bigger bite.

"Rhea, this isn't a joke," the visitor said.

"Look, whoever you are, wherever you came from, I'm really not in the mood for any shenanigans. I'm pregnant and living in a shed eating a bologna sandwich by myself. I'm drawing weird shapes with the mustard to pretend that it makes any of this a fun experience. But none of this was in my life plan. This wasn't my big dream," Penny said.

"And what were your dreams, Rhea?" he said.

"I wish you'd call me Penny," she said. "I'm a little sick of my Hellish name. There's nothing there for me anymore."

"Alright," Not-Paul-Bunyan said. "Penny, what were your dreams?"

Penny dropped the sandwich onto her plate. She screwed up her face and glared at him. She opened her mouth to answer. But strangely, no answering happened. Penny realized she had no idea what to say.

It was the kind of knowledge gap that throws you completely off guard, like the realization that you've completely zoned out and driven past your house. Except in Penny's case, it was as though when she turned around to go home, the house was no longer there.

She should know. It was an obvious answer, wasn't it? What kind of broken person didn't know the answer to an easy question like that?

Apparently me, Penny thought, scowling. She hissed involuntarily and growled an elaborate guttural curse.

"I'm sorry," Penny said, peeling her lips forcibly into a prim smile, "you'll have to forgive me. I just returned from a trip abroad. I'm afraid the Infernal is still spilling out, even though it's no longer appropriate."

"Takes some time to learn how to properly code switch, I'd imagine," Not-Paul-Bunyan observed.

Penny sighed. He was right, but she didn't like him saying it.

"Anyway, the reason I've come —" the visitor began.

"Fucking finally," Penny hissed softly in Infernal under her breath.

"—is because Amarynth is in trouble."

Penny laughed. "Oh yeah, right. Amarynth in trouble. That's a good one."

Not-Paul-Bunyan frowned. "I'm not joking."

"Oh please," Penny said. "This isn't my first time talking to the dead."

"I told you, I'm not dead. I'm only close to death. Close enough to get this message across to you. And even then, it wasn't easy," Not-Paul-Bunyan said.

"Okay, whatever you say, you're not dead," Penny said. "Anyway, I'm used to my special visitors — dead or close to death, whatever that means — having a sort of flexible relationship with the truth. It's understandable, really. When you've left the world, what reason do you have to still be beholden to the world at all? Let alone be beholden to something that most living people can't fully accept, like the truth."

"I'm telling the truth, Penny," he said.

"It just doesn't *sound* right," Penny said. "Amarynth is the most capable person I have ever met. She's downright freaky. Nobody sneaks up on her. Nothing. She's always six steps ahead of everyone. There's no way that she's in danger. Danger just doesn't happen to Amarynth. If anything, we should all be more scared of her."

"What if I told you it wasn't a person that snuck up on Amarynth but a…thing?" Not-Paul-Bunyan said.

"I'd tell you that you sound drunk," Penny admitted.

She closed her eyes and began to visualize a large chunk of rock, a sheer monolith, obsidian black. It stretched up into the sky. She wrapped herself around it mentally, felt her limbs tingle in response to the guided visualization, and began to scale up the monolith, higher and higher, never quite reaching the top.

It was a top that she knew theoretically existed — for it was her own mind, her own construction. But it was also one she knew was an element that she'd never reach.

As she mentally scaled this monolith, she kept her breathing regular, exhaling and inhaling slowly and deeply.

Finally, after a long ascent, she peered down mentally from the heights she'd climbed and saw Not-Paul-Bunyan in her mind's eye as the most minuscule dot. Nodding, she climbed higher until she knew even that small dot would disappear.

When she opened her eyes, she noted her visitor was gone.

That was probably her favorite thing she'd brought back from her recent trip to Hell —the ability to block out her dead (or near-dead, she added derisively with a laugh) visitors. Once upon a time, she'd been forced to see them, forced to interact with them, whether she wanted to or not.

But ever since she had connected with the memory eater and gotten her old memories back, it was quite a simple matter to dismiss unwanted guests. It was as easy as hanging up on a rude caller.

"I never thought I'd learn to set boundaries from a trip to Hell," Penny mused.

She picked up the rest of her sandwich and devoured it.

The Car Breaks Down at an Imposing Mansion on a Dark and Stormy Night

An Exploration of Cognitive Dissonance and Confirmation Bias

As has been noted elsewhere in this book — and throughout public discourse surrounding the emergence of intuitive powers — there does seem to be a strong attitudinal component to psychic potentiation. Namely, a practitioner's relationship to others and their environment can either hamper or strengthen psychic prowess.

Intuitives of all stripes are susceptible to interference because of their personal biases. However, as has been explored in other chapters of this volume, certain subtypes are more prone to these effects than others. At present, precognitionists, intuitives with the ability to see potential future outcomes, are the subtype most profoundly affected by bias. However, nearly all psychic practitioners find bias to be a meaningful complication if not an outright hindrance to the effective functioning of their abilities.

As a response to this, many psychic practitioners make meaningful attempts to mitigate their own biases, through a variety of personal development programs. However, as has been noted, there is little evidence of the efficacy of these purported solutions.

The reason for this is that bias isn't a bug in the human psyche; it is a feature. There are many functional reasons for our brains to round things off in an illogical manner, to make pieces fit into an overall puzzle that otherwise wouldn't accept them.

Furthermore, while bias is often spoken of as a single unitary concept when talking about psychic interference, bias itself is an umbrella category, made up of many distinct concepts — which each pose a distinct individual interference pattern to the psychic practitioner.

Take, for example, the case of cognitive dissonance and confirmation bias.

Human beings crave consistency — and when that consistency is lacking, the result can be very painful.

The state of having conflicting or contradictory thoughts, beliefs, behavior, or attitudes is known as cognitive dissonance.

There are many ways for cognitive dissonance to come about, but one common scenario that people encounter is when they learn something new about the world that contradicts their long-held beliefs. Cognitive dissonance can also result when people learn something about themselves or the consequences of their behavior that contradicts their sense of self or identity.

The inconsistency that results is very painful for individuals, and so they'll often work towards reducing that dissonance by any means necessary.

This can be achieved in multiple ways:

The first potential remedy is by changing inconsistent attitudes, thoughts, beliefs, or behaviors so that they are no longer inconsistent with one another.

Another option is to incorporate new information that provides an explanation that can counteract the dissonant beliefs.

Finally, an individual can dismiss the importance of the conflict, telling themselves it ultimately doesn't matter.

Changing your mind about something and admitting that you were wrong can be truly difficult — and sometimes it's harder than others, in situations where there's a higher resistance to change. This can vary not only from person to person but within the individual, as the dissonance in some situations will cause them more distress than in others.

In addition to all these methods of dealing with cognitive dissonance once it has happened, individuals might find cognitive dissonance such a painful, troubling state that they decide to circumvent the risk of it preemptively — by sticking to channels of relating with others where they're unlikely to ever encounter it. This will often manifest as a cognitive bias called confirmation bias.

In simple terms, confirmation bias is the tendency to not only seek out information that confirms one's existing beliefs (also known as selective exposure) but also to interpret any information that they encounter as confirming those same beliefs.

While useful for humanity's cravings for consistency, confirmation bias is quite a large hindrance for psychic efficacy and particularly so for precognitionists. As one might imagine, it is truly difficult to make future predictions if you're stuck on what you believe at present. It can be far too easy to miss uncomfortable changes that are inevitable when you're primed to look past them.

Of course, confirmation bias isn't the only risk. There are myriad other potential pitfalls. The reader may remember the media frenzy that resulted when self-serving bias took hold of a governmental telepath who misinterpreted a top foreign official's stray thought and nearly started a war.

But confirmation bias seems to be the largest threat for the time being.

Based on some early data coming from the Black Square program, confirmation bias also presents a challenge to memory-based powers. This is because individuals will sometimes rewrite memories to get rid of a change, rewriting history instead of admitting that their views have changed, in an effort to create consistency of beliefs over a lifetime.

The implications of this remain troubling for psychic society.

Some prominent precognitionists have speculated, however, that we may very well soon be moving away from a focus on confirmation bias as a psychic society and instead find ourselves increasingly grappling with pluralistic ignorance —i.e., The Emperor's New Clothes. In this model, no one really believes something but assumes that everyone else believes it. Indeed other prominent theoreticians believe that belief itself is preparing to become a force in its own right, without the counterbalance of reason.

It's a terrifying notion but one which would undoubtedly bring a treasure trove of scientific — and paranormal — discovery.

That is, if the precogs are correct and sufficiently unbiased.

Watch this space.

from Insecta Psychica: Towards an Intuitive Taxonomy by Cloche Macomber

"I'm telling you... she didn't know her Tukey HSD from her MANOVA."

Laughter erupted.

Amarynth shook her head. Researcher talk. Acronyms and
eponyms. Codified passwords likely understood once upon
a time, mastered for the sake of entrance into an elite club.
They were beautiful, corresponded to amazing mathematical
calculations — equations that didn't solve the mysteries of the
universe or anything but often brushed up against their general
vicinity.

And that was certainly better than nothing, wasn't it?

But these terms had been ingested transactionally by these
researchers. Used when they were needed. Long since discarded.

And now those calculations were largely performed by
computerized tools and put-upon assistants — those who were
still angling for their entrance into this society.

It pained Amarynth to see people who treated the gateway to
the mysteries of the universe as merely a set of hoops to jump
through in an obstacle course whose ultimate goal was arriving
at the end and being crowned the victor. Being lauded. And
important.

How small-minded. How wasteful, really. Disrespectful to all
those who had come before and built upon humanity's collective
knowledge and expected that their descendants would do the
same.

Perhaps it had been better in the past, Amarynth mused, before
the Four Families had gotten so powerful. Back when they
moved in the shadows. When academicians could be pretentious
perhaps — but relatively obscure. Before society considered them
rock stars.

Maybe Leigh had been right with all that overjustification effect
business, Amarynth reflected. Maybe things went terribly wrong
when the work itself wasn't the reward.

Was that how everything had gotten so far off track?

Amarynth shook her head. No, it was part of it. But not all of it.

Still, it was quite alarming to see so many Watsons here — in the phylactery — thronged by Macombers, merry-making, relaxed even, acting as if any of this was normal.

The way they all sat at the long dining room table reminded Amarynth of a formal holiday dinner, even if there was no food in sight. Amarynth wished that Gino were still here. Instead, when she'd awoken from sleep, he was gone again, with no explanation.

"And just how is our girl doing?" a familiar face said. It was Dr. Allen Watson, the researcher who discovered the existence of psyons and first speculated their role in psychic activity. He was also her uncle, her mother's older brother by... four years? Five? Amarynth wasn't quite sure. A handful of years.

Amarynth stared at him, blinking. He was the last person she'd expected to find at the table. "Uncle Al," she replied, "I haven't seen you since..."

"Since you were four," Al replied. "That's right." He beamed. "I guess that makes this a sort of family reunion."

"A family reunion?" Amarynth scoffed. "More like a scene from a cheesy B-movie."

Al screwed up his face in surprise. "I'm sorry?"

"It was a dark and stormy night. The car breaks down on the road. 'Come in from the rain,' the urbane but vaguely menacing and unnervingly toothy resident suggests. 'Have dinner with us. And drink.' But of course, the wine is drugged. You wake with fangs in your neck." Amarynth forced a painful smile. "Hardly my idea of a family reunion." She pondered this for a second before adding, "Although I suppose it qualifies when you're related to a bunch of vampires."

Al laughed. "Vampires? Oh c'mon, Amarynth. I heard you started hanging out with those conspiracy theorists, but don't tell me that you believe in vampires."

Amarynth frowned. "Clearly, you've never heard of a metaphor."

"Is that what that was?" Al replied. "Dear girl, I've heard of much more than a metaphor." He began to rail off his professional and academic accomplishments.

Of course, Amarynth thought, *a man like him would memorize his entire curriculum vitae and unleash it like Homeric poetry.* It was the same old posturing, just gussied up a little more, translated into a language that you needed money to learn. It was funny, Amarynth mused, that so many of her family members had aggressively pursued research as a vocation. They had installed themselves in academia in a way that set up generations of Watsons of widely varying talent — from the marginal students all the way up to the very rare and gifted scientist — to dominate its hallowed halls.

Well, they'd set themselves up to engage in never-ending pissing contests with the Skinners — at the very least.

She was a Watson, a child from the black sheep arm of the family to be sure, but a Watson nonetheless. Those same doors would have been open to her, had she only asked to be let through them.

But it hadn't appealed to her. Oh, she'd gone to a few symposiums out of fairness. She had given it the old college try — and in this instance, that phrase was quite literal, wasn't it?

But she had quickly tired of it. Tired of the posturing and the naked insecurity that surrounded her, everyone looking for a straightforward pretension to elevate themselves above others by hiding their flaws under a mantle that anyone could own, provided they had the right money, connections, or both.

True, some quite talented individuals also wore that same cloak. But for the vast majority, it didn't mean what they all pretended it meant.

And countless others were struggling in the wider world without the same protection who were more talented and more worthy and who lived and died in obscurity because they lacked resources.

But Uncle Al would have none of that line of thought. There was nothing Amarynth could ever say to make him see that. He had bought into the power of his thick prestigious cloak of academic achievement hook, line, and sinker. And now that he was the proud owner of it, there was nothing he liked better than to perform a dramatic reading of the legend of what he'd done.

"I can tell from your silence that you're quite impressed, my dear girl," Al said.

Amarynth shook her head. "I think you must have my feelings mixed up with your own."

Al scowled. "Well, what do you know? I imagine the whole thing went right over that pretty head of yours."

Amarynth rolled her eyes.

"Yes, I said you were pretty. I know it's surprising to hear from a man of my caliber, of my talents," Al said.

Amarynth laughed. "I wasn't thinking that. Although I suppose it's noteworthy, that you think I'm pretty — but only because you're my uncle, so it's a little creepy."

Al frowned.

"No," Amarynth continued, "I was thinking that you're awfully condescending for a traitor."

Al met this with a raised eyebrow. "A traitor? How do you figure?"

"What else do you call a Watson dining with the enemy?" Am said.

"Oh, is that what you think of the Macombers? That they're our enemies?"

"They've been fighting with our Family for ages — and the other Noble Families. We've literally killed each other," Am said. "Surely, a man of your great sophistication is familiar with history," she added with a bombastic tone.

If Al knew she was mocking him, he didn't let on. "Oh, that? That was ancient history. There hasn't been significant bloodshed for ages."

Am squinted and railed off a list of a dozen homicide cases from the past decade in which a Macomber assassin had been implicated.

"Oh please," Al said. "I didn't say murders. I said significant bloodshed."

"You don't consider a murder significant bloodshed?" Am said.

"My dear girl," Al said, causing Amarynth to shudder once again at the distinctly boundary-crossing term of affection, "it's clear that you haven't studied as a researcher. Which is a pity because you would be such a good one."

"This seems to be a favorite topic of yours," Am interjected.

Al continued, unabated. "Statistical power is all about large numbers, my dear girl." Amarynth twitched. "The more data points you have, the higher the level of confidence."

"That's all things being equal," Am challenged. "The underlying empirical assumption. If due diligence isn't done, if that equality is only presumed but not calculated, then you can walk away with all the data in the world, a huge number of data points, and still know far less than you think you do."

Al beamed. "Very good, Amarynth." He took a long drink of brandy. "It really is a pity that mother of yours never sent you to a proper school."

"Oh, she did," Am said. "Or, rather, I sent myself. It's just not a school that you're smart enough to recognize."

Al gave her an incredulous look.

"I know you're not used to *anyone* questioning your intelligence," Am said, "and why would they? You spend all your time around two kinds of people. The first kind of people, they're just like you. They're people who have paid into the same system, who are too far into it all, and even if they are dissatisfied with what they got out of their investment, they're not about to admit it. Most of them don't admit it to themselves, much less to peers that are in the same predicament."

"Sunk costs," Al summarized bitterly.

Am nodded.

"And the second kind?"

"Panderers, flatterers, hangers-on," Am said. "People who recognize you as having money and connections. You're a Watson, by golly! What they couldn't do with their lives if they only knew a Watson, someone aristocratic and connected. They're not going to tell you the truth about yourself, how you really are. They're too busy performing for you, trying to garner your approval, in the hopes that you'll throw them a crumb or two of that success that came to you from an accident of birth."

Al scowled.

"Anyway, intelligence isn't your problem. Not really. You have plenty of crystallized intelligence, a large repository of facts that you've saved up your entire life. It's your fluid intelligence that's probably lacking. Your thinking hasn't been flexible for decades — and it shows," Am concluded.

Al considered this and studied her face for a moment.

Am stared back.

"You know," Uncle Al said finally, "I felt a little sorry for you when I heard they weren't letting you go. I thought it must be a lot of pressure for one young girl to manage."

"I'm a full-grown woman," Am corrected him.

"Do girls ever grow up fully?" Al mused, taking another sip of brandy.

"Yes," Am answered.

"That was rhetorical," Al said.

"A question that misguided can't ever be rhetorical — unless of course you're surrounded by fools and panderers, as you often are," Am said.

Al's face flexed into a deep scowl. "As I was saying, I did feel sorry for you."

"And now?" Am prompted him.

"Now," Al said, setting down his glass of brandy, "I hope they torture you."

 "Mr. Boccaccio?" Viv said.

"Dr. Boccaccio," the man said. "Yes, I'm Dr. Boccaccio." His voice was warm and friendly and marked with a thick Italian accent.

"Ambrogino Boccaccio?" Viv said.

"Yes," he said. "It says it right there." He pointed to a plaque that indeed said AMBROGINO BOCCACCIO, Ph.D.

It hadn't been hard to find him. Only took a single call to the switchboard at the community college, the information line. Viv had expected to have to kick up more of a fuss, invoke PsyOps, her rank. But whoever answered the phone wasn't concerned about why she needed the information, and they were also fairly good at piecing together what little Viv knew: "I'm looking for Gino B. He teaches city planning students. Has a long last name. I have trouble saying it."

"Dr. Boccaccio. One moment, and I'll give you his extension."

"Could you tell me where his office is located, too, while you're at it?" Viv had asked.

"Certainly."

And now here they were.

"Dr. Boccaccio, we're here from PsyOps, and we'd like to have a word with you," Viv said.

"I hope this is a convenient time," Karen added.

I don't care if it's a convenient time, Viv thought spitefully, *if he's got Amarynth and he's done something to her, I'd rather talk to the jerk at the least convenient time possible.* But aloud she said nothing.

"Sure," Dr. Boccaccio said. "The Department of Psychic Operations? I have to say that's highly unexpected. It's not every day that an urban planning professor is visited by psychic detectives. What are you doing here? What can I help you with?"

"We want to talk about Amarynth Watson," Viv said.

Dr. Boccaccio stared at her, hesitating as though he expected more explanation to follow. When none arrived, he said, "I'm sorry, who?"

"Amarynth Watson. Our colleague. She's a Connections Agent. We want to talk to you about her whereabouts, the last time you saw her," Viv said.

"I honestly have no idea what you're talking about. Did something happen to her? Did something happen to this... Amethyst?"

"Amarynth," Viv corrected, bristling.

"Well, I don't know her," Dr. Boccaccio said. "I don't know any of the Watson family. With how slim funding is these days, I'd love to know a Watson or two. I'd love to be that well connected. I assure you… if I knew a Watson, any Watson, I'd remember that. It would be top of mind."

"She's not one of *those* Watsons," Viv said. *She is my half-sister though*, a softer voice within her added. Viv scowled at the softer afterthought and ignored it.

"I wish I could help," Dr. Boccaccio said, "but I have no idea what you're talking about."

"Viv," Karen said, "he's not deceiving us. He's either telling the truth or at least thinks he is."

Dr. Boccaccio grinned. "You're an empath, right? Or are you a truth evaluator? No, a truth evaluator would have been more definitive, less hedging of bets. You're an empath, I just know it. Boy, this is just like on TV. Next thing I know, Regina Withers is going to pop up somewhere with a microphone to talk about your case progress."

"Over my dead body," Viv said.

Dr. Boccaccio made a surprised noise.

"She doesn't like Regina Withers," Karen explained.

"You've worked with her?!" Dr. Boccaccio exclaimed.

"She was a person of interest on a former case," Viv replied, "and her production company was a thorn in my side. I'm not convinced they're entirely gone, to tell you the truth."

"You have such glamorous jobs," Dr. Boccaccio said.

"Glad you think so," Viv said dismissively. Her phone rang. She pressed the button to answer the call and put the phone to her ear.

"Hello," Viv said.

"Hey Viv, it's Leigh. Leigh Lines."

"Uh-huh," Viv said.

"After you guys left and I went back to work, I had another idea. I checked the badge-in, badge-out record in the visitors' log at Cambria Towers. It's not perfect. Sometimes people manage to get by us without leaving a record, but it's better than nothing," Leigh said.

"Good thinking," Viv said. "What did you find?"

"Well, according to the log," Leigh said, "neither Gino nor Am has gone through the gate in days. At least... the badges they use haven't."

"Is that as weird as I think it is?" Viv said.

"Yeah," Leigh said. "I mean, so long as you think it's pretty freaking weird."

"Are you on a cell phone? Can you get texts?" Viv asked.

"Yeah, I called you on my mobile. Why?" Leigh said.

"Hey, Leigh, hold on a second. I'm gonna text you a picture. Don't hang up," Viv instructed. She pulled the phone away from her ear and pointed it at Dr. Boccaccio, who was sitting patiently waiting for her to finish her conversation, while Karen awkwardly fidgeted in place by shifting her weight from one foot to the other.

Viv took a picture of the professor and quickly texted it to Leigh.

"You get that?" Viv said into the phone.

"Yeah, I heard a beeping sound like I got a text. Hold on, I'm gonna look," Leigh said.

Viv waited.

"Hey Viv," Leigh said.

"Yeah?"

"Who is that guy in the photo?" Leigh asked.

"You don't recognize him, do you?" Viv said.

"No," Leigh admitted. "I've never seen him before in my life. Who is he?"

"His name is Ambrogino Boccaccio. He teaches urban planning at the community college," Viv said.

"But he looks nothing like Gino," Leigh said.

"Thanks, Leigh," Viv said.

"Hey if you figure out where Amarynth is, can you let—"

"Yes, of course," Viv interrupted, abruptly disconnecting the call.

"What's going on?" Dr. Boccaccio said. "Why did you take my picture? What was that about?"

"I'm sorry, Dr. Boccaccio," Viv said, "but it seems as though someone's stolen your identity."

"Are you there, Megan?" Penny said.

A loud crackling and popping replied. She had no idea what that meant.

"I can't see you on the screen. Do you see that little symbol that looks like a video camera? Feel free to click that. It may not have activated automatically," Penny said into her computer microphone.

An indeterminate mass of crackle and hisses poured out of her computer speakers at her.

"THE CAMERA ICON. CLICK IT," Penny said, raising her voice. It was hard enough to give tech support assistance when you could hear if the other person understood you. But this? This was madness.

Penny cursed herself as she felt her blood pressure rise. It had seemed like such a clear-cut proposition, running seances over video call software. Like the perfect work from home career for a medium stuck in a shed during a pandemic, carrying an illicit pregnancy to term.

But the reality had been far from smooth sailing. Even with the instructions she'd worked so hard on writing, the ones she'd sent to her client, there seemed to be gremlins in her computer — or the client's — thwarting everything.

"Stupid gremlins," Penny muttered, covering her microphone with her hand on the off-chance that Megan McGillicuddy — her monied client — could hear the audio that was coming through and that the sound distortion was only on Penny's end.

"Gremlin's a new one to me," a voice said.

Oh great. Not him. Penny spun around. Not-Paul-Bunyan stood in all his glory, grinning like he was proud of himself.

"What do you want?" Penny said. "I told you to go away. I forced you to leave."

"I came back," Not-Paul-Bunyan said to her with a noncommittal shrug.

"Well, if you want to make yourself useful, I'm having tech difficulties," Penny said.

"Oh, that?" her visitor said. "I think if you look into it, you'll find that everything's fine on both ends of the call. It's just… interference." He grinned even more broadly.

Penny glared at him. "What?"

"I just want you to listen to me, Rhea — err, Penny. Just listen to what I have to say to you, and then I'll be gone, and you can do… whatever it is you're doing here," he said.

"Wait, this is *your fault*? *You're* the reason I can't get video conferencing to work?" Penny said.

"Maybe," he said. Again, that stupid grin. "In my defense, I had to get your attention somehow."

Penny sighed, crossing her arms over her chest. "Okay, well, then get it over with. What was so important that you had to tell me? What was so dire and pressing that you had to threaten my livelihood just to make your point?"

"Your livelihood?" he said. "This is your first seance, and it's already your livelihood? What kind of mad money are you making? Maybe I should get into online seances."

Penny furrowed her brow. "It's a long-term strategy," she said defensively. "Never mind that. Spill it. What's the big news? You have my attention now. You might as well tell me."

"They've got Amarynth," Not-Paul-Bunyan said.

"What?" Penny said.

"Amarynth has been captured. She's being held against her will," he said.

"Against her will? Where?" Penny pressed.

"The same place I am," he replied.

"And just where is that?" Penny asked.

"I don't know," he admitted. "We are both with the lich now. I am bound to him. She is here, too, though. And all of us... we're all near death. Death is with us."

Penny frowned. At times like these, she wished she had supernatural powers to affect the dead — or the near-death as this fellow claimed to be — and not just to commune with them. It would be infinitely more helpful when presented with this kind of distressing information to be able to destroy the undead like the clerics of fiction. "The power of Christ compels you," a cross held aloft, and hordes of undead exploding into smithereens. Too bad that was bogus, Penny cursed. And even if it were true, she was far from devout enough to qualify, especially given her dubious origins — a former princess of Hell that couldn't stop hissing and snarling at the slightest inconvenience.

But boy, would it come in handy to be able to put the screws to this visitor and get some real information. Instead, she was left with her normal set of tools — your standard psychological warfare. The dead had little to lose so were typically resistant to your normal forms of persuasion. What was left was confusion. It didn't always work.

"Oh, okay," Penny said, affecting a fake outer calm. "Thanks for letting me know." She closed her eyes and leaned back in her chair, acting as though she were about to banish her unwanted guest again by climbing the monolith.

"Wait!" he cried. "Don't you want to know more?"

"I suppose." Penny shrugged. "Although you said you don't know where you are, so I'm not sure how much help you could be anyway."

"I know someone who might be able to help," the near-death lumberjack said in a frantic tone.

Penny yawned. "Oh, really?" she said.

"Yes."

"And just who would that be?"

"The memory eater of Whisper Street," Not-Paul-Bunyan said.

Penny twitched involuntarily. Oh, no... not...

"She has many names, but I believe she's going by Gretchen Mills at the moment," he explained.

"I know exactly who she is," Penny said. She had a sinking feeling.

Why does everything lead back to her? Penny wondered. If there were one person that Penny would like to never see again, it would be Gretchen Mills, and yet... their paths kept crossing.

And there was another problem with this story. "Why are you telling me this?" Penny asked her visitor.

"Can't it just be to be helpful?" he said.

Penny shook her head. "It never is with your kind."

"Well, that's unfair," he protested.

"But accurate. There's no reason for you to care about Amarynth. No reason for you to warn me. What does it matter to you? The dead aren't invested in what happens with the living," Penny said.

"Well, maybe the dead aren't — but perhaps those who are near death still care," he said.

Penny sighed. She shook her head. "Doesn't have the ring of truth, I'm afraid."

He frowned. "Okay, you got me."

"What is it?" Penny prompted.

"If Amarynth is destroyed, then the rest of us have no hope," he said.

"Destroyed?" Penny said.

He nodded. "She's in great danger."

The words hung in the air heavily. The two stared at one another in the silence. Finally, Penny broke it.

"What do you want? A tip?" Penny shot at her visitor, who was still standing there awkwardly.

"I—no, I... just," he stammered.

"If you're quite finished, I need to convey this information to someone who can do something about it," Penny said, "and I also have a séance to conduct, so if you don't mind."

"O-o-oh, uhh, sure," Not-Paul-Bunyan said. He waved goodbye at her, but nothing happened.

"You're still here," Penny said.

"Um," Not-Paul-Bunyan said, "if it wouldn't be too much trouble, could you send me off?"

"Send you off?"

Not-Paul-Bunyan nodded. "Whatever you did last time."

"Or you could just leave," Penny suggested.

"Well, that's the thing…" he confessed. "I don't know how."

Penny sighed dramatically. "Fine," she said. She closed her eyes and scaled the infinite monolith. When she opened them, he was gone.

She turned to her computer. "Can you hear me, Mrs. McGillicuddy? Megan?"

"Yes, dearie," the familiar voice poured out of her computer. "Loud and clear. And what a relief! I was beginning to think we should reschedule."

"Oh, no need for that," Penny said, beaming her brightest smile at her webcam and seeing her client's image shimmer into place as the video feedback finally decided to display properly. "Ah, there you are." Penny waved at her webcam.

The client waved back.

"Thank you for your patience. I'm just going to take care of something quickly. If you could gather as many votive candles as you have and get them set up on your end, I'll be with you in just a moment," Penny instructed.

The client flashed a thumbs up at her and wandered away from her computer, presumably to fetch those candles.

Penny minimized the video conferencing call and opened a chat program. Frantically, she typed a message to Viv about the situation, that she'd been visited by some kind of spirit (or near-spirit, Penny corrected herself mentally, giggling all the while), who told her that Amarynth was being held against her will and was in danger.

He couldn't tell me where she was, Penny concluded, *only that Gretchen Mills would know.*

She had almost called her "the memory eater of Whisper Street," but those words belonged to a much longer conversation than she was willing to have at the moment — and pointed at a lot of other things she hadn't told Viv and Karen about her recent trip home.

Penny's background was embarrassing to her. And the ritual to send her home in the first place was even more embarrassing, how Gretchen had melded with her completely for a few exquisite moments — mind, body, and soul — before everything had been consumed by flame.

Anyway, as hard as it would be to explain to anyone else that might ask, Penny knew deep down that she needed to keep a few secrets, to have pieces of her life that only she knew. It was selfish. And it probably made true intimacy impossible. But it was an addiction — arguably a form of self-care but even more, it was something that made her feel alive.

"I have the candles!" Mrs. McGillicuddy's voice poured out of the speakers.

Penny switched back to the video chat program. "Wonderful!" Her client was lighting them with a matchbook and placing them around her desk, just within Penny's line of sight via webcam. The client positioned the votives gingerly, as though she were trying to place them as equidistantly as possible.

"That good?" the client called at her.

"Wonderful," Penny affirmed.

Her client beamed and sat down in her desk chair.

"Okay," Penny said, "now who do we want to contact today?"

It'll Be Just Like Da Camera

All dualism does is reveal a ghost facing a skeleton. All real bodies shimmer like watered silk. They are hazy surfaces, mixtures of body and soul.

-Michel Serres

Julia Fantasio, *née* Macomber, squealed at the head of the table. "Oh, Duckie!" she said. "Look what Espoir dragged in."

"Duckie" was her husband, Squire Fantasio. Not born of one of the Four Families but within spitting distance of it for generations, until he happened to land himself a Macomber.

Unfortunately, it was Julia — who had all the eccentricities and annoying features of high society and none of its graces. Even more unfortunately, she had no psychic powers. This was a particularly striking and rare condition within the Macomber matriarchy, as even servants — or adopted, hired muscle like Espoir — usually had some kind of talent.

Poor Squire had landed the dud of the family. No matter. His Julia's name opened doors.

And today it had led to having a grand dinner at the phylactery — of all places!

How many opportunities did a person get to have a full-course meal while the life force of a powerful magical entity swirled all around them?

It was his lucky day.

Squire couldn't wait to hear what his country club friends would have to say when he showed up to play 18 holes and casually dropped that he'd been rubbing elbows with the Macomber lich. That would sure beat their usual brags by a mile. Bunch of insufferable gits, Squire thought resolutely, nodding to no one in particular as he sat at the dining table.

Like many people, Squire spent a considerable amount of time, money, and energy trying to impress people he didn't even like.

Amarynth — also known as "what Espoir dragged in" — groaned at the sight of this hideous couple. They had been in her mother's book, too. Empty-headed flatterers. Enemies. Not just because they were from a rival Family, but because they were insipid.

Am avoided Julia's fawning gaze as she sat at her assigned place at the table. She stared down into her plate, which was set with an ostentatious table service that featured a staggering number of spoons and forks, fanning out for an improbable distance.

It was a large table with many empty seats. One by one, they began to fill. Most of the dinner guests were Macombers but not all. There were many Watsons in attendance. Her Uncle Al of course — and other opportunistic Watsons her mother had warned her about.

It was like a prophecy now, those sessions in which her mother had alerted her of the bad seeds of the Four Families, by guiding her through old photo albums.

Those were all the faces that surrounded her now.

All seemed to be delighted to be there. This was a magnificent event — a fine dinner in the presence of a powerful captive, bathed in the strange energy of the Macomber lich.

Two seats remained empty until right before the service began.

At that moment, Espoir strode in escorting the very unsteady but highly ornamented Macomber lich. She kept one burly arm forever over his. Her other arm remained tucked behind his back. They shambled forward as if doing a strange dance.

The lich wore voluminous burgundy robes that were iridescent as they hit the light and subtle gold-dappled overlay sparked into prominence.

Atop his head was a pointy cap that matched his robes. The sartorial effect was not unlike a priest's vestments on high holy days. He sat at the head of the table, just to Amarynth's right.

"Thank you for coming," Espoir spoke after the guest of honor had been seated. "His undead majesty asked that I speak to you all. He communicated his wishes via telepathy. When you are in a state such as his, you must do everything you can to conserve your energy, you see."

There was polite laughter at this. Nearly every head in the room bobbed obsequiously in unison.

"We will feast," Espoir said, "but that is not all. Tonight, we will also trade stories. Of triumph, hardship, and heartache. Any story at all. Any one you can think of. The first one that comes to mind."

"Oh, I don't know if that's such a good idea!" Julia exclaimed.

Espoir gave her a withering gaze.

"I... I... mean...." Julia said. She shot a helpless look to Squire. "Help me out here, Duckie."

"Dear lady," Squire said, tipping his chin to Espoir, "I do believe my wife means to say that she is not much of a storyteller."

"It doesn't matter," Espoir said. "Everyone must participate. We're going to go around the table, and one by one, you're each going to tell a different story." She looked to Amarynth. "That means your story will be last, Amarynth."

"What makes you think I'm going to tell you a story?" Amarynth said.

"Well," Espoir said, "if you don't, you'll die."

Amarynth frowned.

"Don't believe me?" Espoir said. "Fine." She stood, walked across the dining room, and opened the door. "We're ready for him," she called outside.

Espoir returned to her chair.

In walked Gino.

"Oohh Duckie, it's some kind of entertainment," Julia cried. "Is this man a comedian?"

"Hush, Julia," Squire said. "Just watch."

"Hi Amarynth," Gino said. "Look, I know none of this makes any sense right now, but the best thing for you to do is to go along with this. Tell your story. It's the only way anything gets fixed. It's how you get out of here."

"Gino, what are you doing here?" Am said. "Are you working for them?"

Espoir scoffed at this. "Hardly. We were wondering if *you* knew how he got in here. We figured he was part of your little break-in."

Amarynth shook her head.

"Amarynth," Gino said. "Just go along with it."

"No," Amarynth said. "I can't. I won't."

"Fine then," Espoir said. "Have it your way." To Gino, she said, "Kneel before the great lich. He will render punishment."

"No, not on Gino," Amarynth said. "Punish me. I'm the one who deserves it."

"The wicked don't get to decide who gets punished for their crimes," Espoir said. To Gino, she said, "Kneel."

He did. Amarynth wanted to run over and shake him, to tell him to snap out of it, to not go so passively into this unknown punishment, to fight, to resist. But she found herself frozen in place. She didn't know if it were a panic attack or the effects of the lich's lifeforce, but she couldn't move.

The lich raised one bony finger and pointed it at Gino. A few moments later, Gino fell over.

"He's dead," Espoir said. She sounded almost surprised by it herself.

Amarynth screamed.

"Oh calm down," Espoir said. "He's not fully dead."

"Not... fully... dead?" Amarynth said.

"He's just near death. Dead enough that you round up but not completely dead," she explained. "The lich is fully capable of restoring him to life if he wants to." She paused a moment as if listening to the lich's thoughts. "And he will. So long as you tell the best story you've ever told."

Amarynth was crying now. "Yes, anything," she said. "I'm ready."

"In good time," Espoir said, grinning. "You'll have to wait your turn."

Servants shuffled in with the bread course. Espoir motioned to the man on her right, a stodgy, red-faced individual who should have been indicted twelve times over for embezzlement from charities. Amarynth would have recognized him from television where his misdeeds were often featured but never prosecuted by the Psychic State, even if she had never seen him in her mother's photo albums. "We start with you, my good fellow," Espoir said, misusing the term "good" as a descriptor.

"Oh goody!" Uncle Al erupted before the first storyteller could begin. "This will be just like *The Decameron*!"

"Did you hear that, Duckie? It'll be just like da camera," Julia crowed.

"Not da camera, you vainglorious pillock!" Uncle Al sneered. "*The Decameron.*"

"Oh," Julia said shrilly, "I knew that."

Uncle Al rolled his eyes, unconvinced. "It's a book from the fourteenth century. A party of ten people flees from Florence, which is overrun by the plague, to the Italian countryside, where they hole up for two weeks. While there, they tell stories to pass the time. It's incredibly fitting, given our current situation. Why, there's even a plague outside. Not the Black Death of course. Nothing so impressive as that. But we do have PTI, don't we, playing the role of our romantic plague?" He grinned for a few moments before his face fell into a scowl. "I can't believe you called it 'da camera.' What an outrage! Such an insult to Boccaccio! I'm disappointed with the state of public education these days. And the state of private education, too, since you ostensibly had access to the best one money could buy, Julia."

"Oh, go ostensibly yourself," Julia retorted. "Do you hear how this little man speaks to me, Duckie?"

"You'll have to excuse my wife," Squire said to Uncle Al. "The... nuances of social niceties elude her."

"That's not the only thing that eludes her," Uncle Al grumbled. He coughed briefly to clear his throat. "Never mind me. My apologies, Espoir. Let the story-telling begin."

And while the rest of the table buttered rolls, the first story began.

As it did, the lich turned briefly to Amarynth. He lifted the mask that rested over his eyes for a split second, revealing... eyes that were very familiar to her indeed.

It was Change. Amarynth didn't know what it meant. But suddenly, she was filled with hope. It made the clumsy story being told sound much better to her ears.

Although... if the lich was just that foolish shapeshifter, then who was going to save Gino from death?

The Curse of Knowledge

Karen could feel a mix of excitement and sick dread emanating off Viv as she rapped on the door of 659 Whisper Street.

It was the same thing Karen had sensed when Viv's phone chimed and she glanced at the screen. Karen hadn't asked any questions, figuring Viv would fill her in. She was still waiting for that clarification.

"Damn it," Viv said. "She's not answering." She rapped again.

"Gretchen Mills?" Karen said.

"Yeah," Viv replied. "Penny texted me. Apparently, Gretchen knows where Amarynth is."

Really? Viv had written back to Penny. *That's all he said, that Gretchen would know?*

Well... Penny had written, followed by a series of "I'm typing" ellipses that seemed to bounce in place for ages, *there's a lich there? A litch? I dunno how you spell lich/litch.*

Lich, Viv had replied. *Thanks.* The chat dots had moved no more.

"Is Amarynth in there?" Karen said to Viv, as Viv pounded on the door once again, even harder.

"Not unless Gretchen has a lich," Viv replied.

"I don't," said a voice that came from behind them.

"Oh, there you are," Viv said. "I was wondering why you didn't answer. Or why any of your... residents... didn't."

"They know better than to open the door to strangers," Gretchen Mills replied. "It's one of the first things they're taught."

Gretchen Mills was the house mother here at 659 Whisper Street, also known as The Warrens of Persephone, an organization that took in any woman who came to them, purportedly supporting them and helping them improve their lives — offering a staggering array of services, such as housing, job training, and even meditation.

That was what they liked to tell people they did anyway — in glossy brochures and their public appeals for funding.

Underneath it all, Viv and Karen had always suspected it was some kind of cult. The question, however, was what exactly they worshipped.

"If I had the stomach for it, I'd go undercover and infiltrate them, see what's really going on," Viv had told Karen the last time they'd visited the place, investigating a murder case.

"I'd do it, but they'd probably recognize me," Karen had replied. "I don't imagine I'd get far."

It would be hard to pull any sort of con on Gretchen Mills, Karen thought, as she regarded her now. There was a certain knowing look in Gretchen's well-made-up eyes as she regarded the two detectives standing next to her door. She wore a tight-fitting tan pencil skirt and a multicolored tie-dyed fluorescent blouse. Her hair was dyed a vibrant red and heaped on top of her head in a perfect dome.

She looked like a walking sherbet cone topped with a maraschino cherry.

"So girls," Gretchen said, "what can I help you with?"

"You already know," Karen said. It sounded like an observation, not an accusation.

"I do," Gretchen said, nodding. "I suppose we should go for a walk."

"You're not going to invite us inside?" Viv pressed.

"Do you have a search warrant?" Gretchen countered.

Viv shook her head.

"Anyway, there's nothing that you want in there." Gretchen thought for a moment. "Nothing you want professionally anyway. I usually have *something* people want." She grinned broadly. "It's why I lock my doors, you know."

The three began to stroll down Whisper Street. It wasn't the best neighborhood in Skinner, but Gretchen seemed unperturbed, as they sidled by a couple who were screaming at one another in their driveway. The woman was barefoot, wearing a large muumuu, and hurling glassware at the man's head.

Gretchen stopped. "Shouldn't you be doing something about that?"

Viv shook her head. "Not our department. We don't deal with domestic disputes."

"Not unless there's some kind of psychic angle," Karen added.

"Ah, so if they were throwing psychic energy or something..." Gretchen let her voice trail off.

She led them to a park. It was late in the evening. The sun was going down. "This is the best time to come here," she said. "The children are gone. No families playing. But it's not quite the time for what goes on in the park at night. Still a bit early for drug deals and hookups."

"Pity," Viv said.

"Well, it's not like you'd do much about them anyway," Gretchen said. "And it's not like the normal cops do much either, other than hurt people and strut around like they're important."

Viv sighed. She couldn't argue with that. While some citizens put PsyOps and Skinner PD under the same general umbrella, thinking that cops were cops, their everyday realities were different.

And Viv, like every other intuitive she knew (and half the normal citizens), was terrified of the normal police.

The Real Police, her mother had called them, underscoring that Viv's own career wasn't real. It was more like a badly paying internship. A bit of cultural flair.

Viv walked to the swing set. She sat on a swing.

"Penny's telling the truth," Gretchen continued. "She got good information."

Viv nodded. "I figured. But I bet that's not all you know."

Gretchen shook her head. "I know a lot more than that. But I'm not sure how much of it will help you."

"Try me," Viv said.

"What if I told you that Amarynth had learned how to travel through mirrors and landed herself in a magical prison?" Gretchen said.

"Through the looking glass? That's very *Alice in Wonderland*," Viv said.

Gretchen snorted.

"Where does the lich come in?" Viv pressed.

"The lich? You know about the lich?" Gretchen said. She laughed.

"I don't see what's so funny," Viv said.

"Why aren't you nervous?" Karen said to Gretchen suddenly.

"I'm sorry," Gretchen said. "Should I be?"

"Well, you're being interviewed by PsyOps about something very serious. And from the sound of it, Amarynth's in quite a dangerous situation. You're usually not that coldhearted. Why aren't you more worried? You'd think you'd be a little on edge about us showing up to interview you. And if not that, you'd think you'd be worried about Amarynth."

"Especially because if anything happens to her, I'm going to make your life miserable. Bureaucratically miserable," Viv said. "I don't have much actual power, but I do know how to be a nuisance."

Gretchen laughed. "Oh, I'm sure of that." She walked behind Viv and pushed her swing.

"Hey!" Viv cried.

"Just enjoy it," Gretchen urged her.

And Viv did, in spite of herself. There was something about a swing that brought you back to a place and time when things were simpler. To a time when swinging in the air with your legs hanging free was about the most exciting scenario you could imagine.

Karen watched them in fascination. Viv's hair appeared to be quite short most of the time, but streaking through the air at this speed, her flame-red hair trailed behind her, flickering like tiny flames. Her ever-changing eyes graduated through the color spectrum even more quickly than normal, like a frenetic rainbow lightshow.

But that wasn't the only striking aspect of watching them. There was something utterly maternal about Gretchen pushing Viv on the swing. Something quite unexpected. Perhaps this was why she was such an effective house mother. Still, it made Karen wonder just how many sides did this woman have.

Finally, Gretchen stopped pushing, and Viv's swing came to a rest.

"The truth is that Amarynth has been captured by people who want her to figure out what the source of PTI is and to stop it," Gretchen explained.

"That's... ridiculous," Viv said. "How is Am supposed to know all that?"

Gretchen shrugged. "I don't know how, but she does. She doesn't know she does. Not yet. But she does."

Viv frowned.

"Anyway," Gretchen said, "Amarynth is going to be fine. She's capable of much more than she knows — and certainly more than you give her credit for, Viv." Gretchen turned to Karen. "And that's why I'm not worried. You don't need to protect her. She can fend for herself." Gretchen smiled. "If anything, she's going to be the one to protect the rest of us."

"You know," Viv said, "I'm awfully sick of Amarynth being the one who protects all of us."

"I'm sure she is, too," Gretchen replied.

Curse of Knowledge

While there is still a lot left for researchers to discover about intuitive taxonomy and the origins of the Psychic Phenomenon, every day scientific inquiry yields exciting new insights into the intuitive experience, not simply broadening but also deepening our collective understanding of the psychic population.

For example, it's long been noted that intuitives of all types are more prone to mental health challenges. While it does seem that certain subtypes suffer these effects more than others (empaths come to mind as a particularly vulnerable group, a phenomenon explored more fully elsewhere in this text), anecdotal observation quickly notes that no type is completely immune to this pervasive finding.

Empirical exploration of this observation unsurprisingly confirms what is common knowledge: It is depressing to have psychic powers.

However, until recently, although both laypeople and government agencies frequently guessed at why (and were content to declare this as fact, without any backing scientific support), the scientific community was at a loss to explain it.

However, new studies point at a cognitive bias that has been a known psychological phenomenon for decades — although never applied to understanding the intuitive experience.

This is called the curse of knowledge.

The curse of knowledge is a cognitive bias in which the person mistakenly thinks the individuals they're communicating with already know the things that they do.

This illusion has been known to cause many problems among even a population of normal citizens. For example, an expert can confuse an audience of laypeople if they assume that their audience knows enough to understand them and therefore don't tailor their talk appropriately. This author can remember such a predicament all too well herself as a student sitting in a lecture hall while a guest expert filled the instruction with words that nobody in attendance knew and never provided an explanation.

In the days before smartphones and before laptops in classrooms were all that common, this typically resulted in bewilderment as no one could look anything up mid-lecture. The best a student could hope for was that the regular professor would interject with appeals for the guest lecturer to define basic concepts.

But that's not the only way the curse of knowledge can cause problems: An individual can also assume that everyone knows what they know and that no one would be interested in hearing what is in reality quite a fascinating perspective.

While the curse of knowledge is known to affect practically everyone to some degree at a certain point in life, regardless of their psychic or normal status, intuitives are particularly prone to the bias. Their powers put them repeatedly in situations where things are obvious to them that aren't to other people (and depending on the subtype, this can happen more frequently and/or profoundly).

Multiple studies in this area show a strong inverse relationship between this phenomenon and mental health and wellbeing, most marked in the psychic population.

from Insecta Psychica: Towards an Intuitive Taxonomy
by Cloche Macomber

The fear had long receded. In fact, Amarynth wasn't feeling much of anything. Her emotions had been swept away by a towering wave of boredom. And then another. And another.

At times during the story-telling session, it had frankly been difficult to keep her eyes open. It was probably telling that Uncle Al's turn as storyteller had been the sole standout — if for no other reason than listening to him try to recite Homeric epics from memory and pass them off as his own struck her as pretty comical.

He probably would have pulled off the con if he didn't keep stumbling every time he made a modernizing substitution.

Well, semi-modern. He had made Penelope — the wife of Odysseus, left behind when he went to war, beset with a flurry of unwanted suitors as all presumed her husband dead — a flapper for some reason.

This had been distracting to Uncle Al of course, as he invented some lines on the fly about the beads on her short shimmery dancing costume and got swept away in a lascivious train of thought that left him salivating and stuttering.

But that brief blip of comedy and unintentional tragedy had long passed. Amarynth had been lulled to semi-hypnosis by the speaker to her direct left, Petunia Eck, the mousy "just for show" wife of one of the notorious Eck brothers. She was the political wife, there primarily for photo ops and to lend an air of respectability to a future Eck bid for office, while her husband was free to carouse when the cameras were off and would-be donors well out of sight.

Of course, she had attended this dinner alone.

Amarynth had felt sorry for this poor, clearly put-upon woman at first, but as the night had progressed, Petunia had revealed herself as quite a calculated callous creature herself. Petunia

hunched in on herself and spoke in a quiet, high sing-song voice
— but this shrinking violent stature was an affectation.

She really could be quite nasty. Quite cold.

Amarynth had been treated to her bitchy asides during the
entire session. She never would have guessed such vitriol would
come in such a tiny meek package. But it had. Petunia Eck was
the human equivalent of poisoned *eau de toilette*, perfume that
smelled faintly botanical and sweet but would kill you if applied
too liberally.

Her turn as storyteller had been dreary. Amarynth found herself
falling nearly asleep but starting as her body slumped forward,
jarring her awake. Each time she sat up ramrod straight.

She was mid-cycle when her dreadful neighbor's story ended
and twitched as she brought her head up to see all eyes on her,
staring.

*If I cared at all what these miserable people thought of me, I might
actually be embarrassed*, Amarynth thought.

"Your turn, Amarynth," Espoir urged her.

Amarynth nodded. She looked down at Gino's body crumpled on
the floor. As she stared at him, she found the words. She opened
her mouth, and they poured from her. The story took over.

"There once was a very beautiful young girl," Amarynth began.

 There once was a very beautiful young girl from a wealthy
family. Her parents were always prim and proper and made sure
that she was always the same way. This little girl was the sole
heiress to a great fortune, and her parents constantly reminded
her that she needed to personify that, to embody greatness — not
just in the large ways or the ways that clearly stood out but in the
small ways, too. Her pinafores must always be pressed. Her hair
must never be mussed.

It was a great preoccupation, memorizing the various rules of etiquette, committing them to memory, and monitoring herself to make sure she always complied, but her dear parents never failed to remind her when she strayed. And so with time and practice, it became second nature to her.

It had in the beginning, however, been extraordinarily stressful to her. Perhaps in a less active mind, learning would have been less painful, more rote — but her little mind was always moving. Always guessing, second-guessing, third-guessing. Doubting, undoubting, redoubting. Because not only was this little girl beautiful, but she was also intelligent — so intelligent that it got her into trouble.

She was perpetually looking at the same problems other people saw, and instead of working through them methodically, piece by piece, her mind would rush through everything and leap to a solution.

This caused a lot of confusion when she was small, as those who knew her always doubted what she said. However, when they worked through those same problems, they would be confronted with the truth — that her calculations were correct.

She had correctly solved problems that fast. Faster than should be possible.

If pressed, this young girl couldn't explain to other people how she solved problems that fast. If it were possible for her to pinpoint it and explain, it would take longer to detail how she had arrived at the solution than to figure out the problem in the first place. The reality, however, was that she didn't know how she did it. She just knew.

This was far from a satisfactory answer.

"You'll have a blessed life," her mother told her. "One free of pain. Free of the struggles that normal people go through — because you are gifted. You are special. And life always rewards people with your gifts. It's known."

And the young girl smiled at this. Felt great comfort.

She was one of the lucky ones, she told herself. She prepared herself for this easy life that everyone around her assured her was simply inevitable.

And yet… the easy life never came. Instead, she wasn't surrounded by shortcuts to the top — or even admirers. No, this little girl was flanked with jealous saboteurs.

"It's not enough that you were born beautiful, Bella Watson," her schoolmates said, "you had to be a smartass, too. A know-it-all."

For they never spoke kindly of her intelligence. No, her natural gifts were always framed as pretension, as something she did on purpose — something she affected —to harm other people, to make them feel small.

Her gifts were never her blessing — or even her shield. They were always considered weapons.

And so those early attacks came — before Bella could even think of striking — and more followed.

Many of her peers who had been beautiful as children became awkward when puberty struck. Some of these gawky teens would once again grow into beautiful adults — but not all of them.

Bella never had an awkward phase. Well, not externally anyway. Her face stayed clear. Her figure grew a bit larger but only in flattering places. If anything, her hair became more lustrous as she aged.

Internally, however, she was a mess.

Nothing about being born with a "skip past the obvious parts" brain prepared her for the onslaught she'd endured. And she may have been pretty, but her skin was quite a bit thinner than she would have chosen when it came to insults.

And despite her gifts — arguably because of her gifts — she grew into a young lady with few friends, none that she fully trusted, knowing that at any minute they could turn their backs on her, betray her at the exact moment they had earned her trust.

But then she met Mal, and everything changed.

Mal had seemed different, from the very beginning. He was someone she could relax around.

Later, she would look back and realize that was primarily because Mal was secretly a demotivator — an intuitive whose psychic power was making everyone around him act extremely lazy. But this was a simpler time — before the Psychic Phenomenon was a known quantity — before precognitionists were seen on every daytime talk show, being paraded around like circus acts.

No, back in those days, she just knew she'd finally met someone she could feel relaxed around. And she couldn't help noticing that he stood out everywhere he went. In reality, this was because Mal sapped the abilities and energies of everyone he encountered.

But it wasn't until many years later that Bella would connect those dots, that the reason he stood out wasn't that he was particularly lofty but because he dragged everyone else down.

She fell for him. Fell hard. How could she not, with his dark delicate features? His tall, fit physique. And his hands... Well, the first time she'd ever met him, she found herself involuntarily envisioning those giant hands working their way over every inch of her body — and a small piece of her would never be satisfied until this fantasy was realized.

This is how Bella Watson found herself pursuing a goal for the first time in her life. Mal wasn't a prize she could simply have handed to her. No, Mal would take some work. He didn't seem naturally interested in her. Perhaps it was his easy, relaxed way — he seemed to drift, to never quite attach to anything or anyone.

Bella pursued him relentlessly for months, for years. They grew into adults and a bit beyond before she finally bedded him. From Mal's point of view, the lovemaking had been a whim they'd both had and acted on. Something fun and physical had transpired. Nothing meaningful.

After all, he was working hard on his professional life, building a name for himself. His easy way with others set him up well for a career as a public speaker. In the early days, he called himself a motivational speaker. After the Psychic Phenomenon changed everyone's idea of what was possible, he was the first to rebrand to a demotivational speaker. Too clever by half perhaps, but accurate. He was widely mocked at first, but imitators soon followed. Before the close of the year, a union was formed for this new occupation.

That was Mal. That was the way he would always be. A trailblazer. A visionary. Mocked at first but then copied.

A more insecure man, one who was desperate for the approval of others, would have been destroyed long ago.

But not Mal. No, for that, Mal would have to care about something. Actually care about something.

That was, you see, Mal's greatest strength and greatest flaw: He just didn't care about anything. Not really.

Oh, he could adopt a caring face when it was socially or financially expedient. He could pretend to be concerned when it was appropriate.

But deep down inside, there was nothing that mattered to him. Not really.

It was his biggest advantage in business. And it also made him irresistible to women.

Bella fumed as she watched Mal move from lover to lover, as he spun carefree with joy, as though this were simply a complicated dance he was performing — and not toying with women's hearts, the fate of families.

She soon discovered she was carrying his child. And she was far from the only one.

Most disturbing was that trashy Euphemia Tender Lee. Tender — or "Tenny" as she liked to be called — claimed to be the descendant of Confederate leadership, descended from Robert E. Lee himself. What a thing to be proud of! Descended from traitors.

It was gauche enough that Tenny was proud of such a thing. Further, she seemed to have no proof of this heritage. What a thing to lie about!

Hardly surprising though, as there was nothing authentic about that woman. Anything she'd ever been had been bricked over, repainted, shaped to an image that she cynically thought the world wanted.

And maybe she's right, Bella Watson thought many times, wiling away the lonely hours, heavy with child.

Instead of reacting to her pregnancy with joy, Bella's parents had been disgusted by the news. Mal wasn't of noble birth. He was just some lowbrow entertainer. How could their daughter have given up her body to a commoner? Especially without a commitment?

They had been further outraged to learn their beautiful, otherwise intelligent daughter was insistent on *keeping* the product of this unholy union.

"But dear," her mother had said, "everyone makes mistakes. I know people who could take care of this for you. It could just be our little secret."

For the first time in her life, Bella said no to her parents. The prim façade began to fall brick by brick. Each time she repeated the no, more distance crept in between the heiress and her formerly proud parents.

Her father wanted to disown her completely, disinherit her, cut off all financial support.

But her mother argued for a middle path. They would disown her socially, pretend she had never been their child, but Bella would get her own home to live in and access to a bank account that would have more money than she and their grandchild would ever need.

Grumbling, Bella's father made it happen.

Bella stared out of her window for months waiting for her lover to return, but Mal didn't.

The labor was long and painful. Bella was surrounded by strangers, professionals paid to help her. They were wonderful and competent. They did their best, but she felt so alone.

Until the moment her daughter was born. Amarynth, Bella called her. It had been a princess's name in a story she loved a long time ago, when she was a little girl, before everything had become so messy and complicated.

Perhaps this little girl would grow up the way that *she* should have. Hopefully, she would steer clear of all her mother's mistakes and become the elegant, flawless heiress everyone had meant her to be.

But such was not Amarynth's fate. From the beginning, she seemed awkward, helpless, imperfect. Her hair grew in unruly clumps, never behaved. She was fussy about foods. Suffered from colic.

"You are your father's daughter," Bella would scold her infant and then catch herself and scold her own words instead. As the months progressed and little Amarynth continued to grow and change, Bella came to realize that the hopes that had oppressed her were not ones she wanted to imprison her daughter with.

Her infant daughter's face was often smudged with half-eaten breakfast that dried before Bella could wipe it and lingered for far longer, as the tiny infant went to improbable lengths to avoid face-washing for as long as possible. The child could be quite fussy, quite unruly. But there was nothing that made Bella's heart swell so much as the sight of that tiny face, however smudged.

Still, a deep unhappiness lingered. A loneliness.

The love she felt for her child was deep, profound. But another part of her longed for a partner — and more specifically, longed for Mal.

The longer he was gone, the more she realized he was never coming back.

That was why she was so shocked to discover him at her door one dark night.

"Hey Bella, you look good," Mal said casually, leaning diagonally against her doorframe, with his head cocked at a flirtatious angle.

"I, uh, wasn't expecting company," Bella replied, pulling her worn bathrobe tighter around her and nervously smoothing down the hairs she knew must be sticking up from her head.

Long gone were the days of primness and propriety. Amarynth's hair needed so much tending — and seemed bent on evading that caretaking — that Bella seldom paid much attention to her own appearance anymore.

As Mal stood there backlit by the lights that flooded her courtyard, Bella realized she couldn't remember when she had last brushed her hair.

You wouldn't know it by the way he was looking at her, however.

He looks like he's starving. Like I'm the first bit of food he's seen in days.

Intensity of some kind was bubbling beneath the surface. Whether it was carnal or emotional energy remained to be seen. In any event, Mal managed to keep it together. She invited him in. They sat together civilly and traded old stories.

Later, Bella would not remember what they talked about that evening. She was too lost in the rhythm of his voice to absorb the small talk that they bandied back and forth, back and forth, back and forth... like a swinging pendulum.

It was like a spell, she'd later write in her diary. *At the time I thought the spell metaphorical — as though it were my own emotions captivating me, casting magic. Looking back, I'm not so sure it was metaphorical.*

Hearing that voice again was hypnotic. She fell into a kind of stupor, a drunken haze. Before she knew it, they were in her bedroom, naked, engaged in a familiar old dance — one that to her thinking had ended much too soon.

She passed out blissful, at peace, thinking *Perhaps Amarynth will have a sibling.*

It was her daughter's voice that finally woke her — a shrill interruption to her dreams. Bella smiled as she left Mal's sleeping form behind, where he lay ensconced in rumpled sheets. He looked positively Renaissance that way, didn't he? Like something one of the Masters would paint.

Her heart soared as she tended to her child, who needed a diaper change but was soon put back down to sleep in her crib.

When she returned to her bedroom expecting to see her lover, however, that sleeping vision was gone.

The bed was empty.

"Mal," Bella called firmly but not too loudly, so as not to wake the baby.

The room began to vibrate, just as a porch does when a large truck drives by.

And then smoke started to pour in through the vents, thick black smoke that was as opaque as soot. It swirled into the center of the room, each eddy dancing around another until the individual streams began to coalesce.

A strangely humanoid form materialized out of this inky incorporeal matter. He was tall and pale. There was no hair upon his head. His entire form was covered under a robe.

The room was still.

His dark eyes peered directly at her, uncomfortably intense, as though they not only saw her but well beyond her.

"I am not Mal," the pale man said, his voice reverberating and shaking the room once more. He didn't speak as a normal man but in chords — as though hundreds of voices were speaking through him all at once at different tonalities.

It was a very wide voice.

"That much is clear," Bella said. "What have you done with him?"

"It was me all along," the wide voice said, shaking the floor.

Bella frowned. Her heart sank. "So Mal..." she began, before becoming choked up and unable to finish.

"He never came," the pale man with the wide voice said. "It was me all along." His pale lips turned into a terrifying grin, revealing teeth so angular it seemed as though they'd been ground into fine points.

"And just who are you?" Bella said, afraid of the answer.

"I am Death," the pale man said.

Bella shook her head.

"It's true," Death said. He closed his bleak eyes and sent a vision into Bella's head.

It happened too quickly for her to fully process it, but in microseconds, Bella saw a horrific flurry of images. A bird carcass left on the sidewalk to rot while people simply stepped around it. The last breath of a widower. Maggots. A mess hall exploding into flame.

"Don't hurt me. Take anything you want. Just leave me and my daughter alone!" she cried.

Death's expression softened. "You're so suspicious of me, Bella Watson. I know you're afraid of me, but I'm not your enemy. An unwelcome guest maybe — but at the end of the day, at the end of all days, I am the best friend that you, or anyone else, will ever have."

"Don't hurt me," Bella repeated, her lip quivering. "Don't hurt my baby."

"Surely, you want more from life than to avoid me," Death ventured.

"Well, it's at the top of the list," Bella admitted.

"Bella Watson, you haven't been happy for a very long time. What's the point of living if the best you can say is that you've escaped Death for another day?" he said.

Bella's lip continued to quiver. The vision he had sent was horrifying. She knew everything he was capable of. Everything he was responsible for. It was peculiar to call such a powerful force "he," although he had assumed this simple form. He was much larger than anything she could truly understand. That casual telepathic message more than affirmed it.

This was a problem she didn't instantly know the answer to. What was a young mother supposed to do when Death visited her home?

And, she thought with a shudder, after you've made love to Death, what's left for you?

"You see, Bella Watson," Death continued, "I'm not here to hurt you. And I'm not here to end your life. Nor am I here to end your daughter's life."

Bella wanted to be relieved but still felt quite anxious. "Then why are you here?" she said, dreading the answer.

"I need you to do me a favor," Death said, curling his lips back again. The daggers in his mouth glistened.

Bella frowned. "I'm sorry," she said. "You're an omnipotent, omnipresent abstract force... what could you possibly want from me?"

"Nothing much," Death said. "All you have to do is keep something for me. Never give it away. Keep it in the family."

"Well, that sounds simple," Bella said. "Obviously, there's a catch. What's the catch?"

Death waved his hand in the air dismissively as though this were pure nonsense. "No catch. No need to be suspicious."

"I have a right to be," Bella said. "I was just betrayed, after all."

"Betrayed?" Death said, sounding more than a bit wounded.

"You violated me," Bella said. "I only went to bed with you because I thought you were someone else."

"The French call it *la petite mort,* you know. The Little Death," he said defensively.

"I know," Bella said pointedly. "Still doesn't make it okay."

"Well, I'd say I'm sorry," Death said, "but Death makes no apologies."

"Of course not," Bella replied huffily. "You have that in common with Mal."

Death gave a little laugh. It sounded like an old engine trying but failing to start.

"You're a shapeshifter," Bella said.

"I suppose," Death said. "Although that's not giving me credit for all of my achievements."

"Are there more of you?" Bella said.

"More shapeshifters, more Deaths, or more... eidolons?" Death said, searching for better ways to describe himself.

"Yes," Bella said vaguely.

"Yes," Death replied just as obliquely.

"You can't blame me for being suspicious, given who you are and what you just did to me," Bella said.

"No," Death replied, "I suppose I can't." He hesitated. "So you won't help me?"

"It just sounds too dangerous. Like the man who tells you to watch his suitcase for him at the airport, and it turns out to be bombs or drugs he's trying to smuggle," Bella explained.

"I'm not smuggling drugs," Death said.

"No, you might kill someone that way," Bella joked.

Death made that feeble engine-rattling noise again. "Well, I suppose it's a good thing I'm offering payment then."

Bella's eyes widened. "What do you mean by payment?" She stopped herself. "I have all the money I need, as you can see."

"You're quite correct, Bella Watson. But I'm not offering money. No, I have something you actually want," Death said.

Bella frowned. "I'll believe it when I hear it."

"How did you feel when Mal showed up on your doorstep?" Death said. "When you saw him there, before you knew it was me, how did you feel?"

"I was happy. Unspeakably happy. Excited, flustered. Flushed from head to toe," Bella said.

"And when you made love?" Death prompted.

"It was ineffable. So was seeing him there afterward and letting myself hope that he would be here not only when I woke up but forever," Bella said.

"No one stays forever," Death reminded her.

"You're such a downer," Bella countered.

Death nodded. "I get that a lot."

Bella scowled.

"What if I told you that you could be happy forever, that I could snap my fingers, and from here on out, you would find that you have everything you need right here, right in your home?" Death asked her.

"I would tell you that sounds amazing," Bella said. "I was happy for a moment. And then it ended."

"It doesn't have to end, Bella Watson," Death said. "What would you do for that?"

"Anything," Bella admitted. "I would do anything."

"How about holding on to something for a friend?" Death replied.

"Okay, you win," Bella said. "What is it?"

Death fished a tiny mirror out of the pocket of his robe. It was a toy mirror, rimmed with magenta plastic. He held it out to Bella.

"This?" Bella said. "Is that all?"

"That's all," Death said.

She took the small mirror from him. "Hold on a moment," she told him. She went to her infant daughter's room and affixed the mirror to the mobile that hung over her crib. It clipped on easily and spun around slowly. It looked so natural hanging there that it was as though it had been custom made.

"Over your daughter's crib?" Death said.

"It's as good of a place as any," Bella said. "This way it won't get lost or broken, since it's somewhere safe. I know where it is, but it's just out of her reach."

"I suppose it's your decision, where you keep it," Death said.

"Do you have a problem with my decision?" Bella pressed.

"No," Death said. "It is fine with me. I'm just surprised."

"Why are you surprised?" Bella said.

"I can't think of another mother who would decide the best place for a cursed object is over her child's bed," Death confessed.

"A cursed object? Who said anything about a cursed object?" Bella protested.

"Bella Watson, you said it yourself. There's no reason for a stranger — or near-stranger — to ask you to hold on to something for them if it's completely on the level. You compared it to smuggled drugs and bombs. I can assure you the item is neither. But those are cursed objects, are they not?"

"In a sense," Bella conceded.

"If Death gives you something, you must assume it cursed," Death explained.

"Whatever," Bella said. "It's in my house. I did what you said." Her eyes gleamed. "Don't you owe me something?"

Death hung his head. "I suppose I do. Very well. The placement of the cursed object is fine. More than satisfactory for my aims. You have fulfilled the bargain. And you shall be rendered payment."

He raised one pale hand slowly, moving his fingers into position as though he were about to snap them.

And for a long moment, everything froze in time.

Later, Bella would write in her diary that hours had passed, hours she couldn't account for.

And in that temporal interstice, nothing moved.

Then Death snapped. He dissipated into the same disparate flows of black smoke that he had materialized from. The black smoke flowed out of the same vents that it had used to enter the room.

At that moment, Bella was filled with a deep profound happiness. Mal was nowhere to be found of course.

But she suddenly decided she never wanted to leave her house again. All her happiness could be found at home.

Later, this would be diagnosed as agoraphobia.

Death had fulfilled his bargain. Bella had indeed suddenly decided she had everything she needed right here.

The profound unhappiness never returned. Occasionally, there was bitterness, a sense that she had been done wrong by others.

But a strange contentment with her surroundings, one so deep and perfect that she would never want to go anywhere — a contentment that would strike others as perfectly pathological — flooded into the void where deep loneliness had been.

My dear child, the voice over the crib said to the infant sleeping below. The mirror's voice was silent, not meant to be heard by human ears. No lemma, the word found in the dictionary — that would be heard and turned into a lexeme, the unit of meaning. Instead, the voice skipped steps and spoke completely in lexemes. No sound, no words, only meaning delivered directly to the child's brain.

Amarynth opened her eyes and stared at the mirror hanging down from her mobile. It glistened in the moonlight spilling in via her bedroom window.

Can you hear me, child? The mirror said to her.

The child's mind responded for her. *Yes, I can hear you. Of course.*

We will be best friends, you and I, the mirror continued. *In fact, I will be your only friend. The only voice you fully hear. The only voice you fully understand. And I will be the only one who fully hears and understands your voice.*

I understand, the infant's mind responded. The child lay on her back and listened to the strange conversation taking place between her automatic mind and the mirror. She did so passively with utter curiosity and without fear or judgment. It never occurred to her to interfere. Those nighttime conversations would seem utterly natural, harmless as they occurred. They were no different to her than the other ambient noises she'd hear in her home, like the boards creaking in her house, the rumbling of HVAC, stray barks of dogs walked through the neighborhood, the sound of her mother scissoring her legs through a web of sheets in her empty bed, or the birdsongs. So many birdsongs.

A part of her would always remember, of course, that a voice spoke to her from the mirror and that it claimed her. That part of her would remember that the voice in the mirror was Death and that he would invade her mind, giving her powers that would remain sealed deep inside of her until the day that Death was needed.

You are Death's Mirror, the mobile called to her, as it spun above her head like a scintillating dervish, a confusing blur of primary colors and sparkles as the light hit the planes and twisted. *You will become Death's reflection. You are not Death, little one. No. You are life itself. On one hand, you are my opposite. This is the same as any mirror. On another hand, you are Death's vessel and its portal. You are the reflection and the road.*

It is a great responsibility, child, said the mirror.

The infant lay on her back. She raised her feet further in the air and admired her wriggling toes. As the mirror spoke to her, she attempted to put one of her tiny feet in her mouth.

The mirror had no face to frown. *Very well*, it said, *I can see that you will need a great deal more power to fulfill your duty. I will grant you great power. I will give you knowledge. This knowledge will protect and guide you.*

The mirror imbued her with knowledge — and as an afterthought, it hid what it had done, storing the memories deep within the recesses of her unconscious mind. It was safer for the child to not know where this knowledge came from. This way she wouldn't inadvertently risk revealing herself and her strange origins — and become a subject of persecution for her gifts.

But knowledge will not be enough, the mirror concluded. Death reached through the mirror and poured more of his soul into the child, who cooed as the transfer took place, as though being tickled.

The rest will be sealed until later.

Until when? The child's automatic mind asked, while her memory slept. *How will I know when you're needed?*

I will come, the mirror said. *For now, you should sleep.*

As the years wound on, the little girl outgrew that crib and that set of toys, but she never got rid of the tiny mirror. She hid it among her things, and when she finally left her childhood home, it was one of the only possessions she took with her.

She could never explain it to other people — like a lot of other things—but it wasn't just a tchotchke to her. A cheap knickknack you might find at a yard sale. For some reason, she couldn't bear to part with it.

When she got a pet bird, she'd clipped it in the cage without a thought.

And now and then, she'd find herself taking the mirror out and admiring herself in the low-fidelity reflection and feeling a strange breeze blow through her.

"What ever happened to that child?" Gino said.

Amarynth spun around. Not only was Gino's body no longer lying crumpled on the floor, but he had also suddenly appeared behind her. It used to drive her nuts, how easy it was for him to sneak up on her. But it was starting to make an awful lot of sense. Because why would an eidolon bother with walking?

"It's me," Amarynth said, finishing her story.

"Yes," Gino said. "Very good, my girl. You are Death's Mirror."

"I am Death's Mirror," Amarynth repeated.

The guests watched in rapt fascination as Amarynth stood up from her place at the table. When she played the scene back in her mind later — as she would many times — she never quite understood why they all just sat there in their chairs watching. Surely, they must have sensed that they were in danger.

The room practically vibrated. Whatever ambient energy floated through the phylactery began to thicken. A purple mist descended.

And yet, the entire dinner party sat, fixated.

Of course, Julia Fantasio still found a way to talk. It would appear that her freeze response (of fight-flight-freeze fame) also featured some talking.

"Ohhh Duckie, look! It's a bit of magic, I think," Julia said to her husband Squire.

Squire didn't respond.

Amarynth outstretched both hands, with her palms facing away from her, as though she were pushing on an invisible wall.

The purple mist color shifted and thickened further, filling the room with blinding light. Everything shook. A loud screech sounded and sustained, stabbing deep into Amarynth's brain before she had a chance to thrust her fingers protectively into her ear canals.

After a few moments, the mist cleared and took the glare with it. Amarynth looked to all sides and saw the bodies of everyone who had been at dinner. Some were slumped over in their chairs, and others had slid enough that they were lying on the floor. The bodies barely even looked human at that moment. The ones still seated struck Amarynth like Hollywood corpse dummies, and the ones that had landed on the floor resembled piles of discarded clothing more closely than actual expired living things.

"They're all dead," said Gino, who was now standing in front of her. He hadn't moved there by normal means. Of course not. What was the point of pretending now? Amarynth sighed, and her chest ached.

"Not me," said Change, who was still in lich form. "I'm quite alive. Not sure if that's a good thing or a bad thing. But I'm alive."

Amarynth ignored Change and turned to Gino. "Then you're…" She couldn't bring herself to say it.

"Yes, I'm Death," Gino said. "I've been with you for years. In a different way these past few months —"

"You could say that again," Amarynth muttered.

"—but I've never left you. I've been inside of you all this time. I am a part of you," Gino said.

"Is that why... I know things?" Amarynth ventured.

Gino nodded. "You always knew, too, on some level that I lived in you. But it was a deep level, buried down where you could pretend it wasn't so. It took an incredible amount of energy to stay that in denial."

Amarynth shook her head. It was all too much.

Gino continued. "This is why you could never express yourself, Amarynth. It was never because you didn't have the words. It was because if you said too much, this particular story might also come out, and it would change everything. You always had something to say. It was just the wrong thing. It was too soon for others to hear it." He looked around at the bodies that surrounded them. "You had to be pushed to tell this story."

"I never wanted any of this to happen," Am said softly.

"I know," Gino said. "You wanted to live a normal life. But normal life has never been for you. It never will be."

"I don't want you around anymore," Amarynth said. "I never got a choice. You were forced on me."

"It can't be helped," Gino said. "It's too late now. It can't be undone."

Amarynth scowled.

"But now that your story is told, now that you know, things are going to be different, Amarynth, I promise," Gino assured her.

"Different how?" she said.

"You're going to be even more powerful than before," Gino told her.

"Great," Amarynth said bitterly. "Exactly what I need. Even more power than I asked for."

"More powerful?" Change interjected.

"Yes," Gino said.

"Amarynth, stop moping for two seconds and get to the bottom of this," Change said.

Am glared at him.

"Fine," Change said, "if you're too emo to ask, I'll do it. Why is she more powerful now? And how?"

Gino smiled. "Bless your heart," he said to Change. Gino turned to Amarynth. "This is why I don't like to get lumped in with shapeshifters," he explained to her. In spite of herself, Amarynth broke into a grin.

"I heard that!" Change said. "And I have feelings!"

"But it's a good question," Gino admitted. "Amarynth, you're free now. There was so much of your power that was inaccessible, locked up tight, secured in psychic chains — because for that power to be unleashed, you'd also have to accept the rest of it. You'd have to accept the truth about yourself. Now that you have... well... there's no limit to you."

"Oh really?" Am said. "Boy, that sounds fantastic. Are you telling me I traumatized myself so I can have enough power to, oh, do things like accidentally kill a bunch of people?"

"They were assholes," Change offered helpfully.

"Maybe," Am said. "But they were people."

"Just barely," Change said.

"Yes," Gino said, "you killed them, Amarynth. You did that. But not just that."

"What do you mean?" Amarynth said.

"You also ended the plague," Gino said in an even voice.

"Excuse me?" Am said.

"PTI is gone. It's over," Gino said.

"Just like that?" Am said.

"Just like that," Gino said.

Amarynth didn't know what to say to that.

"Remind me to stay on your good side," Change said. But neither Am nor Gino was listening to him.

"You're leaving now," Amarynth said. She knew it as a certainty. Only this time it didn't come to her as a small internal voice — now it was her own voice. It was much crisper, much clearer. Much quicker.

Gino nodded. "Yes. In a way." He shrugged. "We both know I'll never really leave you. It doesn't work that way. It can't work that way. We're bound forever. No matter what happens, it can't be undone."

"I know," Am said.

"But yes, this human form is leaving you," Gino said.

"And you're never coming back," Amarynth said.

"Never's a long time, Amarynth," Gino said.

"You can't lie to me anymore, Gino," Am said.

"I know."

Gino stepped back from her a few steps. He waved at her playfully, smiling in a lighthearted way. It reminded Am for all the world of the sort of casual wave a parent might give their child as the school bus pulls away.

His image began to shimmer like a reflection in water. In a moment, the center distorted, like a stone had been dropped in that reflection. As the waves of obscurity spread to his distal limits, he dissipated into a wall of shining nothingness.

And after a few breaths in and out, that wall dropped away too.

It was as though he'd never been there.

And like he didn't really leave, Amarynth added silently.

"Okay, so now that he's gone—" Change said.

"He's not really gone," Amarynth corrected.

"Okay, now that he's differently here," Change began again, "I just want to thank you."

"Thank me?" Am said. "For what?"

"For cleaning house," Change said.

Amarynth groaned. "I can't believe you'd say that about murder. Or manslaughter. Or whatever it is that I've done."

"It had to be done," Change said.

"Is that why you helped me?" Amarynth said. "Where's the real lich anyway?"

"Oh, shoved in some backroom. Relieved of his clothes," Change said.

"You didn't!" Amarynth said.

"Of course I did. Do I strike you as someone who has any shame?" Change said.

"No," Am said, for it was quite true. "You think you're unlikable, but I'd say that is the one likable thing about you."

"That I don't have any shame?" Change said. "Hold on a second while I put that on my dating profile."

Amarynth laughed. "Well, I have to admit, your lack of shame makes you... challenging... sometimes..."

"That's putting it diplomatically," Change said.

"But it's also pretty refreshing," Am said. "There's enough shame in the world. Maybe an overabundance."

"There's probably the right amount of shame in the world," Change said. "It just ends up pooling in the wrong places. It's like money that way. There's enough to go around if everyone would just share equally, but that's not how it works. Lots of inequality. Some have all the money. Some have all the shame. Rarely does anyone have a lot of both."

"Yeah," Amarynth said. "Anyway, hanging out with you is like taking a vacation from shame, Change — for better or worse."

"Bit of a backhanded compliment," Change said, "but I'll take it."

"He's gonna be really mad, isn't he, when we let him out?" Am said.

"Who?" Change said.

"The real Macomber lich," Am said.

"Oh probably," Change said. "But it won't matter."

"No?" Am said.

"The real one is pretty pathetic, too. I'm more powerful than that guy. And you *certainly* are. That's part of why you spooked Espoir so badly. The real Macomber lich is all smoke and mirrors," Change said.

Smoke and mirrors. Amarynth's face fell reflexively. Those were two of her least favorite things at the moment. And the phrase had been on the causality board she and Leigh had prepared.

"Oh hey, I didn't mean anything by that," Change said. "It just came out. The expression. I wasn't trying to…"

"It's fine," Am said.

"I don't have a lot of experience being around freshly traumatized people. Anyone who is even a little bit sensitive seems to be done with me before I've even opened my mouth," Change confessed. "So I'm a little ham-handed here. I don't know what I'm doing."

"Well, the first thing we're going to do is let the lich out. And then we're going to get the hell out of this place," Amarynth said.

"How?" Change said. He studied her face.

Amarynth smirked.

"Oh, you little devil, you can teleport now, can't you? I can tell. You have that teleportation sheen just coming off you. You are a changed woman," Change said, his all-too-familiar eyes gleaming.

"Maaaaaybe," Amarynth said coyly. "Teleportation is handy for situations like these, but I'm not sure how much I'll use it."

"I'm impressed. Even I can only travel a little that way. In short bursts. Too much, and it doesn't work," Change said.

"Yes, but I can't exactly go around teleporting all the time. Not if I want to fit into human society," Am said.

"I use my powers all the time though," Change said, "just to disappear dramatically… to confuse people or make a point."

"Exactly," Amarynth said. "And you don't exactly fit in seamlessly, do you?"

Change sighed. It was a painful but well-made point.

"Anyway, I'm still amazed you helped me. It was... very unexpected," Am said. "And as you know, I'm not used to being surprised by much of anything."

Change smiled. "I'm a professional of course, but... well, let's just say that they had that coming. And then some. Not the best work environment."

Amarynth nodded.

"Don't get me wrong," Change continued, "a freelancer takes any work they can get. That's the gig economy for you. But at a certain point, enough is enough. Not sure what I'll do next. But I'll figure something out, I suppose."

"It's a good thing you weren't here then," Amarynth said. "I'll send you away and release the lich myself."

Change stared at her in disbelief. "Amarynth..." he said.

"You said it yourself, Change. I can handle him on my own. There's no reason you have to soil your reputation by having the Macomber Family know you played any part in this," Amarynth said. "You leave now, and nothing has to change for you. The rest of the witnesses are dead. It's a pathetic lich. I'm betting he doesn't have any form of second sight."

"He doesn't," Change said. "He barely has first sight even. But you don't have to do this, you know. I knew what I was signing up for when I did this. I've been prepared to accept the consequences of my actions."

"You were never here, Change," Amarynth said. "I mean it."

"Thank you," Change said. He paused for a few moments, before adding, "Everything they wrote about you in the library is true."

"Who wrote about me?" said Amarynth. "In what library?"

"Never mind about that," Change said, instantly regretting bringing it up. "It's not all that important. Anyway, I'm surprised you don't know."

Amarynth shook her head. Finally, she said, "I used to think I knew everything. Now I'm not so sure." Her face bloomed into a smile. "And what a relief that is."

"Yes, yes, I know I'm freaking out," Viv said.

"I didn't say anything," Karen replied.

"You didn't have to," Viv said. "I know you can feel this mood. I'm feeling a little guilty about it."

"Guilty?" said Karen. "Why?"

"Because I can see how it's affecting you," Viv said.

Karen shrugged. "It's all just part of being an empath."

Viv shook her head. "I'm just glad it's not me. I don't know how you deal with it. How you keep going with all that emotional stress bombarding you every day."

"I don't know either," Karen admitted. "For a while, I didn't. I was in the hospital when you met me, after all."

Viv nodded. "How do you have room for your own feelings?"

"What do you mean?" Karen said.

"Like right now. I'm a nervous wreck, and you're carrying that, too. Doesn't that crowd your own feelings out?" Viv asked.

Karen shook her head. "Not at all. Right now, I'm feeling your anxiety, and it's making me nervous, so I'm feeling that, too." She thought for a moment. "It's a bit like chords."

"Chords?" Viv said.

"Yes," Karen said. "If you play two, three, or more tones at once, there's a unique sound produced. To a lot of people, it's a singular unit. But a trained musician can hear the individual tones. I'm the same way when it comes to emotions. I'm a bit like a singer who can harmonize well."

Viv grinned. Her mood lightened a bit, and so did Karen's. A bell sounded to let them know they had arrived.

The lift doors opened to the familiar sight of the subterranean level. Skinner PsyOps HQ lay before them.

"Okay, Karen, let's see what Martin wants," Viv replied. The dread descended again upon them.

Neither of them was prepared for Martin's expression as they entered the office. Their boss, their notoriously stressed out and frustrated little boss, he was.... smiling?

"Hey, Martin," Viv greeted him. "Did you win the lottery or something?"

Martin laughed heartily.

"I see the body snatchers have been here," Viv said to Karen.

Karen giggled. "Clearly."

"I don't know how you did it, team," Martin said.

"Did what?" Viv said. "I mean... we've been working our butts off, but it hasn't exactly been our finest hour. We don't have much to report. I was honestly pretty nervous when you told us to come in."

Martin stared at her incredulously. "Haven't you turned on a television?" he said.

"No.... why?" Karen asked.

"Hit the lights, Karen," Martin said.

And she did.

Martin pressed a few buttons on the side of his desk, and a raggedy screen unfolded itself on the back wall of the office. A light shone projecting an image onto it. At this very moment, it was a soup commercial.

"I didn't know you could get live television on this relic," Viv murmured.

Martin shrugged. "Doesn't come up much." He leaned forward. "Shh… it's coming back on." The local news logo crashed onto the screen and the fanfare played with postapocalyptic splendor, as news themes did.

"All over the city — all over the State — hospital patients are waking up. PTI wards have completely emptied," a hyperactive news anchor announced.

Footage of the empty wards panned across the screen as the reporter continued talking.

"I'm here with Dr. Marin Chiver, psychic expert, to discuss the possible long-term effects of PTI infection and the impacts on society."

Dr. Chiver nodded affably but with reserve. A seasoned professional.

"Dr. Chiver, do you think this is the last we've heard of PTI?" the reporter asked.

"That's a question probably best left for the epidemiologists," Dr. Chiver said. "Or perhaps the precogs. It's difficult to know how a virus will behave in the future. But for the time being, it's taken its leave. The sensory losses have reversed themselves. The afflicted patients can all see again, smell again, hear again. Just like that."

"What about the new psychic powers, the ones that were a side effect of the illness? Are those gone as well?" the reporter asked.

"Reports on that matter are mixed," Dr. Chiver said. "Many individuals are claiming that they no longer have psychic powers now that they've been 'cured.'"

"Claiming you say?" the reporter interrupted. "So there's some doubt there?"

Dr. Chiver nodded. "Understandably. There's a stigma that accompanies psychic powers, after all. I suspect there will be many people who retain those powers and conceal them from others."

"Well," the reporter said, "I suppose there will be a huge call for your psychic detection services then."

"Oh yes," said Dr. Chiver, grateful for the plug for her business.

Martin turned off the feed as the "expert's" contact information flashed on to the screen. Karen turned the lights back on.

"Wonderful news, right?" Martin said, rubbing his eyes. But he noted that neither Karen nor Viv looked thrilled. "Okay, you look nervous. What's going on?"

"I wasted a lot of gas," Viv admitted. They'd been driving around, trying not to worry about Amarynth. "I've gone way over our normal expense budget."

"Never mind about that. We can deal with that," Martin said. "The plague is over. This is huge. This changes everything." Martin rubbed his forehead. "Please tell me you had something to do with it."

Viv shook her head. "I don't think so."

"It was Amarynth," Karen said.

"Amarynth?" Martin frowned. Leave it to his team members to be more effective while on suspension than on duty. Martin wondered — not for the first time —what he had ever done to deserve everything his employees put him through.

"We went to consult with her on the case. You know how Amarynth is... she just... knows things," Viv said, as though it pained her to admit that Amarynth was as knowledgeable as she claimed to be.

"Aw, Viv," Karen said, reinforcing Viv's kind words. "She does. Amarynth does know things — it's nice to hear you say it for a change."

"Whatever," Viv replied dismissively. "Don't make a big deal out of it." She flushed as red as her hair.

"Okay," Martin said, "so you sought out Amarynth for a consult, and she cracked the case for you?"

Viv shook her head. "No, that's just it. We went to go find her at her apartment, and she had disappeared."

"Disappeared?"

Karen nodded. "We've been looking for her all this time. Chasing leads. We've been hunting down a new boyfriend who also disappeared and seems to be an identity thief."

"There was this creepy blackened mirror in her bathroom that looks way too much like a crime scene chalk outline," Viv added.

"We weren't getting anywhere," Karen admitted. "More questions were raised than answers."

"Sounds about right," Martin grumbled.

"Martin!" Karen protested. "Maybe we don't work like other teams, but that's because we're thorough!"

"You're something," Martin joked. He stuck out his tongue.

Karen made a frustrated noise. It was so cute and squeaky that Viv laughed. Martin did, too.

"Anyway," Viv continued, "we were just looking into the identity theft angle when Penny got in touch with us."

"Yes, Penny," Martin said deliberately, sweeping his eyes up dramatically to an inconspicuous corner of his office that he knew housed a hidden camera and giving a little half-nod to both detectives to remind them of PsyOps's monitoring procedures. "Penny is on *medical leave*," he said purposefully.

"Yeah, yeah, yeah," Viv said, waving Martin's words away with her hand. "She's just hanging out at home. Set up in her own little place. Anyway, Penny had one of her visitors, and she said we should ask Gretchen Mills about Amarynth."

"Okay," Martin said, "so you followed up with her obviously?"

Viv nodded.

"And what did she say?" Martin asked.

"She said that Amarynth was going to be just fine," Viv said.

"Is that all?" Martin prompted.

"We went to the playground, and Gretchen pushed Viv on the swing set," Karen offered. She clapped a hand over her mouth.

"KAREN!" Viv said.

Martin laughed so hard his shoulders shook. It took him a bit to regain his composure. He was having trouble breathing.

"Okay," Martin said finally. "What then?"

"Well," Viv admitted, "we drove around for a while."

"Looking for leads?"

Viv nodded at the same time that Karen said, "No, we were worried about Amarynth, and Viv was looking for an easy way to calm down."

"KAREN!" Viv said again.

"Somebody, help me," Karen said. "It's like I have a death wish today."

Martin laughed until he was out of breath again. He made a mental note to start up his couch to 5K again. He was going to need it if he stayed in this job any longer.

Heck, he'd need a lot more than that.

"Okay, so where's Amarynth?" Martin asked. "It sounds like she probably has the missing pieces to this bizarre puzzle."

"That's just it," Viv said. "We don't know. We haven't heard anything. You're saying the plague is over, but we're still in the dark. Haven't heard from Am."

Martin frowned. He picked up his telephone receiver and quickly dialed the Connections Agent's cell phone number. Several seconds later, he hung up the phone. His forehead wrinkled.

"It went to voicemail," Martin said. "That's so unlike her. Half the time, she answers before it even has a chance to ring once. The other times, she calls you first."

Viv shrugged expansively with both palms upturned.

Back in her apartment, Amarynth wandered over to the birdcage. She opened the door and took out the toy mirror hanging in her parakeet's cage. Perhaps later she would cover the reflective surface with blue painter's tape. It seemed the safest idea.

For now, she placed the mirror reflection-side down on the window ledge.

She examined Tesla's food dish, expecting the level to be low, and was surprised to note that *someone* had filled it in her absence.

Closing the door, she looked at her cell phone. So many missed calls. She scrolled down her history and read it, feeling all the while like it was a very short play.

Her eyes lingered over the final missed call. It had come in just a few minutes ago. Right before her arrival home.

Martin at PsyOps.

Her finger hovered over the icon she could press to call him back. It would just take a single movement of her finger to start the call. She shook her head, backed out of the call history screen, and locked her phone.

He could wait.

The Accursed Truth

That is happiness; to be dissolved into something complete and great.

-Willa Cather

Psychometry

Not to be confused with psychometrics (the detection and measuring of psychic powers via standardized testing), psychometry is a strangely subtle though powerful intuitive power.

A practitioner of psychometry can learn many facts about people, places, or events simply by touching certain objects.

However, the confusion between psychometrics and psychometry is confounded by the reality that practitioners of both disciplines are known as psychometrists. For the following passage, please be advised that all subsequent mentions of psychometrists relate to intuitives who practice psychometry and not normals who administer psychometric tests.

Interestingly, PsyOps has not to date employed psychometrists in their attempts to solve crimes. This is quite puzzling as it would seem to be greatly beneficial to the public good to have detectives who can make the most use of physical evidence associated with a crime. However, psychometrists need to touch objects directly with their skin and cannot make their predictions while wearing gloves, and the State says this greatly limits their ability to work as detectives. Since touching evidence alters it, by depositing biological and fingerprint evidence on the object in question and/or disturbing any that is presently there, any insights gleaned from the potential employment of psychometry would simultaneously also damage the court admissibility of physical evidence.

At that point, many cases would quickly devolve into a situation where it was the psychometrist's word against someone else's. Hardly an ideal way for the legal process to unfold.

This, however, is the official story. Unofficially, some have speculated that the true reason that the Psychic State has not employed psychometrists at PsyOps is that they are not interested in discovering who actually committed the crimes. These skeptics claim that the State is more concerned with keeping up the appearance of propriety and sticking to modes of operating that ensure bureaucratic safety.

In fact, a discipline like psychometry could potentially make it more difficult for PsyOps teams to engage in less-than-factual arrests — such as those that are politically motivated by key government players. This author would caution the reader — and any relevant law enforcement agencies — that this is not the point of view of the author, the editors, or the publisher of this volume. However, it is a point of view that is of public and academic interest and therefore worth mentioning in passing.

In any event, psychometrists are found chiefly in the private sector, working not as Green Stars but typically as Blue River class when properly registered. As many intuitives remain unregistered — despite extensive public efforts to rectify the situation — there are a great number of psychometrists working informally or "off the books."

However, judging by the limited public information available on them, psychometrists are typically employed either as private investigators or in service to investigative firms, and in that capacity, they can often be quite helpful to private citizens.

from Insecta Psychica: Towards an Intuitive Taxonomy by Cloche Macomber

"It was really good of you to come on such short notice," Amarynth said, as she welcomed her guest in the lobby.

"Of course," the psychometrist replied. "Anything for your mother. Bella Watson saved my life, you know."

Amarynth pushed the insecurities out of her head, the ones that told her that she was nothing without her mother. A nobody. These insecurities were loud, but they weren't helping her become anything else, were they? It was time to start actively rejecting them.

She led the psychometrist into the elevator, and together they rode in silence as the lift reached Amarynth's floor. As the doors opened, the package concierge stood almost directly in front of them, delivering something to one of Amarynth's neighbors, his mail cart blocking their path.

Amarynth nodded her head and said, "Excuse me," to him as she did a semi-acrobatic maneuver to get around the cart.

The psychometrist, however, laid one hand on the cart as she steadied herself to move past. When she did, she froze.

"There's good news coming for you, sir," she said to the package concierge.

He stared at her for a few moments, blinking, confused. Finally, he said, "Thank you, ma'am. I appreciate that."

"Your youngest will get better. The surgery will be a success," the psychometrist elaborated.

At this, the package concierge's mouth dropped open. Amarynth and the psychometrist walked away.

"That was kind of you," Am said. "To do a reading without charging anything."

The psychometrist shrugged. "When the information just comes to me like that, I say what's the harm in giving a freebie?"

Amarynth smiled as she opened the door. As they stepped in, Tesla sang happily.

"You have a bird?" the psychometrist asked.

Am nodded.

"I'm a bird person, too," the psychometrist offered. "We're our own breed, really. Bird people are okay with a mystery. With not knowing all the answers."

"If you say so," Amarynth said. But she had to admit the psychometrist had a point.

"Bella said you had a particular object for me to analyze," the psychometrist prompted.

"Yes!" Am said. "I do. An old toy." She walked to the windowsill where it was lying face down and picked it up.

She presented the toy to the psychometrist, a set of plastic plinks with a mirror attached on the end. "It's part of the mobile I had when I was a baby. It hung over my crib."

The psychometrist accepted the object and let her hand curl around the mirror, completely enveloping it. She closed her eyes and groaned as if she were in great pain. She kept her eyes closed for several seconds before she opened them and sighed.

"I don't know how to tell you this, Ms. Watson," the psychometrist said, "but you're cursed."

"Cursed?"

The psychometrist nodded. "This is a cursed object you handed me. Whoever gave it to your mother intended something quite malicious for her. And it would seem that when she hung it over your crib that you ended up bearing the weight of the curse in her stead."

Amarynth frowned.

"You are riddled with malicious supernatural forces," the psychometrist said. "It's a wonder that you haven't accidentally destroyed the world."

Amarynth laughed. "Well, if I destroyed the world, I'd be a lot more effective than I am now."

"Pardon?" the psychometrist said.

"I'm suspended from work. The only people I really know are my coworkers — and I'm not sure any of them would call me friends, even though one is related to me, it turns out. And I thought this one guy was into me, but it turns out he's an eidolon. And not just any eidolon, mind you. He might be Death itself." Amarynth sighed. "Although at this point, I'm not exactly sure what to believe. He told me so many lies. And now I'm so exhausted and confused, I don't know if I care which ones are true or why he lied."

"Well, I don't know what to tell you, Ms. Watson, other than that you spent your entire infancy sleeping under Death's Mirror."

"Excuse me?" Amarynth said.

"This cursed object. That's its name. Death's Mirror," the psychometrist said. "As painful as it was to touch it, and as much cleansing I'll have to undergo as a result, I feel honored to have had the opportunity. It's quite famous, you know. Or infamous, I suppose."

"Gino called me Death's Mirror," Amarynth said.

"Gino?"

"My ex-boyfriend. The eidolon. Possibly Death itself, but he was such a liar that who knows," Amarynth explained.

"Well, that's something he told the truth about then," the psychometrist said. "This artifact is part of you now. You've melded with it."

"So what do I do now?" Amarynth asked.

"I'm sorry?" the psychometrist said.

"How do I break the curse? Do I need to destroy the object?" Am said.

The psychometrist shook her head. "No, don't destroy the object. There's no need for that. It won't do anything."

"Then how do I break the curse?" Amarynth asked.

"You don't," the psychometrist explained. "You're just cursed."

"Wait," Am said, "you're telling me I'm cursed, that I've been cursed my whole life, that I'm Death's Mirror, and that there's nothing I can do about it?"

The psychometrist nodded. "Nothing to break the curse. Although..."

"Although?" Am said.

"Well, let's just say that there are many ways to live with a curse. And *that* is something you do get a choice about," the psychometrist offered.

"Oh, great," Am said. "I get the worst news of my life, and it's followed by a motivational speech."

"I'm just being honest," the psychometrist said.

"I know," Am said. "You know... as mad as I am at Gino for lying so much, it did make me feel good. His lies were so much better than the truth."

"Anyway, say hi to your mother for me," the psychometrist said. "I have another appointment to get to. I know the way, so don't worry about showing me out."

Amarynth wasn't worried about that at all of course. Even though she knew it was immature to shoot the messenger, she was still glad to see the bearer of bad news leave her home and didn't care in that moment how stressful or confusing said exit would be for her.

After the psychometrist left, Amarynth was grateful that she hadn't asked for payment. Let her mother take care of that, too. Because her mother had taken care of an awful lot in her life, hadn't she? Including some things she really shouldn't have.

What had possessed her mother to pass the curse onto her infant instead of accepting it herself?

"I used to think I owed everything to her," Amarynth said to Tesla, who responded by jumping from perch to perch in his cage in a frenetic fashion. "Today I learned it's the other way around. My mother owes me. She passed a cursed object onto me when I was a defenseless baby.... and shielded herself in the process."

Tesla tweeted at max volume.

"Well, little buddy, I guess we're cursed," Am said. "Whatever that means."

On the Psychic-Paranormal Conflation Problem

Many obstacles obstruct the work of even our most enterprising intuitive taxonomists. Participant noncompliance has been formerly discussed in this work as a major hurdle. Even taken alone, this is quite a vexing problem — as it is difficult indeed to study a population that resists every attempt for a researcher to do so.

However, our field has been greatly assisted by the cooperation of the Psychic State via both its PsyOps teams as well as through research conducted within the Black Square detention program.

As the number of available participants has started to rise, the taxonomic community has increasingly been forced to contend with a new obstacle. This has come to be known as the Psychic-Paranormal Conflation Problem.

To summarize, there does seem to be a variety of paranormal activity found within our young country. Some of this aligns squarely with what taxonomers and laypeople alike think of psychic phenomena. The origin points of these activities are easily tested and confirmed as intuitive in nature — either by psychometric batteries and/or via the presence of psyon traces.

However, we are increasingly discovering events that rival intuitive activity in their strangeness and break from normal possibility that are not covered under the current definition of psychic activity. While able to perform feats that humans should theoretically not be able to achieve, these beings also do not show any of the hallmark signs of being intuitives.

This raises the question of whether such individuals are humans at all... or if they are something else beyond the parameters our scientific community would use to come to a consensus understanding.

Some critics find our approach tautological and nondescriptive, but for the time being, convention dictates that we label this population — whether hypothetical or actual — as paranormals.

While frustrating to some intuitive taxonomers, others have delighted in this possibility, arguing that an adjacent non-normal population — and perhaps one with a diversity that we do not yet comprehend — poses infinite realms of scientific possibility.

This author remains cautiously optimistic.

However, it's worth noting that some controversy surrounds whether a problem such as the Psychic-Paranormal Conflation exists or if it is simply a byproduct of an incomplete understanding of what makes an intuitive individual, intuitive. Those who subscribe to this point of view argue that perhaps it would be better to reexamine our current definitions of "psychic" and "intuitive" rather than to force everything that doesn't belong under the current definitions into a miscellaneous bucket of "paranormal."

In any event, this issue — regardless of how it is ultimately resolved — is likely to keep intuitive taxonomers busy for quite some time whether they argue for a two-party classification system (normals and intuitives) or a three-party one (normals, intuitives, and paranormals).

from Insecta Psychica: Towards an Intuitive Taxonomy
by Cloche Macomber

A pervasive purple mist.

Am I back in the phylactery? Amarynth wondered.

No, that wasn't quite right. The mist was in her apartment. She was standing in her apartment. She shot a worried glance over to Tesla's cage. The thick black drop cloth she always used when it was time for him to go to bed — the avian equivalent of black-out curtains — was covering his cage.

She turned on the ceiling fan and frantically opened her apartment window, hoping to funnel the ever-thickening mist outside.

But it was to no avail. There was more and more mist. She breathed it in, and the mist pulled at her lungs and bronchial tubes as she did so.

It was like breathing water.

And yet... she wasn't struggling to breathe. It wasn't suffocating her. She wasn't drowning.

She was breathing just fine. If anything, she was breathing better than she usually did, due to her mundane struggles with seasonal allergies.

This purple mist — though solid — cleared her lungs like a powerful nebulizer.

Amarynth turned and looked out her open apartment window. It was the same pan-connected platform city she had seen so many times.

The ecumenopolis.

Every building had a road that led to another — and most intersected at multiple levels.

Her own building was connected to another building by a rope drawbridge.

A figure leaned out of a window in this neighboring building. The form waved. It moved too quickly — but for a split second, Amarynth thought she saw Gino.

...*or Death... or whoever that actually was*, she mentally reminded herself.

Amarynth walked to her parakeet cage and raised the dark shroud.

Tesla chirped hello.

"Whaddya think, little guy?" Am asked the bird. "Do you think I should go check it out?'

The bird sang a happy little tune and jumped from perch to perch.

Amarynth smirked. "Of course. Nothing ventured, nothing gained."

Tesla chirped in response.

"Is that farewell or see you later?" Amarynth questioned him.

The bird closed his tiny eyes and fell asleep.

"Ah, it's good night then. I guess I *did* wake you up in the middle of the night," Am replied.

Amarynth walked back to the open window. She climbed out of it onto the hanging platform. It felt steady beneath her feet. Yes, it swayed but not precariously.

But before she could even get halfway to the other building, a sudden gust of wind blew through and knocked her down.

The bridge gave. The distal end broke from its moorings, and the bridge went vertical, hanging in the air like a stray thread from a sweater.

Amarynth clutched feebly onto the boards, but her hands began to sweat.

A bolt of terror rose in Amarynth's chest. She squeezed her eyes shut, not wanting to see what would happen next.

Her fingers slipped, and she lost her grip on the hanging bridge.

But her stomach didn't drop.

...what the?

Amarynth opened her eyes. The bridge was still hanging there uselessly, and she was no longer holding it. But she wasn't falling.

Instead, she was floating. Levitating in place.

"Of course," she said, "Death would never allow me to fall."

"Me neither apparently," a voice said beside her. She turned her head to see familiar eyes. Change was smirking at her. This time he was a brunette, a dead ringer for a singer Amarynth had seen on one of those TV talent shows, although she couldn't remember the name of the singer or the program.

"What are *you* doing here?" Amarynth asked the shapeshifter.

"Oh geez," Change said. "Is that the way you treat all your friends?"

"We're friends now, are we?" Am asked.

Change frowned. "After everything we went through, you're gonna say something like that? Oh sure, we're perfect strangers. Don't pretend you never put my number in your phone, Amarynth. I was there. We both were. I know the phylactery seems like a bad dream, and it probably will for a while, but we were both there. And what happened there, actually happened."

Amarynth laughed. "No... I'm not saying that I don't want to be friends, Change. In fact, I'd be honored to be your friend. I just didn't know the feeling was mutual."

Change grinned, and with that big dopey smile on his face, he looked even younger than the TV idol he was semi-poorly copying. "Oh, it's mutual, Amarynth." He took her hand in his.

Amarynth noted it wasn't as warm as a normal hand — not ice-cold, mind you — there was a bit of warmth there. There was just something... less warm about it. And it was markedly smoother than human skin.

It reminded her of long-tumbled rock that had been sitting in the sun for a while and then removed and left to sit in shade.

"You have very interesting skin," Amarynth observed.

"Skin, huh?" Change asked. "It's convincing as skin?"

"Well, I dunno about convincing... Your skin is very unusual. It doesn't feel like skin," Amarynth said.

Change scowled.

"It feels better than skin," Amarynth added. "More perfect and satisfying somehow."

That dopey grin again.

Holding hands, they flew over the chasm to the next building. When they came to the window, Amarynth looked in to see who had been standing there.

But now there was no one.

"Hey Amarynth," Change said, lingering as they both floated.

"Yes?" she said.

"I was thinking..." Change flushed a strange crimson. The color didn't look quite natural. His blush was a little too defined, too perfect — reminiscent of the painted circles on a doll's cheeks.

Was that a natural response? Had Change been among human beings and living in their culture so long that some of their mannerisms had become ingrained? Amarynth wondered. Or was he affecting humility somehow, conjuring blood flow into his cheeks to charm her?

In either event, her skepticism wasn't protecting her against it. She was charmed either way — since it was a flattering thought that she could affect him that way and arguably an even more flattering thought that he would go to such great lengths, that he would create a blushing effect to impress her.

"Yes?" Am prompted.

"I was thinking," Change started again, "that if you're impressed with my skin that you'd be absolutely blown away by my lips."

Amarynth grinned. "Only one way to find out," she said leaning forward. A deep shudder rose through her body in anticipation of the kiss.

Just as her lips were going to meet Change's, the sound of thousands of birds filled the air, scores of grackles flying at full speed. They were cawing in a terrible cacophony. Amarynth broke away.

The scene around her dissolved. She was back in her apartment, sleeping on the couch. Tesla was squawking his head off.

Amarynth sat up on the sofa, held her head in both hands.

"What the Hell was that dream?" she asked Tesla, who continued to squawk.

Her phone bounced on the windowsill, making an awful scraping noise, as the vibration impacted the flat surface.

Amarynth sidled over and picked up the cell phone. "This thing is the most dangerous mirror of all," she commented to Tesla as she unlocked the screen.

It was a text from Change:

Sleep well, Amarynth?

Amarynth scowled. Furiously, she texted back: *Look, you creepy goon, that wasn't cool. Don't you know that dream invasion is illegal?*

She let out a little shriek of dismay and sent a quick follow-up text: *Seriously? Weren't you the star witness in that trial?*

There was a long, luxurious pause before Change finally texted back.

Don't be mad. It's not my fault. You said you wanted to embrace change from here on out.

Amarynth threw her phone at the sofa.

"Oh, that was a good one," the shapeshifter said. "I'm proud of myself."

You'd Have to Invent the Math First

Leigh Lines did a double-take when she first saw Amarynth in the lobby.

"You're back!" she cried. "Where did you go?"

"Is it important?" Amarynth asked.

"Well, no, I suppose not," Leigh said. She hesitated. "Yes, it's absolutely important."

"It's a long story," Amarynth warned her.

"Well, I'm about to get done work, so your timing couldn't be any better," Leigh replied.

"End of your shift?" Amarynth said.

"Very," Leigh replied. "This is also my last shift here at Cambria Towers."

"Your last shift?" Am asked.

Leigh nodded. "Now that things are back to normal, the psychophobia has quieted down to its usual dull roar, and they're opening the café back up. The owner begged me to go back. I'm getting triple pay."

"Nice," Am said. She led Leigh up to her apartment.

"So about that story?" Leigh prompted her.

Amarynth left nothing out.

Leigh kept her silence during the recap, although her face reacted many times at the strange bits. Am was almost derailed by this but managed to ignore Leigh's expressions sufficiently to get through the tale.

"And then you were back here?" Leigh asked her at the end. "Just like that?"

Amarynth nodded.

"Any other strange things happen since then?" Leigh asked.

Amarynth bit her lip. She hadn't told Leigh about the dream with Change, where they flew together over the ecumenopolis and...

Oh God. It turned her stomach to even think about it, about what almost happened, what she almost did.

Is that because I'm disgusted, Amarynth thought suddenly, *or because I'm disappointed that it didn't happen?*

She screwed up her face and violently pushed the thought out of her brain. My God, it was annoying having access to so much information sometimes. Her mind had a way of serving up things she didn't want to know —insights that other brains would happily bury deep in a mental purgatory of denial.

Her brain struck her sometimes as a clueless hyperactive librarian that ignored context and happily produced relevant resources on a moment's notice, including the traumatizing ones.

Spectacular.

"Are you okay, Amarynth?" Leigh said. "Did something happen?"

Amarynth frantically corralled her composure. "What do you mean 'did something happen?' You heard that story I just told you. Was that not enough happening to one person?"

"Well, no," Leigh said. "That was plenty. You've been through a lot." She paused. "You just seem... I dunno. It seems like there's something else on your mind."

"Leigh," Amarynth said truthfully, "if there's one thing my mind is good at, it's having a lot on it."

Leigh laughed. "Fair."

"Anyway," Am said, desperate to change the subject, "while you're up here, there is something I was hoping you could help me with.

I know you don't work here anymore, but I'm not even sure who to go to in maintenance about an issue I'm having."

"Sure," Leigh replied, her voice chipper. "Lead the way."

Amarynth rose. Leigh followed her.

"I figured I'd show you before I put in a maintenance call. Because you of all people would understand this. You have a much better handle on how the staff would react to this. And also... I figured that you wouldn't judge me." Amarynth said to Leigh as they stood before her strangely charred bathroom mirror.

"Oh, really?" Leigh said. "Why did you think that? Is it because you think I'm just a kook who accepts everything?"

Amarynth frowned.

"You know what I'm talking about. I run the tinfoil hat club. I think I've been abducted by aliens." Leigh grinned. "I've heard it all by this point, you know. It doesn't even hurt my feelings anymore." She paused. "Okay, maybe it still hurts a little. But only if I let it."

"Leigh, I'm sorry about what I said before. I was stupid," Amarynth said.

Leigh stood unmoved.

"I was beyond stupid," Amarynth tried again. "There's a word for how I acted, but I'm so stupid that I not only don't know the word, I also have no idea how to find it or who to ask."

Leigh laughed in spite of herself.

"At least stupid-even-for-stupid people are good for a laugh," Amarynth said.

"Okay, that's enough," Leigh said. "It's not nice to call people stupid. Not even yourself."

"Even if I deserve it?" Amarynth said.

"Even if you deserve it," Leigh replied. "Which you do," she added.

They stood before the charred mirror, a companionable silence descending between them. It wasn't awkward in the slightest. Instead, it felt right. It felt like a deep understanding between close friends, ones who no longer have their guards up, who never worry about performing, and can instead just be in each other's company without doing a darn thing.

It lasted quite a while before Amarynth finally spoke. "I figured I'd ask you — since you're the expert."

"You need an expert with a tin foil hat?" Leigh countered, but the tone was much less sharp than before.

"Something like that," Amarynth said, smiling.

"Okay," Leigh said.

"Is it still seven years of bad luck to break a mirror if you start out cursed?" Amarynth said. "Or does being cursed loop back around at a certain point so that you end up blessed, like an overflow bug?"

Leigh stared back at her with blank bewildered eyes, blinking.

"Oh, I wasn't expecting an answer, Leigh. Don't look so serious," Am said.

"Oh good," Leigh said. "That's a relief. We're in such uncharted territory here, I'm not even sure how to do that kind of math."

Am nodded. "To do that kind of math, you'd have to invent the math first."

A Connection Is Made

The city is wilder than you think and kinder than you think. It is a valley, and you are a horse in it. It is a house, and you are a child in it, safe and warm here in the fire of each other.

-Robert Montgomery, street poet

Amarynth stared at the maintenance request form for a long time after Leigh left, not because it said anything interesting — it didn't — but because she wasn't sure what to do next.

It was a familiar problem. Funemployment lacked purpose.

"You know," Amarynth said to her parakeet, as he vigorously snarfed down millet, "I think I'm the only person who could save the world and feel lost the next day. Like I'm being lazy. Like I haven't done enough."

If Tesla had any thoughts on the matter, he didn't share them.

"Serves me right," Amarynth said. "What did I expect, bringing up such deep philosophical topics while you're at dinner?"

No avian attention was earned. Not a single iota.

She rose and walked to the window. Staring outside, everything looked as it normally did. From her apartment, she could see a great swath of Cambria Square. It was an adorable neighborhood, a charming network of streets — many of them stubbornly resisting modernization. Instead, cobblestones were worked around. The access roads laced in and out in a deft way, like well-hidden seams in a grand garment, while the rest of the ostentatious neighborhood design camouflaged them.

It was a work of art, this neighborhood. A collaborative one.
It was a miracle with all the hands that had been involved that
Cambria Square had stayed so beautiful.

It seemed different to Amarynth than the storytelling session she
had been involved in when trapped in the phylactery. Instead, the
story of Cambria Square was more like one that had been quite
popular as a class game in elementary school.

In those days, the teacher would sit the class in a circle, and each
student would go around speaking a bit of the story at a time. Not
a terrific amount of information. Perhaps a sentence, maybe two,
a paragraph at most.

Amarynth's teacher had a hotel call bell she would ring when it
was time for the next storyteller to give their input. Whatever had
just been said, this new storyteller would have to build off it, to
make the most of it.

Inevitably, whenever the class told one of these collective stories,
there were always saboteurs. These students wouldn't try to build
a cohesive story or a well-developed one. Instead, they would try
to derail the entire exercise, by throwing a wrench into the works,
adding an improbable twist or a confounding complication.
Their goal was to make the next storyteller's turn — and every
subsequent turn — as hard as possible.

Amarynth had been rather good at that game. She found that
whenever it came to her turn that she always knew what to say.
No matter how badly the story had been undermined by those
that came before her, she had an uncanny knack for thinking of a
counterintuitive link that would bring the plot back on course.

This talent had always struck her — and her teacher — as strange,
for Amarynth had difficulty expressing herself in practically
every other context. She was painfully shy, awkward, and terrible
at explaining anything.

But when it came to collaborative storytelling, she was effortless.

Amarynth remembered this, looking down on the neighborhood — which looked alive from this height, with cars and people moving all about, going wherever it was they needed to go. People with plans. People who weren't funemployed.

Amarynth smirked a bit at this.

Anyway, she thought, it's a miracle that so many people worked on this neighborhood — worked on this city, for the entirety of Skinner was a marvel in many ways as well, if not as immaculately planned as Cambria Square — they all participated in this grand, forever-unfolding story.

And no one sabotaged it.

At least not irretrievably, Amarynth added.

Because for all she knew, there *had* been some awkward time when the Square was an eyesore — and she just hadn't been around then.

Perhaps there had been gifted architects with her same knack for rescuing a hopeless cause.

The thought gave her a strange amount of hope.

And it also gave her an idea.

She pulled out her cell phone and made two calls. The first was to Dr. Clark's office; the second was for a driver.

As the car wound its way towards the most psychic-dense neighborhood in Skinner, the Psychic City, Amarynth stared out the window and wondered.

She could tell that everything had changed. And that it wasn't changing back anytime soon.

And not only had the world outside of her changed, but she had as well.

Now that the full story was no longer hidden from her, she could see into the depths of the powers that Death had given her, the ones that had always been there but were only now able to be accessed.

But every time she did, she quickly got overwhelmed. The simple existence of these new abilities frightened her. She wasn't ready for the reality of them — certainly not ready to exercise them just yet.

But there will be time, she thought. She knew that with great confidence.

It was as though a massive shipment had been dropped into her life. She was far from ready to unpack it all — let alone find a home for everything new.

She found herself metaphorically reading the shipping manifest and feeling woozy at how long it was.

"There will be time," she muttered, soothing herself.

"I'm sorry, Miss Watson," the driver said. "Did you need something?"

"No," Amarynth said. "I don't need anything else. I have the opposite problem. The trouble is that I have way too much to handle," she added truthfully.

The driver laughed. "Well, if you ever need help with decluttering, let me know," he added amiably. "My wife is a professional organizer."

"I never knew you were married," Amarynth said.

The driver grinned. "Well, I'm an open book, Miss Watson. Anything you want to know, just ask."

They chatted until the car stopped at their destination.

"It was wonderful talking to you," she told the driver. "I hope I won't be more than a few minutes."

"Take your time, Miss Watson," the driver replied. "Like you said, there will be time."

Amarynth grinned. "I know," she said.

She climbed out of the car and looked up at the little house on Bell — the one where her three favorite coworkers lived.

"Did you call a limo, Karen?" Viv's voice called.

"No," Karen said. "Why?

Viv pointed out the front window. Karen crowded in next to her to look.

"Oh, that?" Karen said. "That isn't a limo."

"Oh, c'mon, Karen," Viv said.

"Well, it isn't. It isn't even stretch. That's just a luxury sedan," Karen continued. "True, there's a driver... oh my God, there's a driver. He's wearing one of those little caps —almost like a pilot."

"Yes, he is," Viv said.

"But it's not a limo," Karen concluded sternly.

"I don't care that it's not a limo," Viv said.

"Oh, really? You were so keen on making sure before that I knew Martin's vehicle was a *panel van*, not a murder van." Karen paused, before adding, "Although murderers use them, so I think I was actually kind of right. More right than you are about this being a limo."

"Karen, the real question isn't what that car is. It's what it's doing here," Viv said.

"Oh," Karen said. "I suppose you're right."

Viv shook her head in frustration. She walked to the door.

"What are you doing?" Karen protested.

"You can hide in here if you want, but I'm going to figure out what's going on," Viv replied.

The front door of the little house flew open.

Two voices argued from behind it — one lower and booming, the other shrill and defensive.

I can't believe how much I've missed that sound, Amarynth thought. *It's like a dog and a cat fighting — but musical.*

Amarynth shook her head and walked up onto the front porch.

Viv stepped outside at just the right moment to see Amarynth standing there, without having seen her approach the house. Viv screamed and jumped a foot in the air. "Er," Viv said, clearing her throat. "Oh, hi, Amarynth." Viv had a fairly low voice, but she said these words in a conspicuously lower tone of voice than she normally used. Viv forced herself to sound casual, but when Amarynth looked at the eideticist's hands, she could see that they were shaking.

"Hey Viv," Amarynth said. She thought about pointing out Viv's obvious fright and apologizing for jumping her, but Viv preemptively soured her on this course of action with a stern glance.

Karen popped out behind Viv. "Am!" she cried. "You're back."

"I am indeed," Amarynth said.

Karen leaped forward and wrapped her arms around Amarynth's neck. Due to the incredible volume of Amarynth's hair, people often thought she was a great deal taller than she was —and a lot taller than Karen — but in reality, they were close to the same height.

"I'm so happy you're safe," Karen said.

I dunno about safe, Amarynth's inner voice added. *Safe for now maybe.* But outwardly Amarynth grinned and said, "Me too."

Viv rolled her eyes. "Oh geez, it wasn't so bad. I always knew you would come back." But there was something subtle and quavering in her voice. Maybe it was leftover adrenaline from having the bejesus scared out of her — or maybe...

She cares, the voice within Amarynth summarized, *even though she pretends she doesn't. That's just how Viv protects herself.*

Amarynth playfully rolled her eyes back at Viv.

Karen laughed.

"Anyway, it's good to see you guys. I've really missed you." Amarynth hesitated. "I'm not sure what Penny's told you."

"You know how Penny is about telling stories," Viv replied. "She leaves a lot of gaps."

"She does," Amarynth said, nodding. "Wait."

"Hm?" said Viv.

"Where is Penny? Don't tell me she ran off again," Amarynth replied. "A woman in her condition shouldn't be traveling..."

"No," Viv said. "She's still out back."

"In the shed?" Amarynth asked.

"Yeah," Viv said.

"Even though the plague is over, and it should be fine to go back to the house?" Amarynth said.

"That's what *I* said!" Viv exclaimed, throwing her hands in the air.

"We went back there and told her that everything was fine. That she could come back to the house now. She screamed at us to go away. I think she has every stick of furniture in that shed pressed up against the door," Karen said.

"I don't know what's gotten into her," Viv said.

"We even emailed her proof!" Karen said. "News articles about how PTI disappeared. How epidemiologists have been confounded by the whole thing, but that the danger seems to be gone. She never replied to any of the emails. She's still in there. Still shut up! Won't let anyone in."

"The last time I went back there and pounded on the door, I *swear* she growled at me. She made noises that didn't sound human," Viv said.

That's because they probably weren't, Amarynth thought. Likely one of the many Hellish dialects Penny — as a native of Hell — could speak fluently.

"Okay," Amarynth said. She walked down the steps and towards the driveway that led back to the backyard shed.

"Where are you going?" Viv asked.

"I'm going to get Penny to come out," Amarynth said.

"How?" Viv said. "She's not coming out. We've tried everything."

"Yeah, how?" Karen piped in.

"I have my ways," Amarynth replied.

After Amarynth had disappeared behind the house, Viv turned to Karen. "She's been back for five minutes, and she's going to get herself killed."

Inside the tiny shed, Penny snarled and swatted at the swirling clouds of imps attacking her.

"You'll never leave this shed," they hissed at her, spitting drops of acid in her face.

Penny felt her skin singe and burn. She cried out — both in incredible physical pain but also with the psychological pain of knowing that she was being hideously deformed with each blast of acid.

She closed her eyes and tried to scale the monolith, but every time she would get even a short distance up the shaft, she would slide back down.

Then the imps invaded her monolith vision.

"YOU CAN'T DISMISS US," they hissed in Impish. Again the acid hit her skin, like small bits of oil splattering from a hot pan on a stove.

The acid sizzled as it burned her face.

Penny heard a loud thumping at the door of the shed.

"GO AWAY!" she screamed in Infernal.

The thumping continued.

She translated it to High Infernal — the language of the court. "GO AWAY!"

Then came the response. It was faint, but she thought she heard her father's voice.

"We've come to get you, Rhea! You can't escape us that easily — and this time we will put you in a place that ensures you never run away. We'll put you somewhere you can't embarrass us. You've broken your mother's heart, you know. It was bad enough that you were such a disappointment. You had to flee to Earth — of all places — and return in even worse condition than you left us. No matter. Every family has a few aunts shut up in the attic that nobody talks about, don't they? Relatives they have to hide from the rest of the world because they want no one to know their shame," her father said.

"I AM IN HIDING FOR A REASON!" Penny cried. "LEAVE ME ALONE."

"You're hiding on Earth," her father's voice replied. "That won't do. We need you somewhere we can keep an eye on you. We need to make sure you don't embarrass us — not just in Hell but on any of the planes."

"GO AWAY!" Penny said. "GO AWAY, GO AWAY, GO AWAY."

She said it so many times, it began to blur into one awful word — a never-ending one, like an infinite pinked seam stretching off into eternity. GOAWAYGOAWAYGOAWAY...

The knocking continued, but so did this stitch. The world began to go dark, as Penny's screaming deprived her of oxygen.

Outside the shed, Amarynth shook her head. No answer. Of course.

Viv and Karen were standing behind her.

"See," Viv said. "What did we tell you? It's no use."

"Sorry for what I'm about to do," Amarynth said. "I'll pay for the damage."

"What you're about to do?" Viv said, as Am spun around and threw her full body weight into the shed door.

"Now just wait a minute, Amarynth," Viv chattered behind her, as Amarynth continued to throw all her weight at the closed door, "Martin worked hard to set all that up. I don't think he'd appreciate you doing that."

Amarynth gave one final heave-ho, and the door gave way. She nearly crashed down onto the floor of the shed due to the momentum but managed to catch herself at the last second, preventing a fall.

It was a good thing, too, because Penny was lying on the floor passed out. The last thing Amarynth wanted to do was to risk falling on top of a pregnant lady.

"Oh, good," Am said.

Viv stepped in front of the now-doorless shed and peered in. "Good?" Viv cried. "What do you mean by good? Penny's sick! She needs help."

"No," Amarynth said. "Penny's gonna be just fine."

"What the Hell are you on?" Viv said. "Just look at her."

Karen stared at them both, confused. "Amarynth," she said finally, "what's going on?"

"This is like morning sickness," Amarynth said.

"I'm sorry?" Viv said.

"You know... how like a lot of pregnant women throw up in the morning?" Am said.

"Yes, Amarynth, I know what morning sickness is," Viv said. "I mean... why does morning sickness have anything to do with this?"

"This is midterm panic. It's normal in Hellish pregnancies," Am explained.

"Midterm panic? You're making that up," Viv accused her.

"It sounds like something college students go through. Finals anxiety. Midterm panic," Karen said.

"I'm not making it up," Am said. "You'll see when she wakes up."

"Since when did you become an expert on Hellish pregnancies?" Viv said skeptically.

Amarynth shrugged "I don't know how I know, Viv. That's always been true of course. And I'm sure you're sick of hearing it."

"You're damn right about that," Viv interjected.

Amarynth turned to face Viv. "All I can tell you is that I know even more than I did before. And that this is one of those things. I don't know why. I do know when it happened. I can guess at how — but I'm not sure."

"Care to share?" Viv said.

"In just a little bit," Amarynth replied. "See? She's waking up."

Penny's form began to stir on the floor. She sat up and looked at Viv, Karen, and Amarynth. "What are you guys doing here?"

"Hey Penny, the plague is over. PTI is gone. Just like that," Amarynth said gently.

"Just like that?" Penny said.

"Yes," Amarynth said.

"Great," Penny said, her face blooming into a smile. "Guess it's time to get out of here." She rose and began to gather the few things that she wanted to bring with her to the house. "Could you help me carry these?" she asked them. "I'm not sure how much I'm supposed to lift in my condition."

Viv stared, a little awestruck and speechless at this quick turnaround, but reached out and grabbed an armful of items — as did Karen and Amarynth.

All four women walked back to the main house in silence. They put Penny's things in the living room.

Finally, Viv spoke. "Penny, why didn't you answer the door?"

Penny's face fell. "So that wasn't a dream?"

"What wasn't a dream, Penny?" Karen prompted her.

"I... saw things that weren't there. But I thought they were at the time. I thought they were after me," Penny explained. "It was terrifying."

"You thought *who* was after you?" Viv asked.

"Does it matter?" Penny snapped.

Viv's face fell.

"I'm sorry, Viv, it's just a little overwhelming," Penny replied.

"I'll bet," Amarynth said. "Midterm panic can make you feel like you're losing your mind — especially the first time you go through it."

Karen and Viv swiveled in her direction and stared.

"No, she's right," said Penny. "I thought I'd be one of the lucky ones — that it wouldn't happen to me." She cast a gaze down at her feet. "Guess I was wrong about that."

"Aw, Penny," Karen said. She sat beside her and put her arm around Penny.

Not to be outdone, Viv quickly took to Penny's other side and cuddled with her. Between the two of them, Penny was suddenly completely enveloped — safe, warm... and loved.

Yes, loved.

She felt a kick within her abdomen. Perhaps a hug from the inside as well, Penny mused. The thought made her happy.

"Anyone hungry?" Amarynth said.

"Starving," Penny confessed.

"I'm always hungry," Viv said. She couldn't remember the last time she felt like she'd had enough to eat.

"Now that things are back to normal, I was thinking we could all go to lunch. Somewhere nice. My treat," Amarynth said.

"How about Ballhaus?" Viv joked. Ballhaus was one of those impossibly luxe places where each course had its own waiter. Viv had heard that some courses had two or three. There were a bread guy and a butter guy, as well as someone whose entire job it was to scrape crumbs off the tablecloth with a blade.

"Sure," Amarynth said.

"Geez," Viv said. "Big spender. Made of money, are we?"

Amarynth shrugged. "I have a lot left to explain to you." She paused. "For the first time, I think I can do it."

"We'll see about that," Viv said suspiciously.

Penny grinned.

"The car's outside," Amarynth said. "Let's go."

"Your car?" Viv said, her eyes widening.

Amarynth nodded.

"Amarynth, if you're in the mafia or something..."

Penny laughed uproariously.

"You're not answering me!" Viv said as the four of them walked outside.

They all climbed into the car.

"I'm one of *those* Watsons," Am confessed as the car pulled away from the curb.

"Wait a second," Viv said. "Hold the phone. Shut the front door."

"Son of a biscuit. Holy flying monkeys," Karen contributed.

"Not now, Karen," Viv said. To Amarynth she said, "After all these years, after all the times you've said, 'Amarynth Watson — not one of *those* Watsons,' it turns out... you were one of *those* Watsons all along."

Amarynth nodded. "Yup."

"You've been *lying* to us for *years*, and all you have to say is 'yup?'" Viv said.

Amarynth considered the question for a few seconds. Finally, she said, "Yup."

"Amarynth Watson — yes, *those* Watsons — if you weren't my half-sister, I do believe I'd kill you," Viv fumed.

"Well, good thing I am then," Am said.

Viv shook her head. "Oh," she said, as the implications of this new information dawned on her, "this means I'm related to the Watson family, doesn't it?"

"Kinda," Amarynth said, tipping her hand back and forth in a "so-so" motion.

"What do you mean, kinda? You're a Watson, and I'm related to you," Viv insisted.

"My mother's a Watson," Amarynth said. "Not our father."

Viv studied her face. "You know who our father is, don't you?"

Amarynth nodded. "And he's not a Watson. He's not noble at all, not in one of the Four Families."

"Well, crap," Viv said. "So who is our father anyway?'

"Maybe if you're nice to me, I'll tell you," Am shot back.

"Amarynth Watson!" Viv said. "That's cruel."

"Hey," Amarynth said, "it's not my fault that you're perfectly incapable of being nice to me on your own. Maybe you just need the proper motivation."

Viv turned to Penny. "Are you *sure* she's not in the mafia?"

Penny laughed so hard that it scared Karen.

"I can't believe you valeted the car," Viv said. "Fancy, fancy."

Amarynth shrugged. "You kind of have to if you're going to Ballhaus. I don't think there's anywhere to park around here. Anyway, I didn't valet it, Viv. The driver talked to the guys at the valet stand, and he's going to park it down the street. I'll text him when we're done here. He was just letting them know his plans, so if anyone saw him loitering, they wouldn't call the cops on him or anything."

"Like they'd call the cops on a limo driver for loitering," Viv said.

"Well, number one, it's not a limo —" Am began.

"Thank you!" Karen cried.

"And number two, yes, they would. They call the cops on everyone for everything around here. The HOA is ruthless in this part of the city. They'll take you to court for not coordinating your shutters with your porch. Forget about doing something really out there like letting your grass grow a millimeter too long," Am continued.

"Or letting your driver loiter without warning people first?" Karen suggested.

"Exactly," Am said to Karen, smiling.

It was late lunch, not during the initial rush, not a typically busy mealtime, and yet the restaurant lobby was milling with people. It reminded Viv of a mosh pit.

"You trying to get in?" one lady said to Amarynth as they entered.

"Yeah," Am said.

"Oh, don't bother. They told me it'd be four hours to get seated, and that's *only* if they have a cancelation."

Amarynth nodded. "Thank you," she said. "That's good information." She turned and proceeded to the host stand.

"Hey, didn't you hear her?" Viv asked Am.

"Loud and clear," Amarynth replied.

Viv shook her head. Amarynth could be so stubborn — so dumb — sometimes. Who did she think she was charging headlong into such a hopeless situation?

"Hello," Amarynth said to the maître d'. "I would like a table."

"Name?" he said in a practiced tone.

"Bella Watson," replied Amarynth.

His face lit up. "Truly? Will Ms. Watson be joining us in person today?" His eyes filled with visions of the headlines — the notorious recluse dining in public for the first time in decades. And at his establishment! He did a quick inventory of which news outlets he had already entered into his phone and made a mental note to look up the numbers of even more.

"No, unfortunately not, I'm afraid," Amarynth said. "I am her daughter — and I'm going to be dining with my three companions. She gestured at Viv, Penny, and Karen.

The maître d' gave them a disapproving once-over. He clucked his tongue. "Well, I can see if I have anything open," he said in that dim tone of voice that foreshadows a negative answer. He took his sweet time flipping through a ridiculous number of pages in the appointment book before him, licking his finger dramatically before turning each page.

"You know, it would be a great shame if my mother found out that we were refused service at a quaint little place like this," Amarynth said to him. She smiled in a bright yet menacing way. "Especially with her... connections. It would be an awful story for the papers, how this... two-bit hovel snubbed the Watson family. A responsible journalist would be careful to mention that it was the black sheep of the Watson family, but journalists are hardly responsible these days, are they?"

The maître d' sighed. "No," he conceded. "They're not." He slammed his appointment book closed. "Follow me," he said, leading the way to their table. His nose was lifted high in the air.

"Okay, she's really in the mafia," Viv said to Penny, who laughed tinnily.

 "The Jagerschnitzel here is so much better fresh," Penny said. She was moaning after every bite. "I used to think they were crazy for making so much sauce — which is how I wound up with it in the first place, since they were dumping the extra out back almost every night, but now I can't believe that there will ever be enough."

"Are you going to order another side of it?" Viv asked, rolling her eyes. Penny did have five ramekins of it so far sitting next to her plate, which was also flooded with sauce.

The poor headwaiter was doing his best — likely tipped off by the maître d' that it'd be a bad idea to tick off these guests, as lowbrow as they might appear. Viv was starting to feel sorry for him, with the number of times Penny had batted her eyelashes and said in her sweetest voice, "I'm sorry, I don't mean to be a bother —"

Yeah, right, thought the waiter each time, that synthetic smile still pinned to his lips.

"But could I just have one more side of this sauce?" Penny finished, punctuating the request with another florid bat of her eyelashes.

"Of course, madam," said the sauce waiter.

Five times so far.

"I think you'd better leave that poor man alone," Viv advised Penny.

"Oh probably," Penny replied, with resignation in her voice. "Honestly, they should serve this sauce as a soup. I'd order four bowls and have it for my meal."

Amarynth laughed. "It is good sauce," she agreed.

"And not just for pregnant ladies who've been stuck in the back yard eating bologna sandwiches," Penny added.

"Oh boy, lay on the guilt," Viv said. "Don't look at us. We tried to get you to come out sooner, but you weren't having it."

Penny shook her head. "The hallucinations seemed real. I swear they did."

"We believe you, Penny," said Karen.

"I don't know what I'm going to do the next time it happens," Penny said.

"Well, if I have any say, there won't be a next time," Am replied.

"Oh?" Penny said.

Amarynth nodded. "After lunch, we're going to see Dr. Clark. You're due for an ultrasound anyway."

Penny smiled, nodding.

"Wait," Viv said, "Dr. Clark is an obstetrician, but what does she know about midterm panic?"

"Nothing," Amarynth admitted.

"Then how is she going to help Penny?" Viv pressed.

"I'll tell her what to do," Am explained. "She can prescribe medicine that should do the trick. It's normally used for other things, but it'll fix Penny's problem."

"An ultrasound," Penny said, slicing into another piece of pork cutlet with her knife and fork. She needed something to go along with the massive lake of creamy mushroom sauce flooding her dinner plate. "That means I'll get to see the baby," she said wistfully.

Amarynth nodded.

"You know, I've been thinking, Viv," Karen piped up.

"Oh yeah?" Viv said, suppressing the urge to say something sarcastic like, "Well, that's a change, isn't it?"

"I was thinking it'd be nice if you painted the nursery," Karen said.

Penny set down her knife and fork, felt a bolt of panic. Now, *why* would Karen ruin a perfectly good meal — at Ballhaus of all places — by bringing up such a touchy subject with Viv?

Viv didn't paint anymore. None of them talked about it. It was a risky move even saying the P-word around her these days.

Viv stared at a dinner roll. The bread waiter had tried to take it from her since it was technically from a previous course, but Viv had glared at him with such intensity that he had violated serving protocol and left it.

"Okay," Viv said finally. "We'll pick out some paints. It'll be Penny's choice of course."

"Of course," Karen replied.

Penny smiled, pleasantly surprised.

"Of course this will mean you'll have to find a place for all that crap you have in there, Penny," Viv continued. While the nursery was technically a second bedroom, it was a rather small room, hardly bigger than a closet, and had never functioned as a normal room in their house. Instead, it was a place that Penny stashed her random finds. Viv was afraid to go in there, worried that the floor-to-ceiling mass would topple onto her if she even looked at it funny.

"I'll take care of it, Viv," Karen promised her. "Penny can tell me what to do, but I'll dig in there and figure it out."

Viv laughed.

"What?" Karen protested. "It's a good plan. It's not like Penny can do it given her condition, and I know that room gives you the creeps."

"I'm sorry," Viv confessed. "I just keep getting these strange visions of you getting buried in a landslide of — well, whatever it is that Penny keeps in there. I can see it now, one tiny arm feebly waving out from underneath the cave-in. Buried alive in a hoarder's house." She lost it.

The others at the table joined her.

"Wait," Karen said suddenly, "is this a jokey vision — or a vision-vision? Like... did you actually see this?"

The rest of the table laughed until they almost passed out.

Karen shook her head. "Rude," she said, but she laughed.

Amarynth's phone began to vibrate on the table.

"Better get that, Amarynth," Viv joked, "could be the don wanting to order another hit."

"She is *not* in the mafia," Penny said, rolling her eyes.

Viv snickered.

Amarynth picked up her phone and looked at the screen. Change was calling her.

She felt an involuntary warmth rush through her at the sight of his name. Ooh boy. This was not the time nor the place for her to even *think* about Change — let alone talk to him. She quickly swiped down to dismiss the call and flipped the phone back over on the table.

"Oooo, now who was that?" Penny said in a teasing voice.

"Nobody special," Amarynth replied. The tips of her ears reddened.

"Nobody special? Amarynth, you're an awful liar," Penny said.

"Well, she fooled me with the Not One of *Those* Watsons thing," Viv said.

Penny shook her head. "That's only because everyone underestimates her. Especially you, Viv. No, you can't fool me on this one, Amarynth." She paused. "Was that Gino?"

"Oh, the identity thief," Viv said.

Am scowled.

"That was kind of rude," Karen said.

"Whatever," Viv said.

"I guess you're never going to get to know your father then," Karen said in a bratty voice.

"She knows him," Amarynth said. "She just doesn't know he's her father."

Viv's eyes grew to the size of dinner plates. "Wait, what? Is Martin my father? Oh God, don't let it be Martin."

Amarynth shook her head. "It's not Martin."

Viv breathed a sigh of relief.

Amarynth turned to Penny. "I'm not seeing Gino anymore."

"You guys broke up?" asked Penny.

Amarynth considered the question. "He left," she said.

"Oh, Amarynth, I'm so sorry," Penny said. "You seemed so happy before."

"Wait, you knew about Gino?" said Viv. "Like before Amarynth disappeared?"

Penny nodded. "She took me shopping for maternity clothes and told me then."

Viv turned to Karen. "Did you know about this?"

Karen shook her head.

"I wonder if he's the one who came to see me," Penny said.

"Came to see you? When?"

"I was trying to get my remote seances up and running, and this annoying man — at least I thought he was a man at first — just randomly showed up in my shed," Penny said.

"What did he look like?" Am asked.

"He was a small man. Dark hair and a beard. Wearing a red and black flannel shirt. Looked like a very small lumberjack," Penny said. "That's what I call him in my head, you see. Not-Paul-Bunyan."

"Should have gone with Can't Believe It's Not Bunyan," Viv offered.

Penny scowled. "That's so much better. I can't believe I didn't think of that."

"Not Gino then. Gino doesn't look like that at all, "Amarynth said. "Although…"

"Although?"

"Well, Gino can change his form. He's not exactly… human," Am said.

"Wait a second," Viv said, "is Gino a shapeshifter?"

"I suppose you could say that," Amarynth said. "Technically, that's true. He can change his form." She paused. "Although that's not giving him credit for all his achievements."

A jolt of fear ripped through her chest. Those were his exact words. It was what he had said to her mother Bella the night he had first appeared to her.

And it was exactly how Amarynth had recounted it when telling the story in the phylactery.

No one else at the table got the significance. They ate in silence for a few moments. Well, they ate in near-silence, as their utensils made clanging sounds against the fine china.

"Holy shit," Viv said, "wait a second… Gino was a shapeshifter. We know another shapeshifter. What was that guy's name?"

"Change," Penny said. "Change Patterson."

"Could that be who visited you, Penny?" Viv said. "And Amarynth, could you have been dating *Change* all along?"

"No," Penny and Amarynth said in unison.

Amarynth gestured at Penny. "You first," Am said.

"I don't know who visited me," Penny said. "But it wasn't Change. His eyes were wrong."

Viv nodded. "I suppose you're right. Unless he's gotten better at doing eyes."

"He hasn't," Amarynth said.

Viv raised an eyebrow.

"I saw Change recently. He was with me and Gino — where we were being held captive. He was impersonating a lich."

"Oh, that's very on-brand for Change," Karen said.

Everyone stared at her.

"What?" Karen said. "The guy knows who he is. You gotta respect that."

"Have you ever met Change?" Viv challenged her.

"No," Karen said, "but you guys talk about him so much, I feel like I have."

"We do *not* talk about Change that much," Viv said.

"Okay, Viv, whatever you say," Karen said, shoveling another large forkful of gourmet food into her mouth.

"Oh!" Penny said. "He did say one thing, the visitor. He said he was near death."

"That he was near-dead?" said Viv.

"No," Penny said. "Not near-dead. Near death."

"Same thing," Viv replied.

Amarynth shook her head. "No, that's not the same thing at all."

"How do you figure?" Viv asked.

"Well, let's say that Gino is an eidolon, a humanoid manifestation of Death — just another way that Death has of affecting this plane," Amarynth began.

"Oh goody, let's just say," Viv said.

Am shot her a stern glance.

"Okay," Viv said. "Is this your working theory?"

Amarynth hesitated. "Yes. The full story is longer. And I promise I'll tell you soon. I've just gotten finished telling it though, and I'm sick of it."

"Okay," Viv said wearily, "you know what, Amarynth? You don't have to explain. Just this one time, I'm going to trust you without seeing the evidence. I'm going to take you at your improbable, spooky-sounding word."

"Finally," Penny and Karen said in unison.

"What?" Viv said, feeling ganged up on.

"All this time, all Amarynth has wanted is for you to believe her," Karen said. "And for that matter, I know how she feels."

Viv nodded soberly.

"Hey, Viv, I know it's been a hard year, what with…" Penny hesitated, not wanting to evoke Viv's mother's crimes or the fact that she was behind bars. She gestured around her instead and said, "Everything that's been happening."

Viv nodded again.

"I bet you feel like you've done a lot of things you can't take back. That's probably a big reason why you fight, isn't it?" Amarynth said, her voice kind.

"Oh my *God*, what is this? Group therapy?" Viv said.

No one said anything.

"Yes," Viv said to Amarynth's question, as her eyes treacherously filled with tears. "No one ever gives you a fresh start. I've been an ass! I admit it. I'm sorry. I want to do better."

"We know you do," Karen reassured her.

"I just don't know how to get from where I am to where I want to be," Viv confessed. "I didn't have the best examples growing up of how to show that I care about people without acting like a total ass. I'm not saying this excuses anything…" Her voice trailed off.

"But it's an explanation," Karen offered.

Viv wiped her face on the fancy embroidered napkin. Amarynth handed her napkin to Viv as well. "Just in case you need another."

Viv nodded her thanks.

"Okay," Amarynth said, picking up from where she'd left off, "so let's say that Gino is an eidolon, a humanoid manifestation of Death — just another way that Death has of affecting this plane. That means everyone who was at the phylactery —"

"The phylactery?" Karen interrupted.

"It's a lich's soul prison. That's where I was being held," Am said.

"You mean, the Macomber lich is *real*?" Karen replied, her eyes growing wide.

"Real, yes, but also a little underwhelming," Am replied.

"What do you mean by that?" Penny asked.

"Well, for starters, Change was able to subdue the lich and leave him tied up in a broom closet," Am said.

They all laughed.

"Anyway, technically everyone in the phylactery that night was near Death. Because they were near Gino. Who is probably Death," Amarynth explained. She looked at her plate. "Although he's a horrible liar, so who knows what's true anymore?"

At the end of the meal, Viv lingered behind with Amarynth for a few moments on the sidewalk after she texted for the car. "Can we talk?" Viv said to Amarynth.

"Go on without us," Amarynth called to Penny and Karen, "we'll be right there."

Penny shot Karen a surprised look, but they wandered out of sight.

"Thank you," Viv said.

"For what?" Amarynth said.

"For everything," Viv replied.

"No problem, Viv," Amarynth said.

"You make it sound like no big deal," Viv said.

Amarynth shrugged. "You don't like it when people make a big deal, do you?"

"Well, no, but..." Viv said.

"What?" Amarynth said.

Viv hesitated. "I wouldn't blame you if you don't want to give me a second chance, Amarynth. I've been a real ass to you."

"You have, Viv, but it's fine. I can look past it," Am said. "Just promise me one thing."

"What's that?" Viv said.

"That you'll start giving me the benefit of the doubt," Amarynth said, "and that you'll at least try to understand me."

"Those are two things," Viv pointed out.

Amarynth nodded. "Yeah, so I'm asking for two things, then." She hesitated, before adding, "So... are you in?"

"Sure," Viv said.

"Good," Amarynth replied, "because I'm tired of being misunderstood. I'd like to finally start connecting with other people."

About the Author

Page Turner is the award-winning author of many books. With a professional background in psychological research and organizational behavioral consulting, Page is best described as a "total nerd." She's been cited as a relationship expert in a variety of media publications including *The Huffington Post*, *Glamour*, *Self*, and *Bustle*.

She clearly can't see the future because she didn't see any of that coming.

Due to her incurable wanderlust, she has lived many places, but these days she calls Dallas home.

Find out more about her at *https://pageturner.ink*